BOOK ONE IN THE ᗡESCENDANTS SERIES

The
Graphic Novel

#1 *New York Times* best-selling author
Melissa de la Cruz
Based on *Descendants* written by
Josann McGibbon & Sara Parriott

Adapted by
ROBERT VENDITTI

Art by
KAT FAJARDO

Lettering by
LEIGH LUNA

Adapted from the novel *The Isle of the Lost*
Copyright © 2018 by Disney Enterprises, Inc.

First Edition, September 2018
10 9 8 7 6 5 4 3 2 1
FAC-038091-18201
Printed in the United States of America

A special thank-you to Krzysztof Chalik for all his help with this book

ISBN (hardcover) 978-1-368-03981-9
ISBN (paperback) 978-1-368-04051-8
Reinforced binding
Visit DisneyBooks.com
and DisneyDescendants.com

SUSTAINABLE
FORESTRY
INITIATIVE

Certified Sourcing
www.sfiprogram.org
SFI-00993

Logo Applies to Text Stock Only

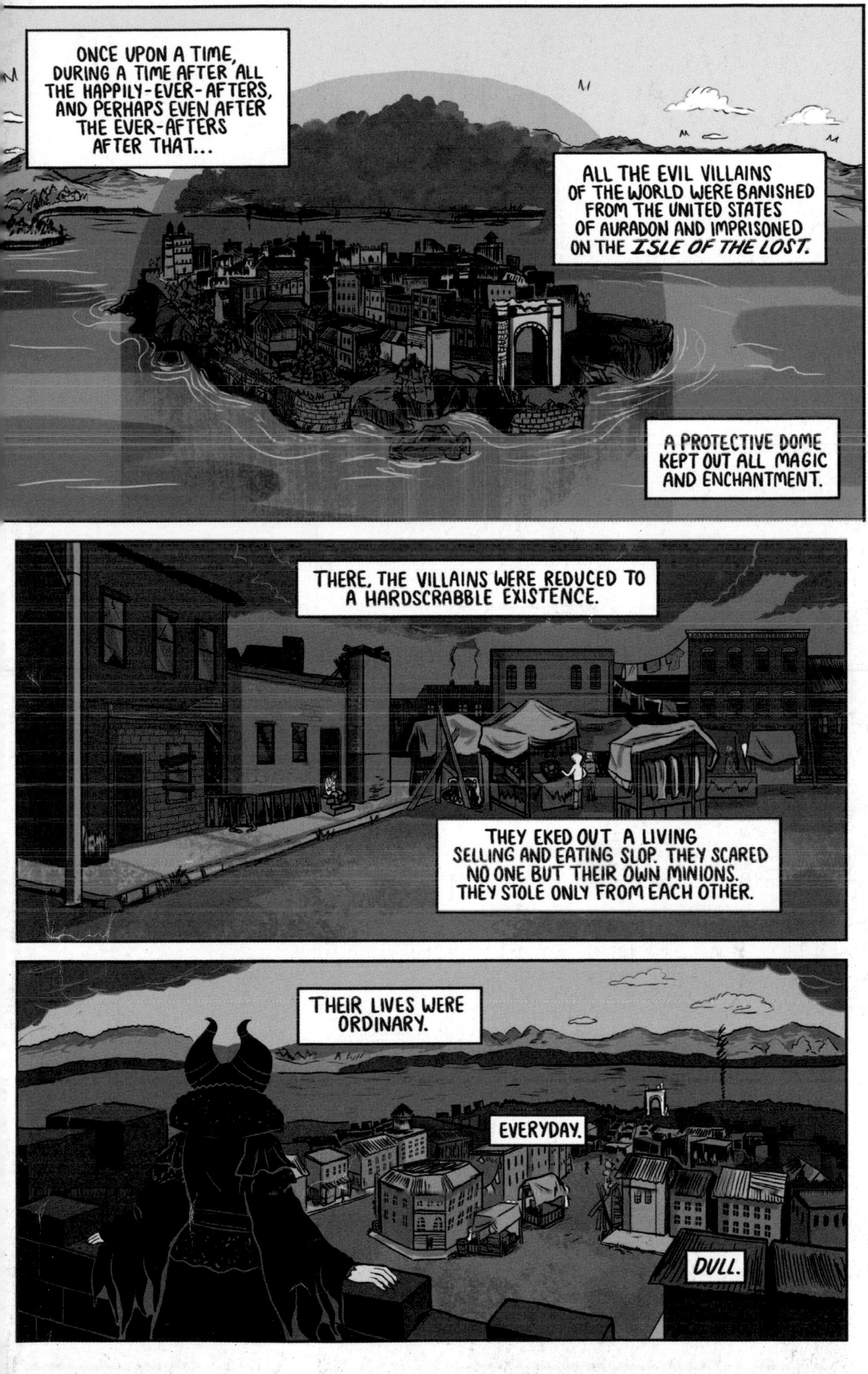
ONCE UPON A TIME, DURING A TIME AFTER ALL THE HAPPILY-EVER-AFTERS, AND PERHAPS EVEN AFTER THE EVER-AFTERS AFTER THAT...
ALL THE EVIL VILLAINS OF THE WORLD WERE BANISHED FROM THE UNITED STATES OF AURADON AND IMPRISONED ON THE *ISLE OF THE LOST.*
A PROTECTIVE DOME KEPT OUT ALL MAGIC AND ENCHANTMENT.
THERE, THE VILLAINS WERE REDUCED TO A HARDSCRABBLE EXISTENCE.
THEY EKED OUT A LIVING SELLING AND EATING SLOP. THEY SCARED NO ONE BUT THEIR OWN MINIONS. THEY STOLE ONLY FROM EACH OTHER.
THEIR LIVES WERE ORDINARY.
EVERYDAY.
DULL.

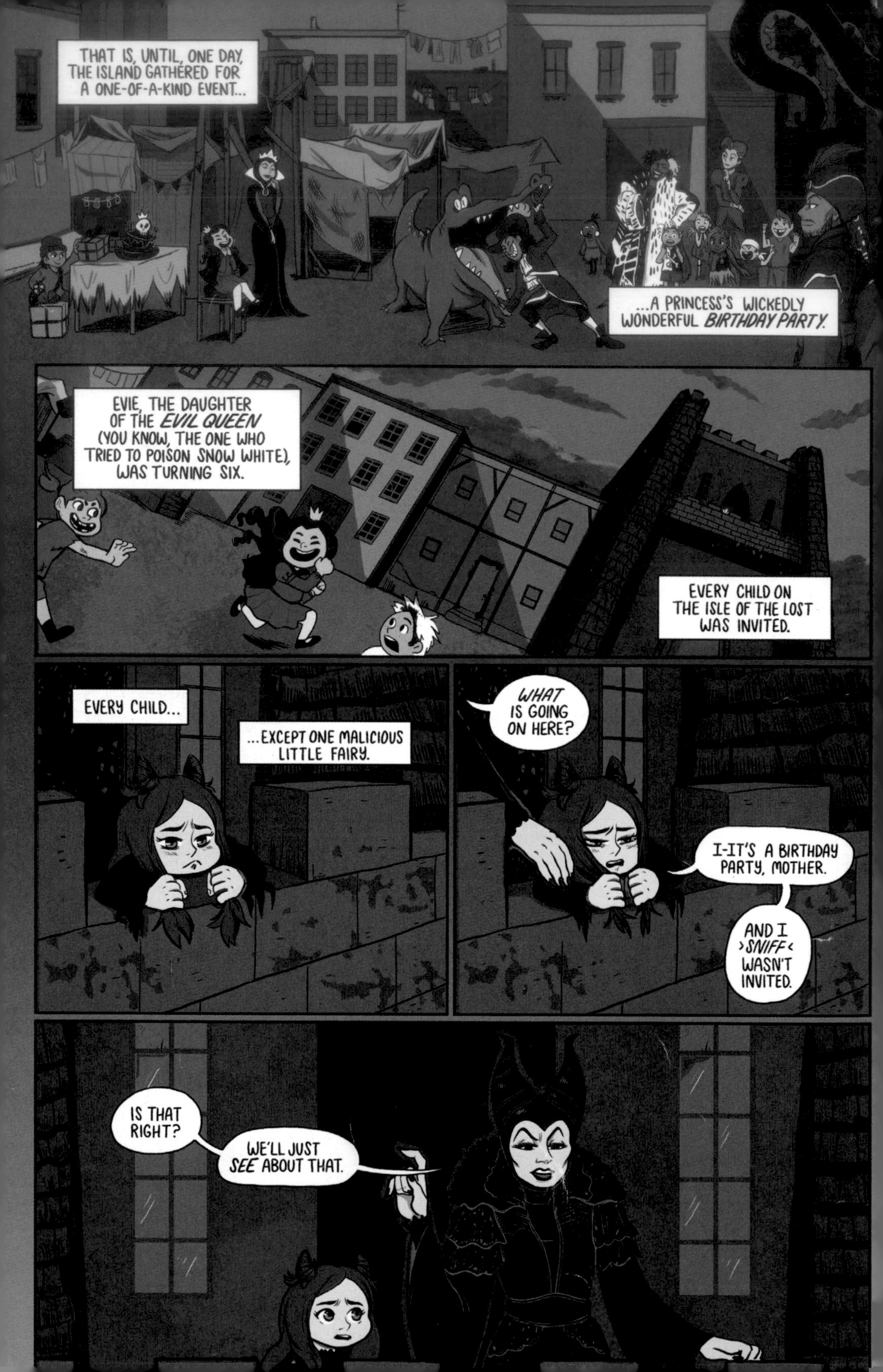
THAT IS, UNTIL, ONE DAY, THE ISLAND GATHERED FOR A ONE-OF-A-KIND EVENT...
...A PRINCESS'S WICKEDLY WONDERFUL *BIRTHDAY PARTY*.
EVIE, THE DAUGHTER OF THE *EVIL QUEEN* (YOU KNOW, THE ONE WHO TRIED TO POISON SNOW WHITE), WAS TURNING SIX.
EVERY CHILD ON THE ISLE OF THE LOST WAS INVITED.
EVERY CHILD...
...EXCEPT ONE MALICIOUS LITTLE FAIRY.
WHAT IS GOING ON HERE?
I-IT'S A BIRTHDAY PARTY, MOTHER.
AND I >*SNIFF*< WASN'T INVITED.
IS THAT RIGHT?
WE'LL JUST *SEE* ABOUT THAT.

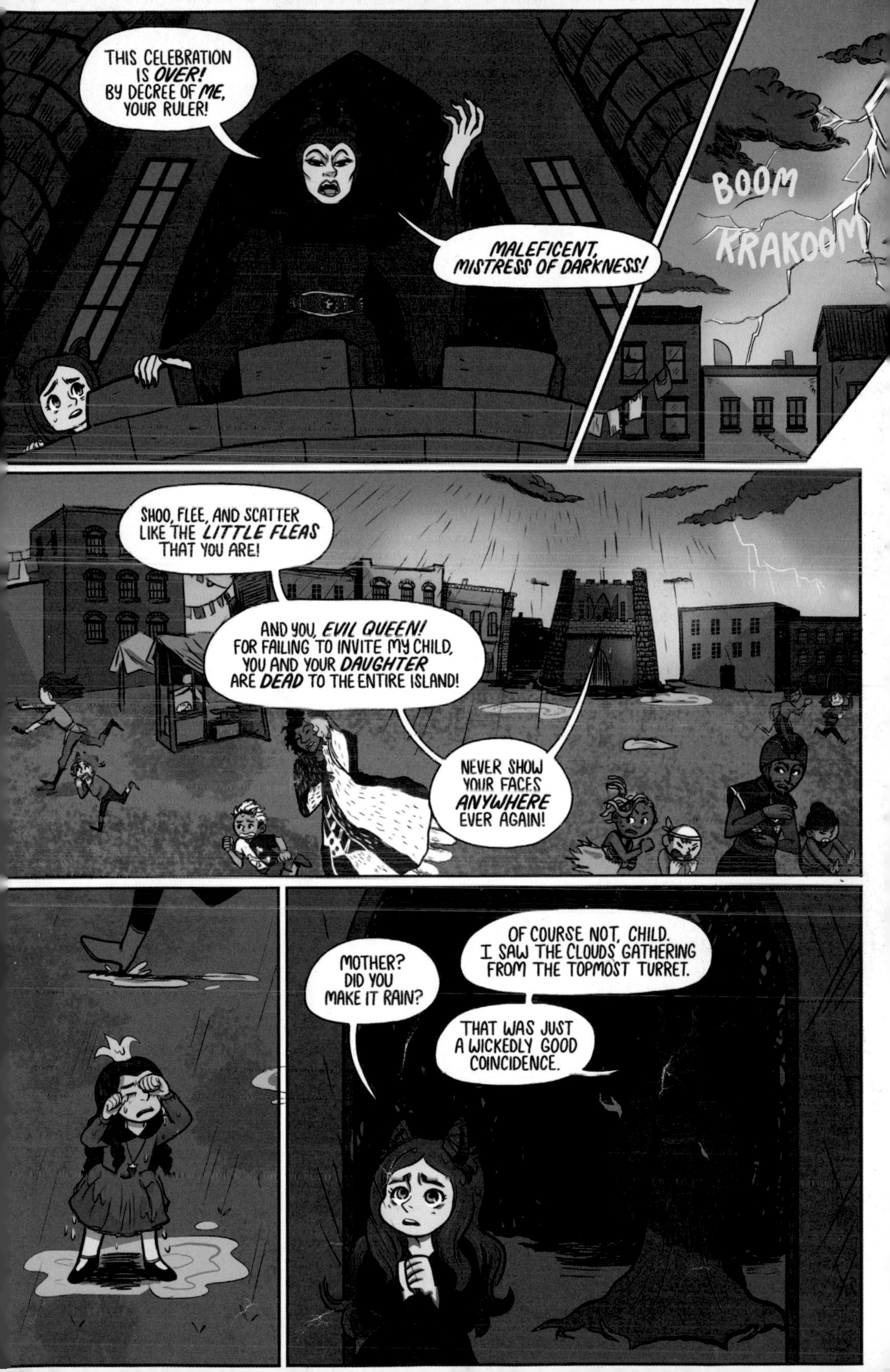
THIS CELEBRATION IS OVER! BY DECREE OF ME, YOUR RULER!
MALEFICENT, MISTRESS OF DARKNESS!
BOOM
KRAKOOM
SHOO, FLEE, AND SCATTER LIKE THE LITTLE FLEAS THAT YOU ARE!
AND YOU, EVIL QUEEN! FOR FAILING TO INVITE MY CHILD, YOU AND YOUR DAUGHTER ARE DEAD TO THE ENTIRE ISLAND!
NEVER SHOW YOUR FACES ANYWHERE EVER AGAIN!
MOTHER? DID YOU MAKE IT RAIN?
OF COURSE NOT, CHILD. I SAW THE CLOUDS GATHERING FROM THE TOPMOST TURRET.
THAT WAS JUST A WICKEDLY GOOD COINCIDENCE.

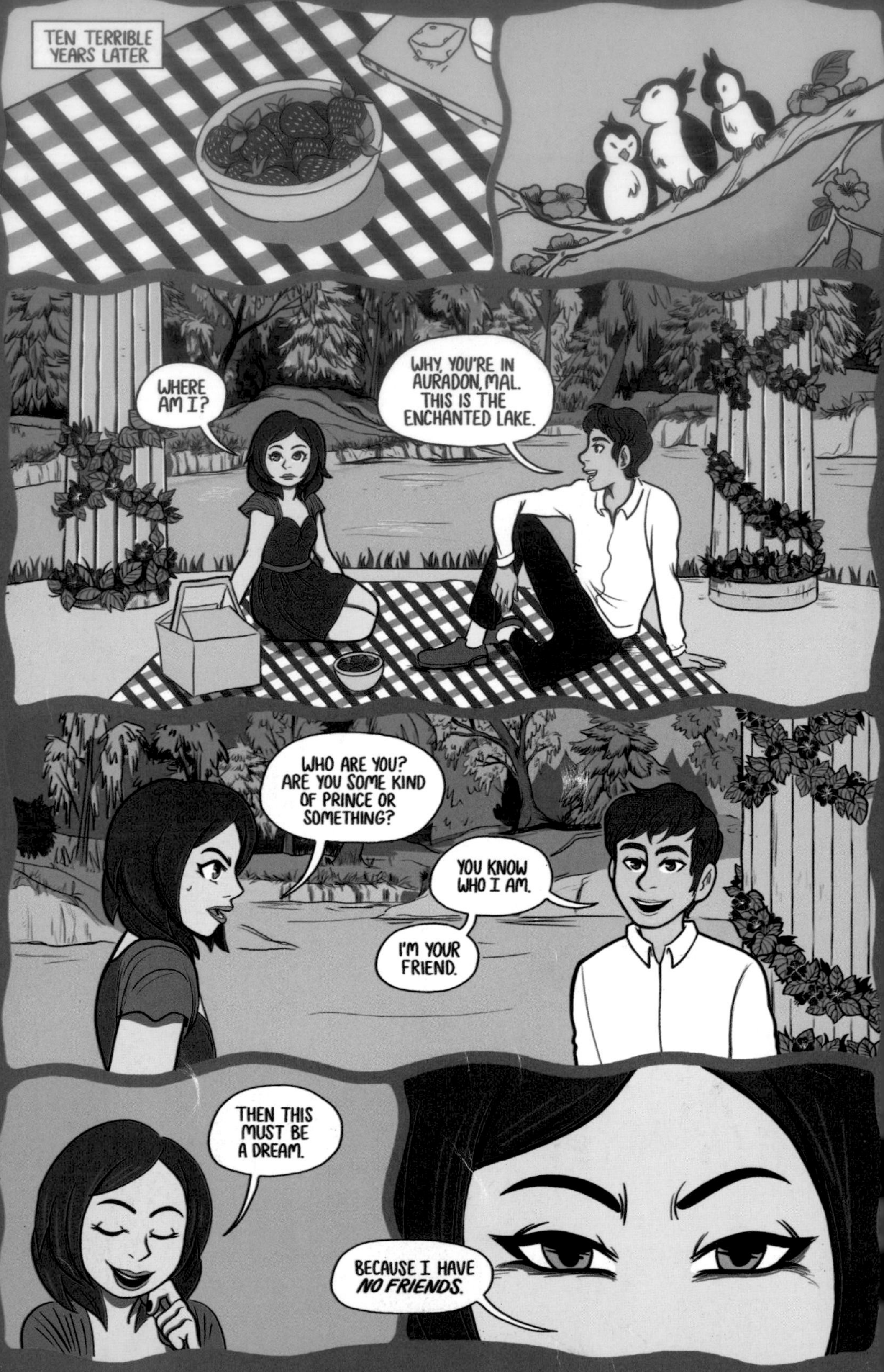

TEN TERRIBLE YEARS LATER
WHERE AM I?
WHY, YOU'RE IN AURADON, MAL. THIS IS THE ENCHANTED LAKE.
WHO ARE YOU? ARE YOU SOME KIND OF PRINCE OR SOMETHING?
YOU KNOW WHO I AM.
I'M YOUR FRIEND.
THEN THIS MUST BE A DREAM.
BECAUSE I HAVE *NO FRIENDS.*

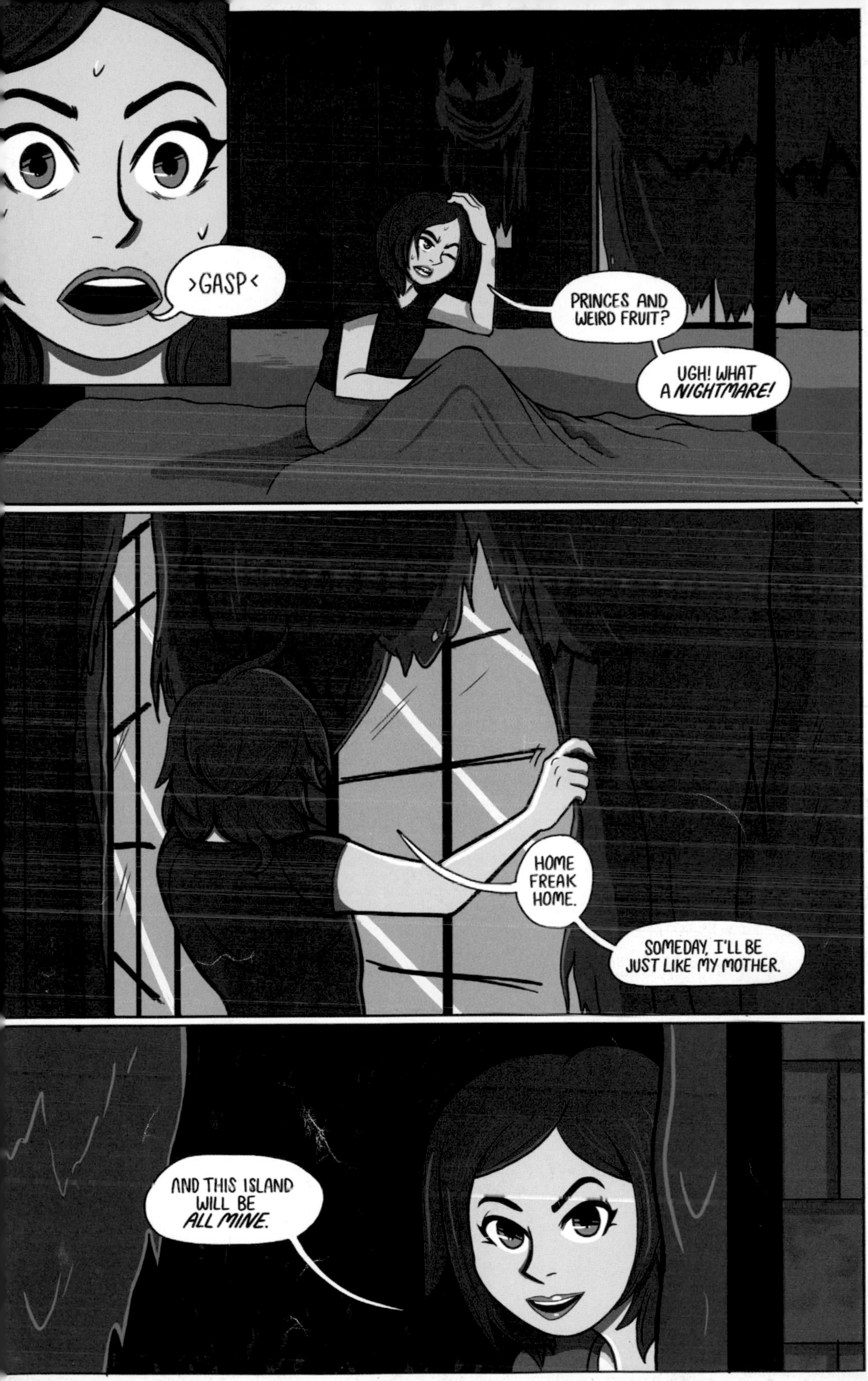
>GASP<
PRINCES AND WEIRD FRUIT?
UGH! WHAT A *NIGHTMARE!*
HOME FREAK HOME.
SOMEDAY, I'LL BE JUST LIKE MY MOTHER.
AND THIS ISLAND WILL BE *ALL MINE.*

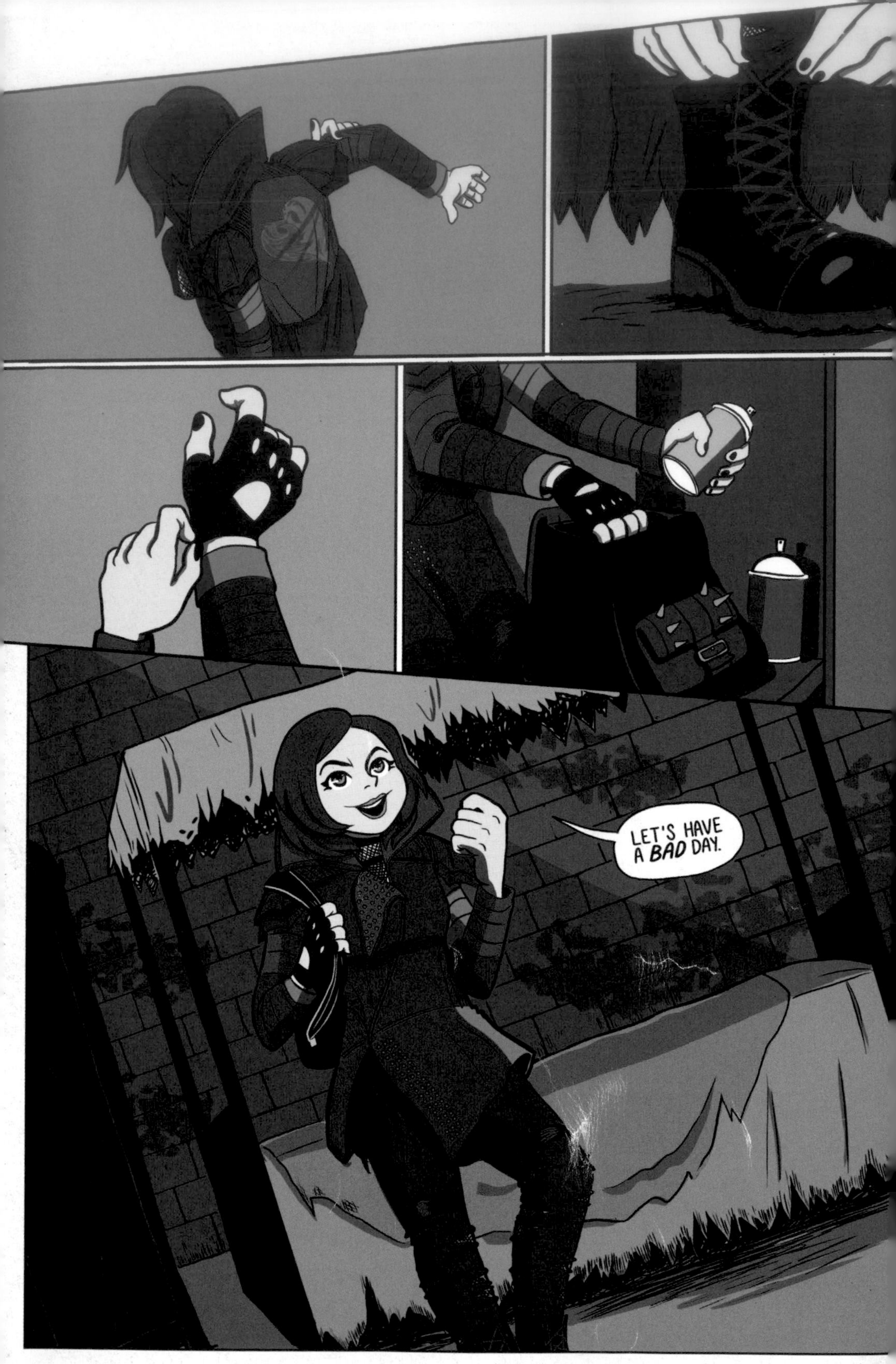
LET'S HAVE A *BAD* DAY.

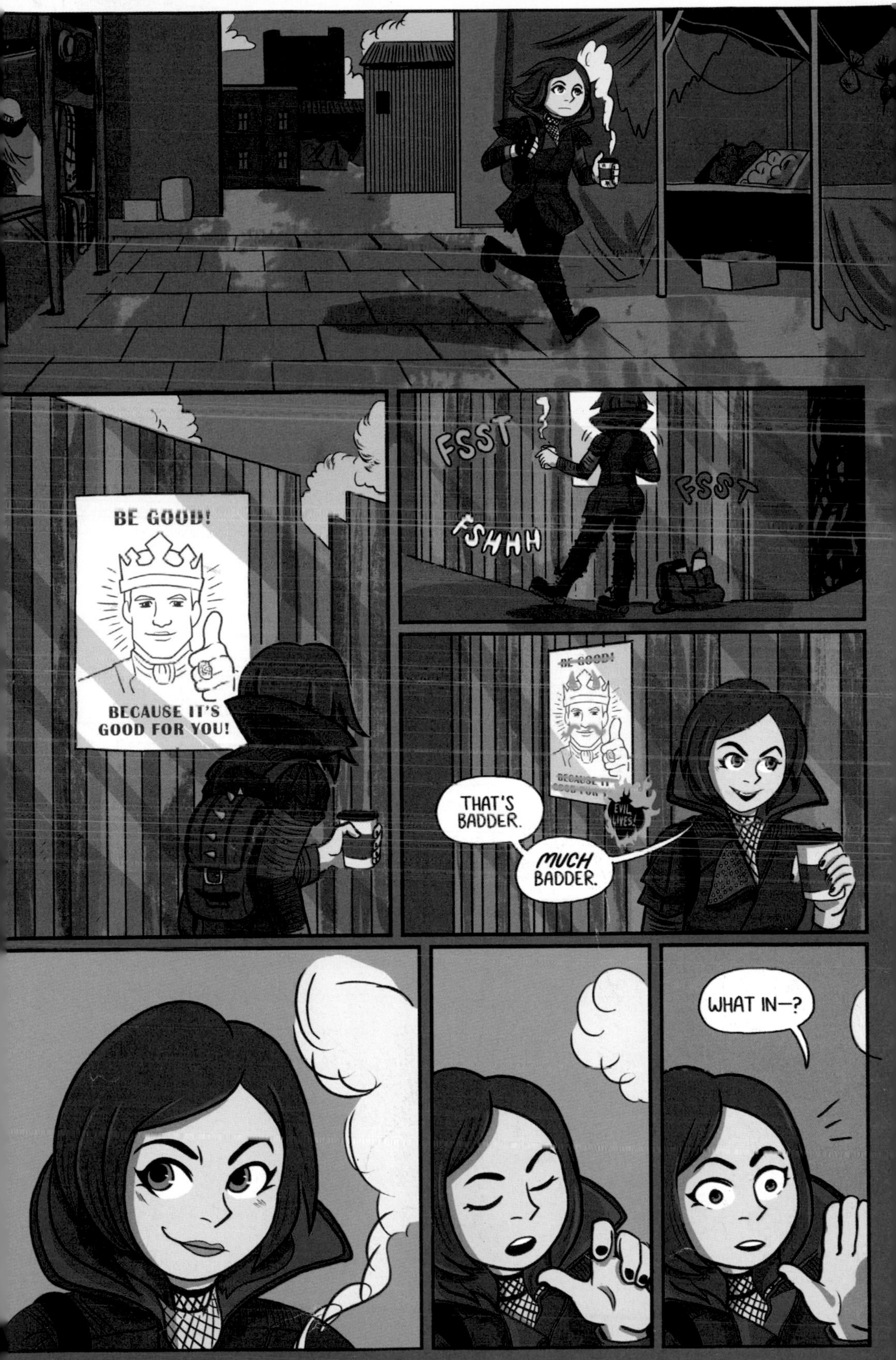

BE GOOD!
BECAUSE IT'S GOOD FOR YOU!
FSST
FSHHH
FSST
EVIL LIVES!
THAT'S BADDER.
MUCH BADDER.
WHAT IN—?

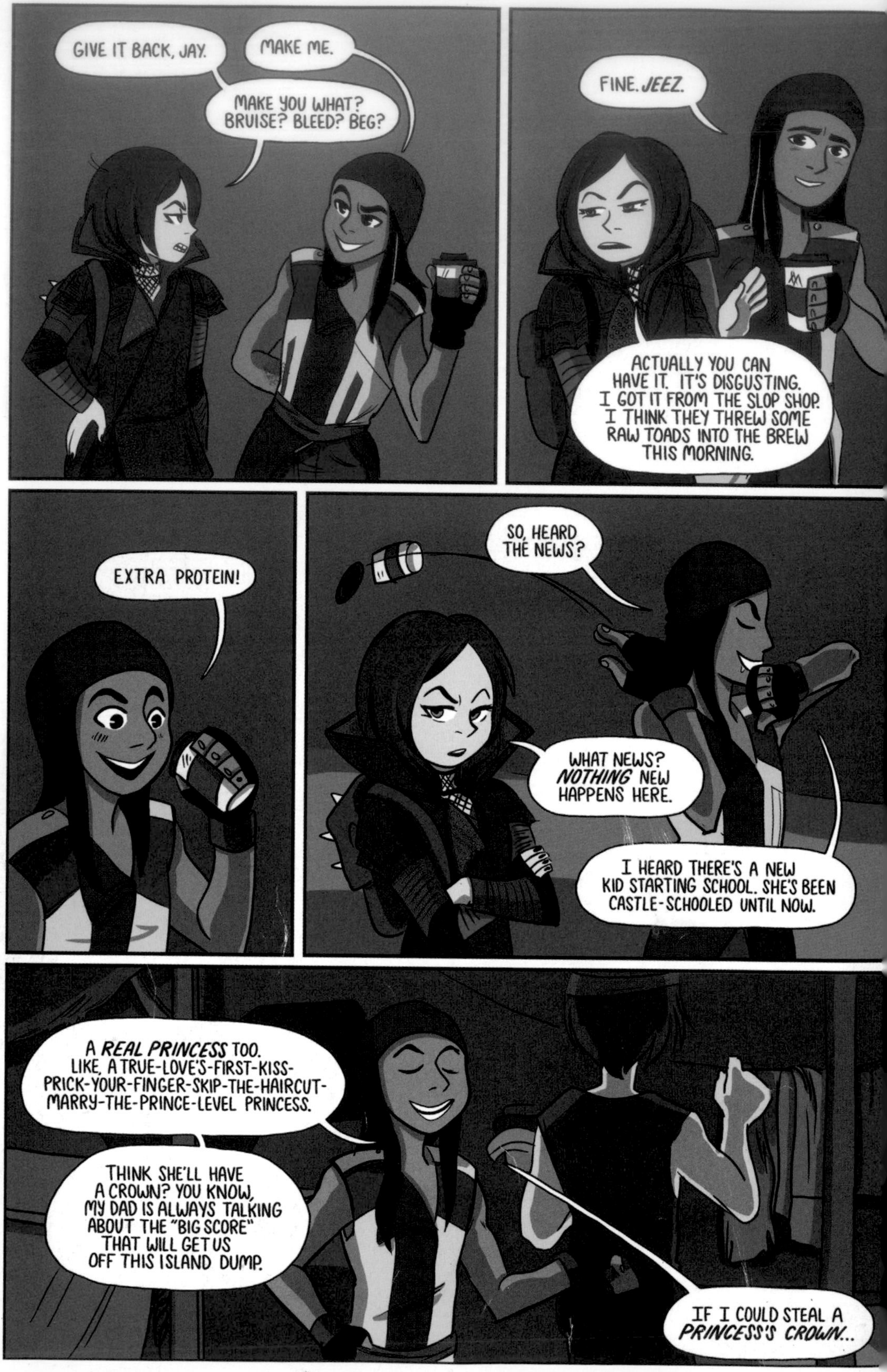
GIVE IT BACK, JAY.
MAKE ME.
MAKE YOU WHAT? BRUISE? BLEED? BEG?
FINE. *JEEZ.*
ACTUALLY YOU CAN HAVE IT. IT'S DISGUSTING. I GOT IT FROM THE SLOP SHOP. I THINK THEY THREW SOME RAW TOADS INTO THE BREW THIS MORNING.
EXTRA PROTEIN!
SO, HEARD THE NEWS?
WHAT NEWS? *NOTHING* NEW HAPPENS HERE.
I HEARD THERE'S A NEW KID STARTING SCHOOL. SHE'S BEEN CASTLE-SCHOOLED UNTIL NOW.
A *REAL PRINCESS* TOO. LIKE, A TRUE-LOVE'S-FIRST-KISS-PRICK-YOUR-FINGER-SKIP-THE-HAIRCUT-MARRY-THE-PRINCE-LEVEL PRINCESS.
THINK SHE'LL HAVE A CROWN? YOU KNOW, MY DAD IS ALWAYS TALKING ABOUT THE "BIG SCORE" THAT WILL GET US OFF THIS ISLAND DUMP.
IF I COULD STEAL A *PRINCESS'S CROWN*...

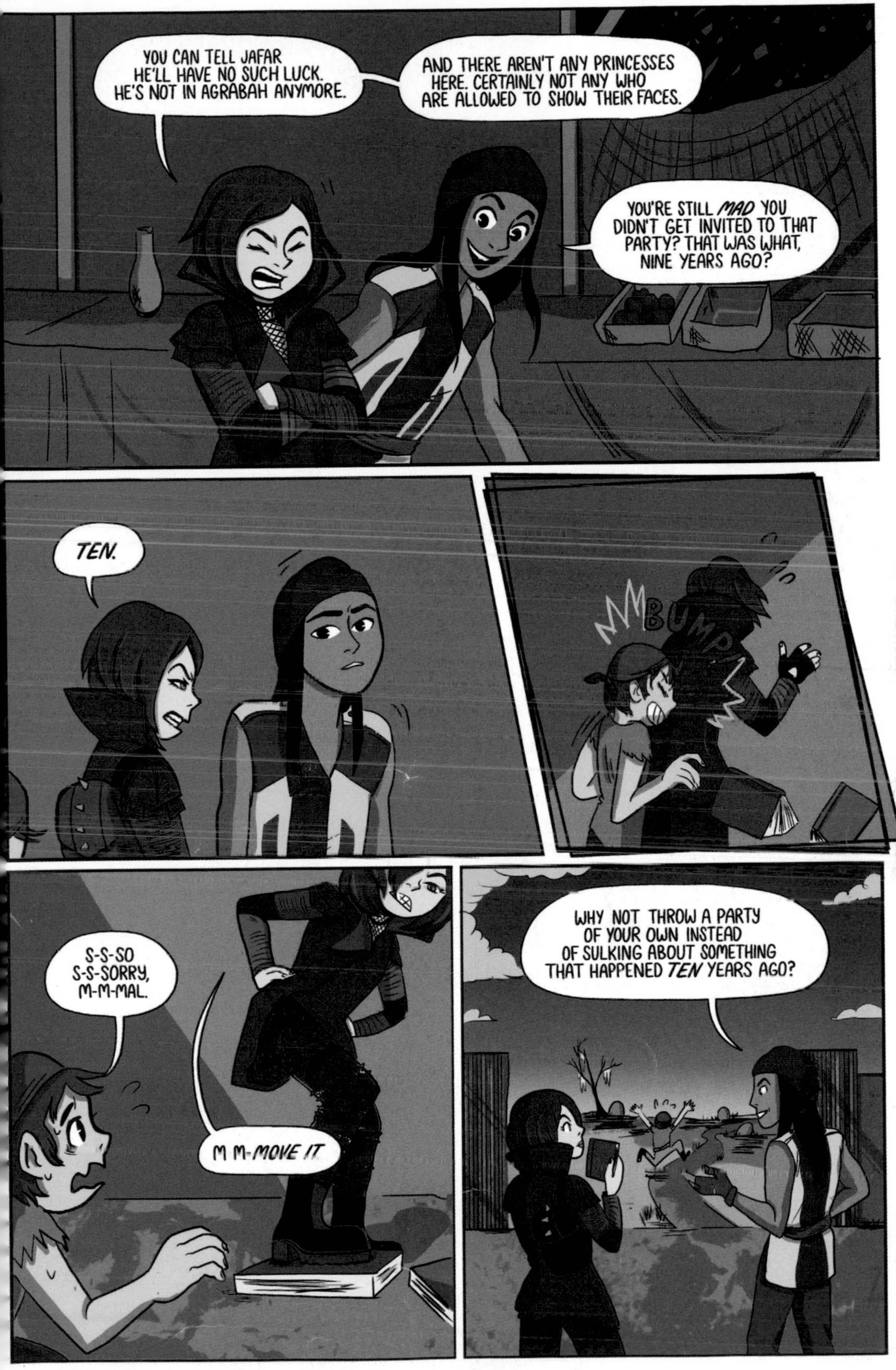
YOU CAN TELL JAFAR HE'LL HAVE NO SUCH LUCK. HE'S NOT IN AGRABAH ANYMORE.
AND THERE AREN'T ANY PRINCESSES HERE. CERTAINLY NOT ANY WHO ARE ALLOWED TO SHOW THEIR FACES.
YOU'RE STILL *MAD* YOU DIDN'T GET INVITED TO THAT PARTY? THAT WAS WHAT, NINE YEARS AGO?
TEN.
BUMP
S-S-SO S-S-SORRY, M-M-MAL.
M M-*MOVE IT.*
WHY NOT THROW A PARTY OF YOUR OWN INSTEAD OF SULKING ABOUT SOMETHING THAT HAPPENED *TEN* YEARS AGO?

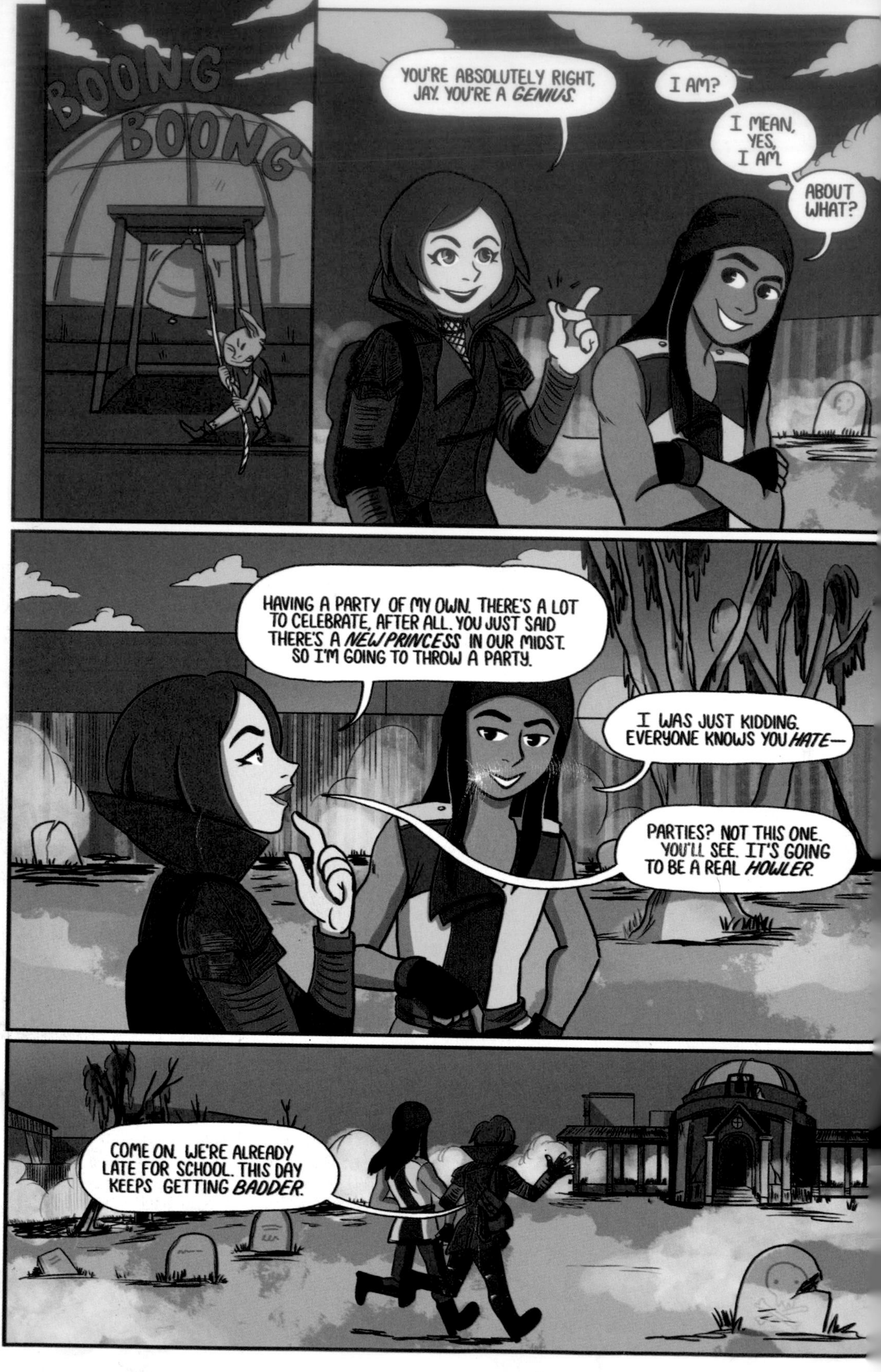
BOONG
BOONG
YOU'RE ABSOLUTELY RIGHT, JAY. YOU'RE A *GENIUS.*
I AM?
I MEAN, YES, I AM.
ABOUT WHAT?
HAVING A PARTY OF MY OWN. THERE'S A LOT TO CELEBRATE, AFTER ALL. YOU JUST SAID THERE'S A *NEW PRINCESS* IN OUR MIDST. SO I'M GOING TO THROW A PARTY.
I WAS JUST KIDDING. EVERYONE KNOWS YOU *HATE*—
PARTIES? NOT THIS ONE. YOU'LL SEE. IT'S GOING TO BE A REAL *HOWLER.*
COME ON. WE'RE ALREADY LATE FOR SCHOOL. THIS DAY KEEPS GETTING *BADDER.*

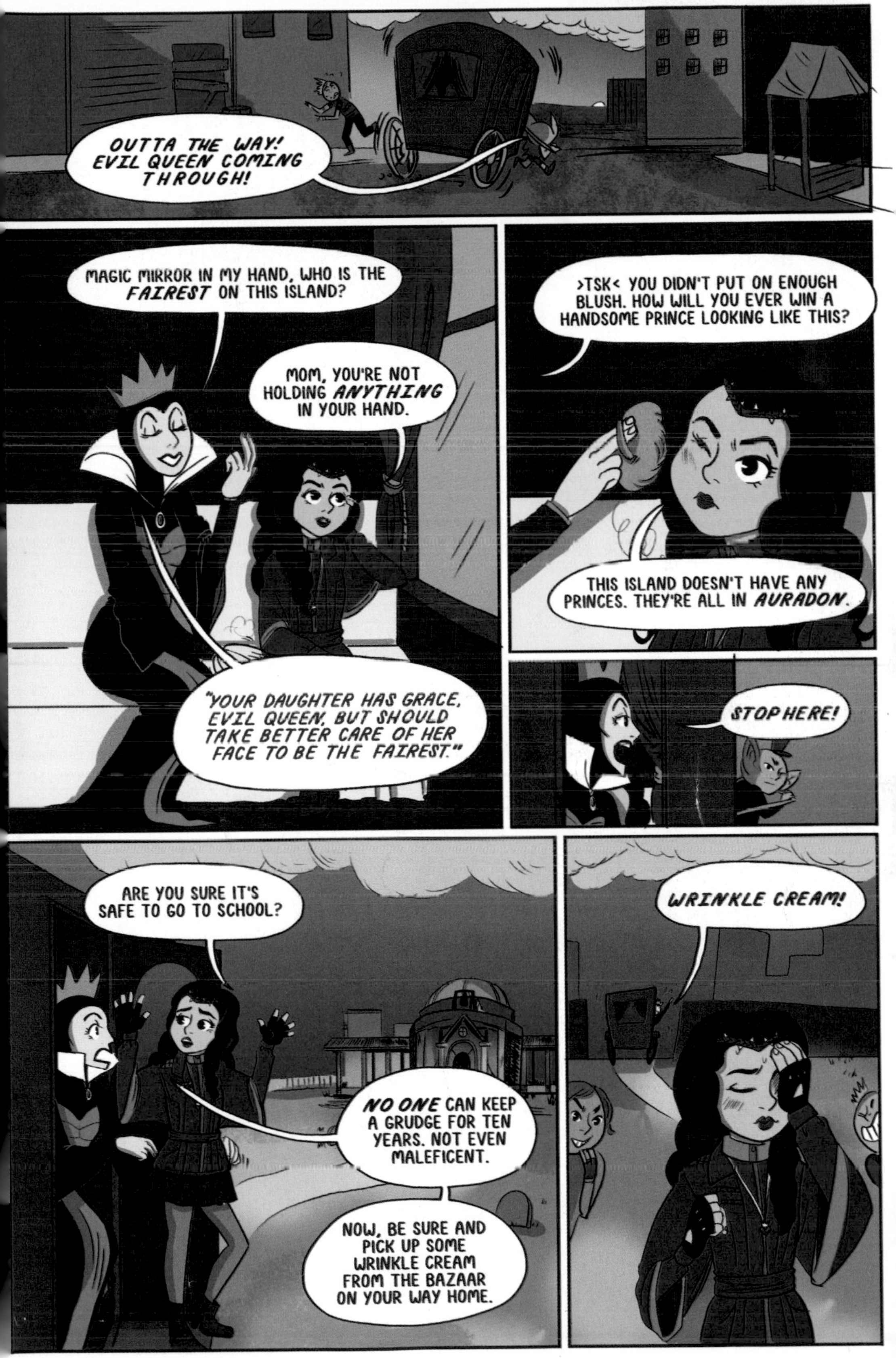
OUTTA THE WAY! EVIL QUEEN COMING THROUGH!
MAGIC MIRROR IN MY HAND, WHO IS THE FAIREST ON THIS ISLAND?
MOM, YOU'RE NOT HOLDING ANYTHING IN YOUR HAND.
"YOUR DAUGHTER HAS GRACE, EVIL QUEEN, BUT SHOULD TAKE BETTER CARE OF HER FACE TO BE THE FAIREST."
>TSK< YOU DIDN'T PUT ON ENOUGH BLUSH. HOW WILL YOU EVER WIN A HANDSOME PRINCE LOOKING LIKE THIS?
THIS ISLAND DOESN'T HAVE ANY PRINCES. THEY'RE ALL IN AURADON.
STOP HERE!
ARE YOU SURE IT'S SAFE TO GO TO SCHOOL?
NO ONE CAN KEEP A GRUDGE FOR TEN YEARS. NOT EVEN MALEFICENT.
NOW, BE SURE AND PICK UP SOME WRINKLE CREAM FROM THE BAZAAR ON YOUR WAY HOME.
WRINKLE CREAM!

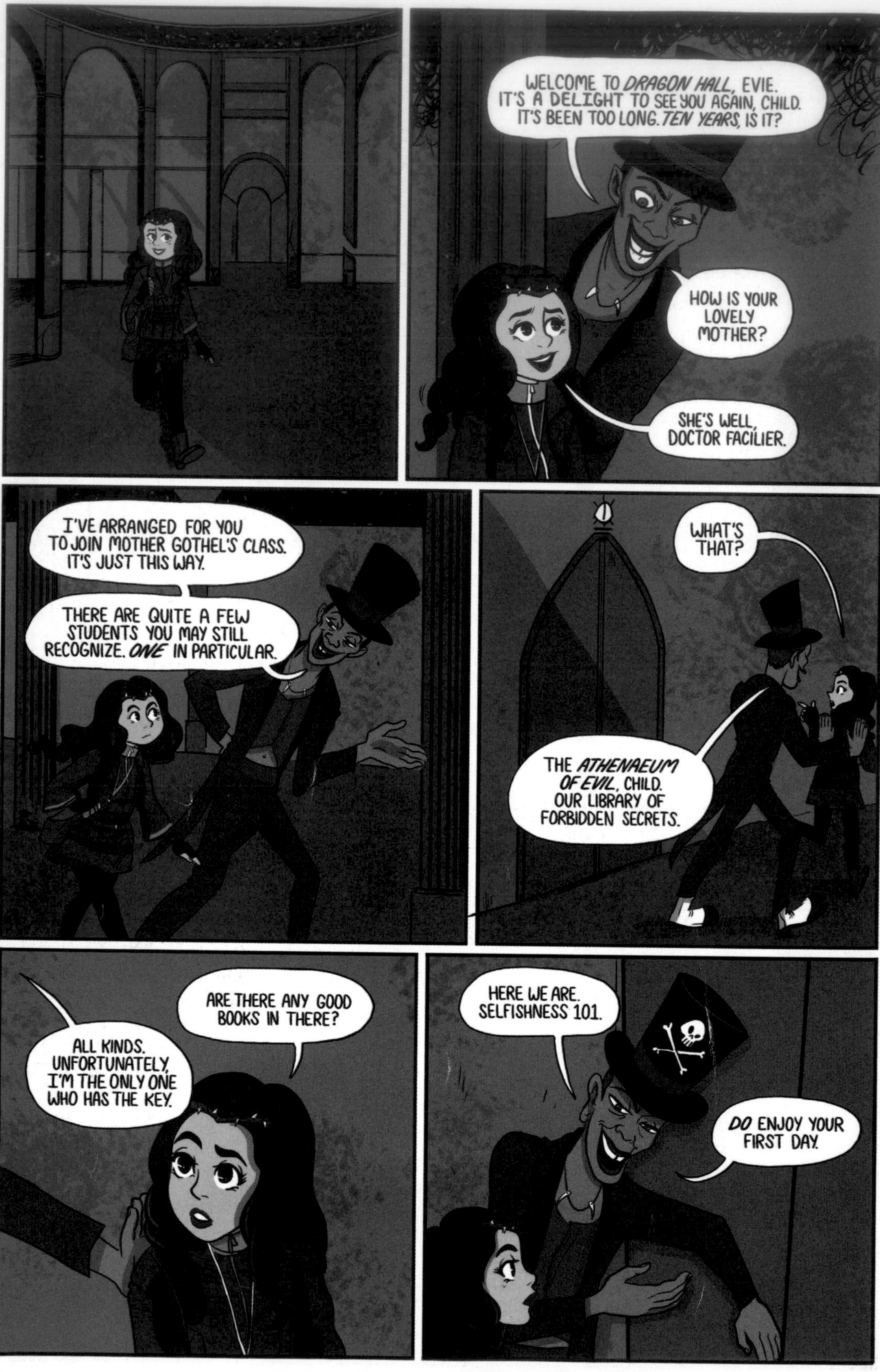
WELCOME TO DRAGON HALL, EVIE. IT'S A DELIGHT TO SEE YOU AGAIN, CHILD. IT'S BEEN TOO LONG. TEN YEARS, IS IT?
HOW IS YOUR LOVELY MOTHER?
SHE'S WELL, DOCTOR FACILIER.
I'VE ARRANGED FOR YOU TO JOIN MOTHER GOTHEL'S CLASS. IT'S JUST THIS WAY.
THERE ARE QUITE A FEW STUDENTS YOU MAY STILL RECOGNIZE. ONE IN PARTICULAR.
WHAT'S THAT?
THE ATHENAEUM OF EVIL, CHILD. OUR LIBRARY OF FORBIDDEN SECRETS.
ARE THERE ANY GOOD BOOKS IN THERE?
ALL KINDS. UNFORTUNATELY, I'M THE ONLY ONE WHO HAS THE KEY.
HERE WE ARE. SELFISHNESS 101.
DO ENJOY YOUR FIRST DAY.

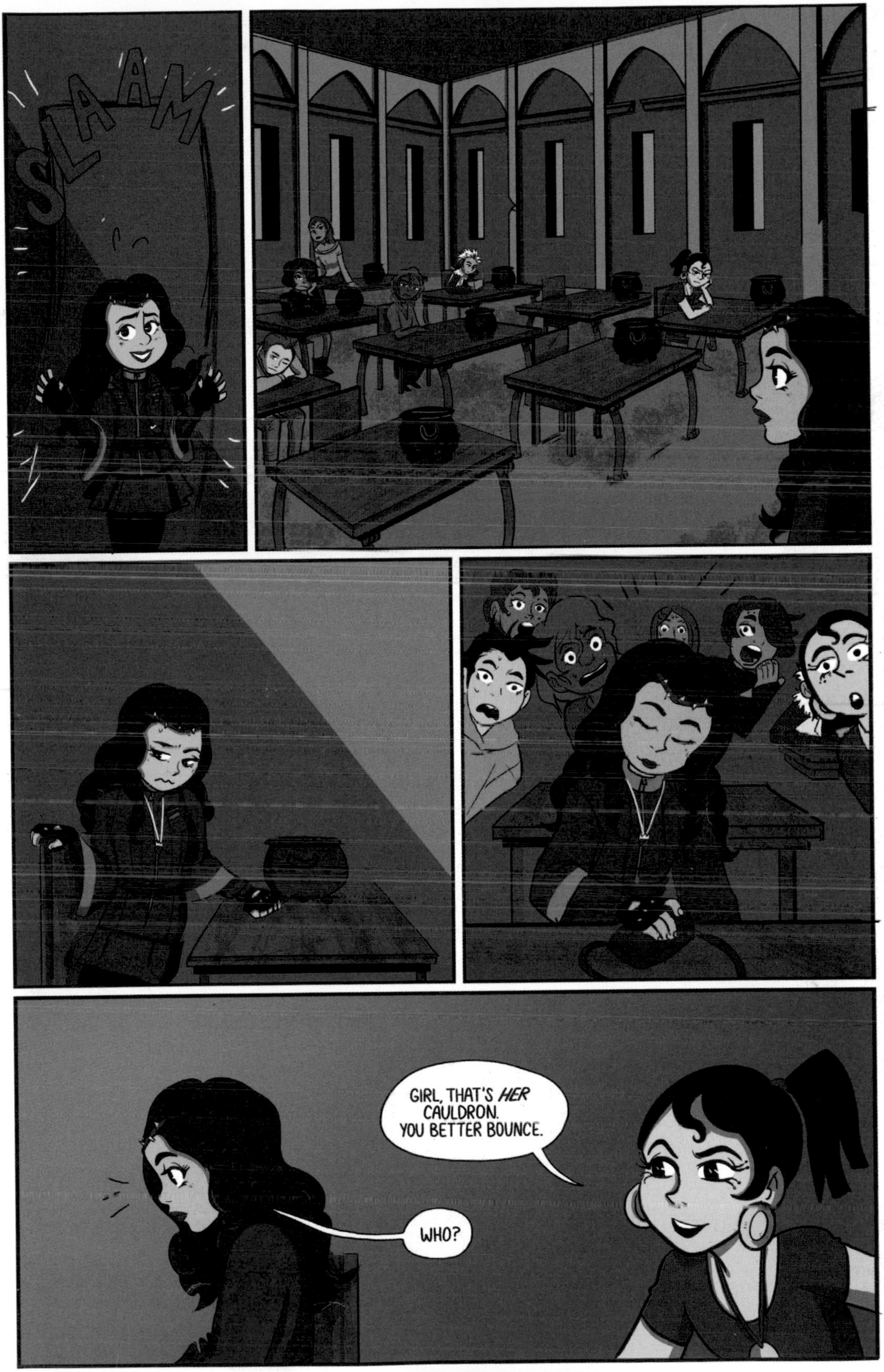
SLAAM
GIRL, THAT'S *HER* CAULDRON. YOU BETTER BOUNCE.
WHO?

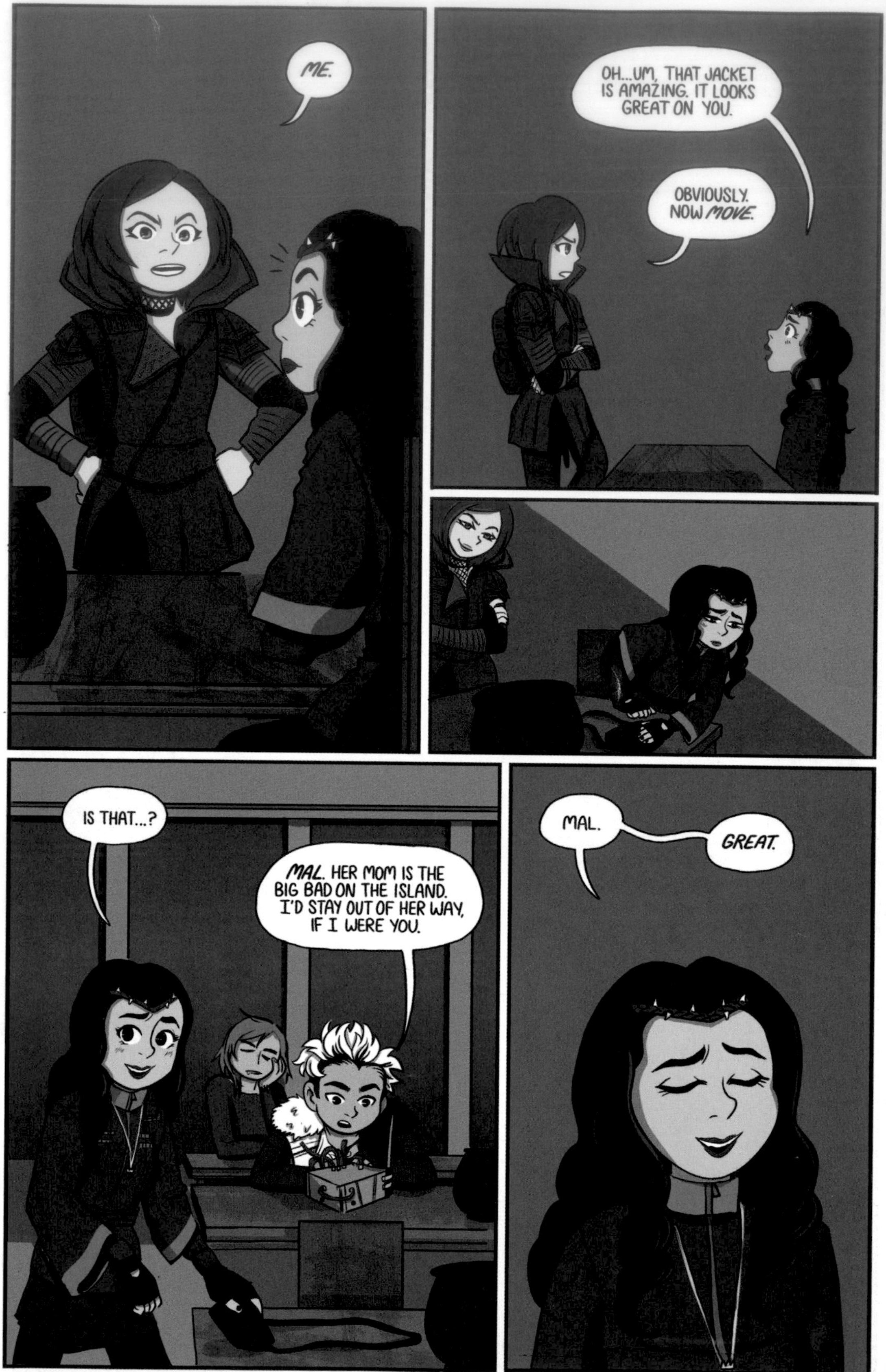
ME.
OH...UM, THAT JACKET IS AMAZING. IT LOOKS GREAT ON YOU.
OBVIOUSLY. NOW *MOVE*.
IS THAT...?
MAL. HER MOM IS THE BIG BAD ON THE ISLAND. I'D STAY OUT OF HER WAY, IF I WERE YOU.
MAL.
GREAT.

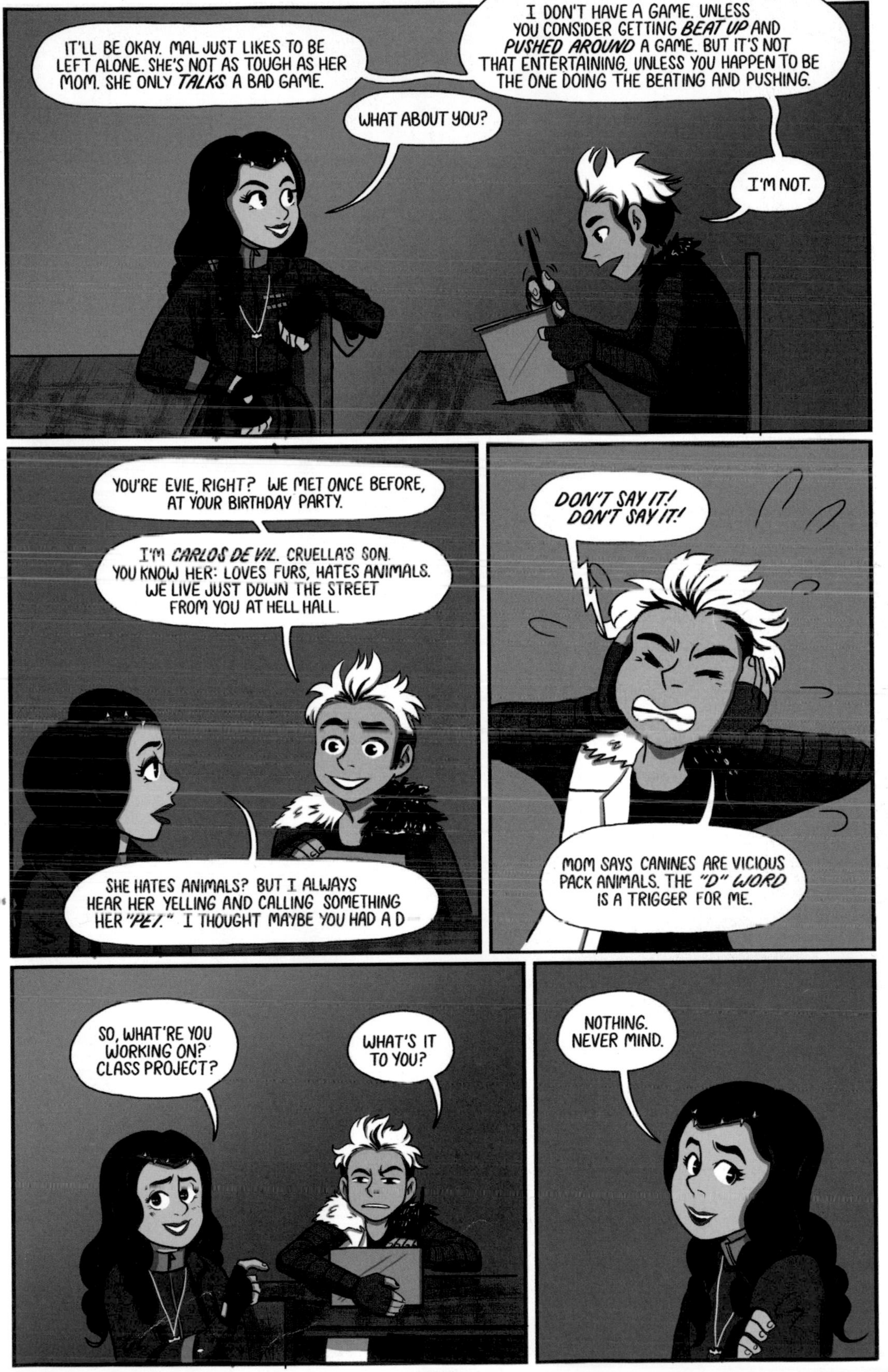
IT'LL BE OKAY. MAL JUST LIKES TO BE LEFT ALONE. SHE'S NOT AS TOUGH AS HER MOM. SHE ONLY TALKS A BAD GAME.
WHAT ABOUT YOU?
I DON'T HAVE A GAME. UNLESS YOU CONSIDER GETTING BEAT UP AND PUSHED AROUND A GAME. BUT IT'S NOT THAT ENTERTAINING, UNLESS YOU HAPPEN TO BE THE ONE DOING THE BEATING AND PUSHING.
I'M NOT.
YOU'RE EVIE, RIGHT? WE MET ONCE BEFORE, AT YOUR BIRTHDAY PARTY.
I'M CARLOS DE VIL. CRUELLA'S SON. YOU KNOW HER: LOVES FURS, HATES ANIMALS. WE LIVE JUST DOWN THE STREET FROM YOU AT HELL HALL.
SHE HATES ANIMALS? BUT I ALWAYS HEAR HER YELLING AND CALLING SOMETHING HER "PET." I THOUGHT MAYBE YOU HAD A D
DON'T SAY IT! DON'T SAY IT!
MOM SAYS CANINES ARE VICIOUS PACK ANIMALS. THE "D" WORD IS A TRIGGER FOR ME.
SO, WHAT'RE YOU WORKING ON? CLASS PROJECT?
WHAT'S IT TO YOU?
NOTHING. NEVER MIND.

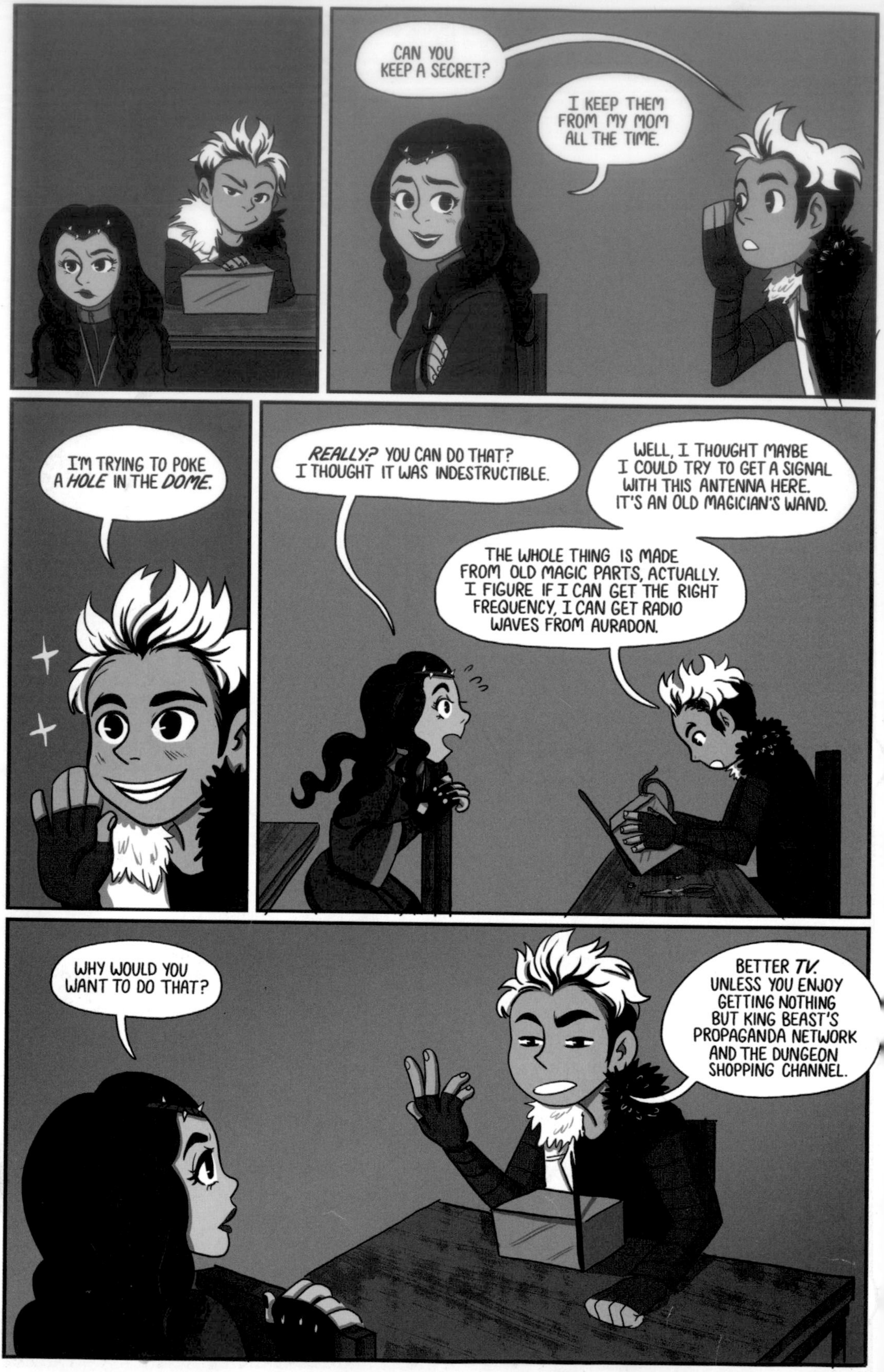
CAN YOU KEEP A SECRET?
I KEEP THEM FROM MY MOM ALL THE TIME.
I'M TRYING TO POKE A *HOLE* IN THE *DOME*.
REALLY? YOU CAN DO THAT? I THOUGHT IT WAS INDESTRUCTIBLE.
WELL, I THOUGHT MAYBE I COULD TRY TO GET A SIGNAL WITH THIS ANTENNA HERE. IT'S AN OLD MAGICIAN'S WAND.
THE WHOLE THING IS MADE FROM OLD MAGIC PARTS, ACTUALLY. I FIGURE IF I CAN GET THE RIGHT FREQUENCY, I CAN GET RADIO WAVES FROM AURADON.
WHY WOULD YOU WANT TO DO THAT?
BETTER *TV*. UNLESS YOU ENJOY GETTING NOTHING BUT KING BEAST'S PROPAGANDA NETWORK AND THE DUNGEON SHOPPING CHANNEL.

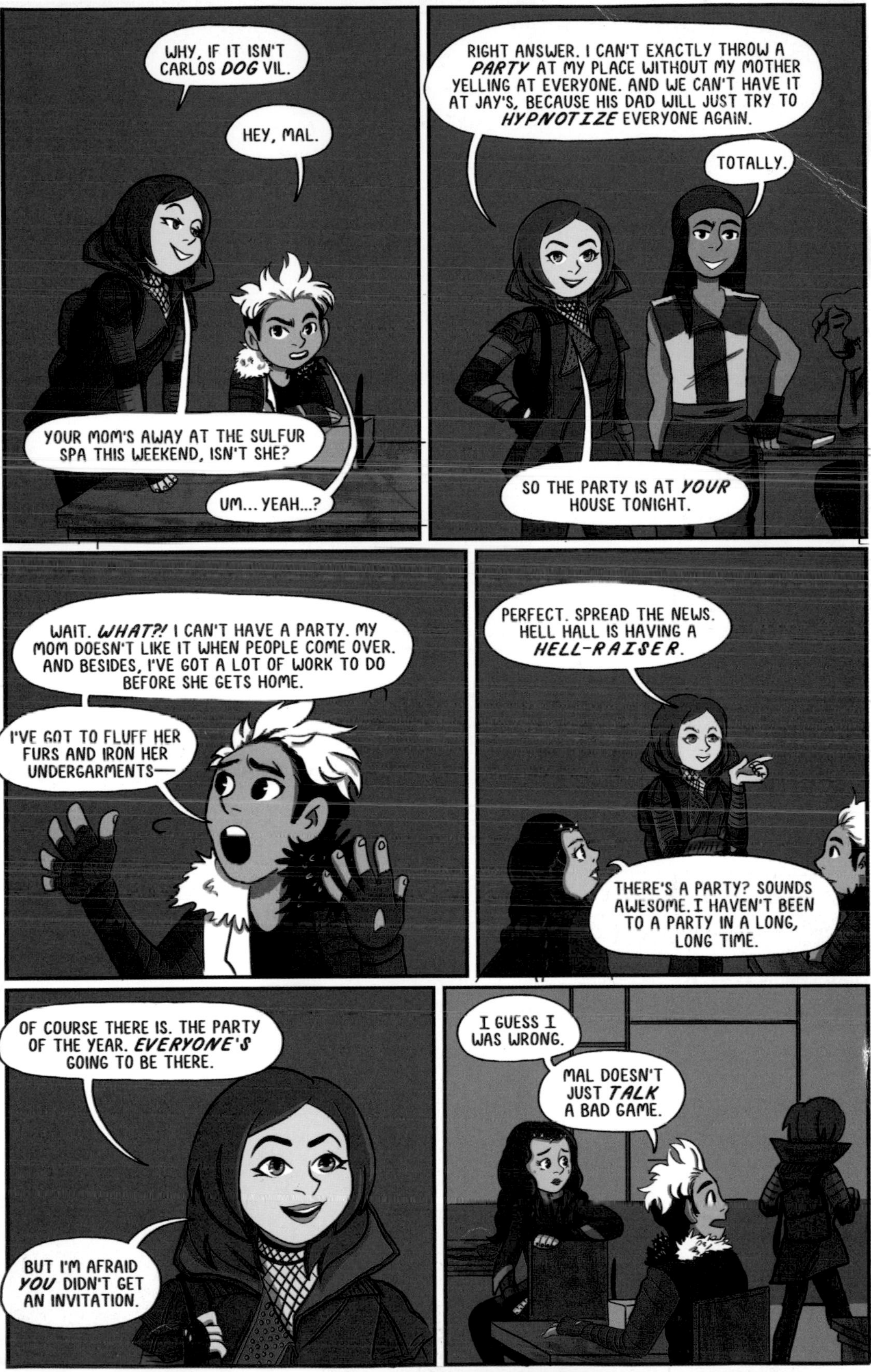
WHY, IF IT ISN'T CARLOS DOG VIL.
HEY, MAL.
YOUR MOM'S AWAY AT THE SULFUR SPA THIS WEEKEND, ISN'T SHE?
UM... YEAH...?
RIGHT ANSWER. I CAN'T EXACTLY THROW A PARTY AT MY PLACE WITHOUT MY MOTHER YELLING AT EVERYONE. AND WE CAN'T HAVE IT AT JAY'S, BECAUSE HIS DAD WILL JUST TRY TO HYPNOTIZE EVERYONE AGAIN.
TOTALLY.
SO THE PARTY IS AT YOUR HOUSE TONIGHT.
WAIT. WHAT?! I CAN'T HAVE A PARTY. MY MOM DOESN'T LIKE IT WHEN PEOPLE COME OVER. AND BESIDES, I'VE GOT A LOT OF WORK TO DO BEFORE SHE GETS HOME.
I'VE GOT TO FLUFF HER FURS AND IRON HER UNDERGARMENTS—
PERFECT. SPREAD THE NEWS. HELL HALL IS HAVING A HELL-RAISER.
THERE'S A PARTY? SOUNDS AWESOME. I HAVEN'T BEEN TO A PARTY IN A LONG, LONG TIME.
OF COURSE THERE IS. THE PARTY OF THE YEAR. EVERYONE'S GOING TO BE THERE.
BUT I'M AFRAID YOU DIDN'T GET AN INVITATION.
I GUESS I WAS WRONG.
MAL DOESN'T JUST TALK A BAD GAME.

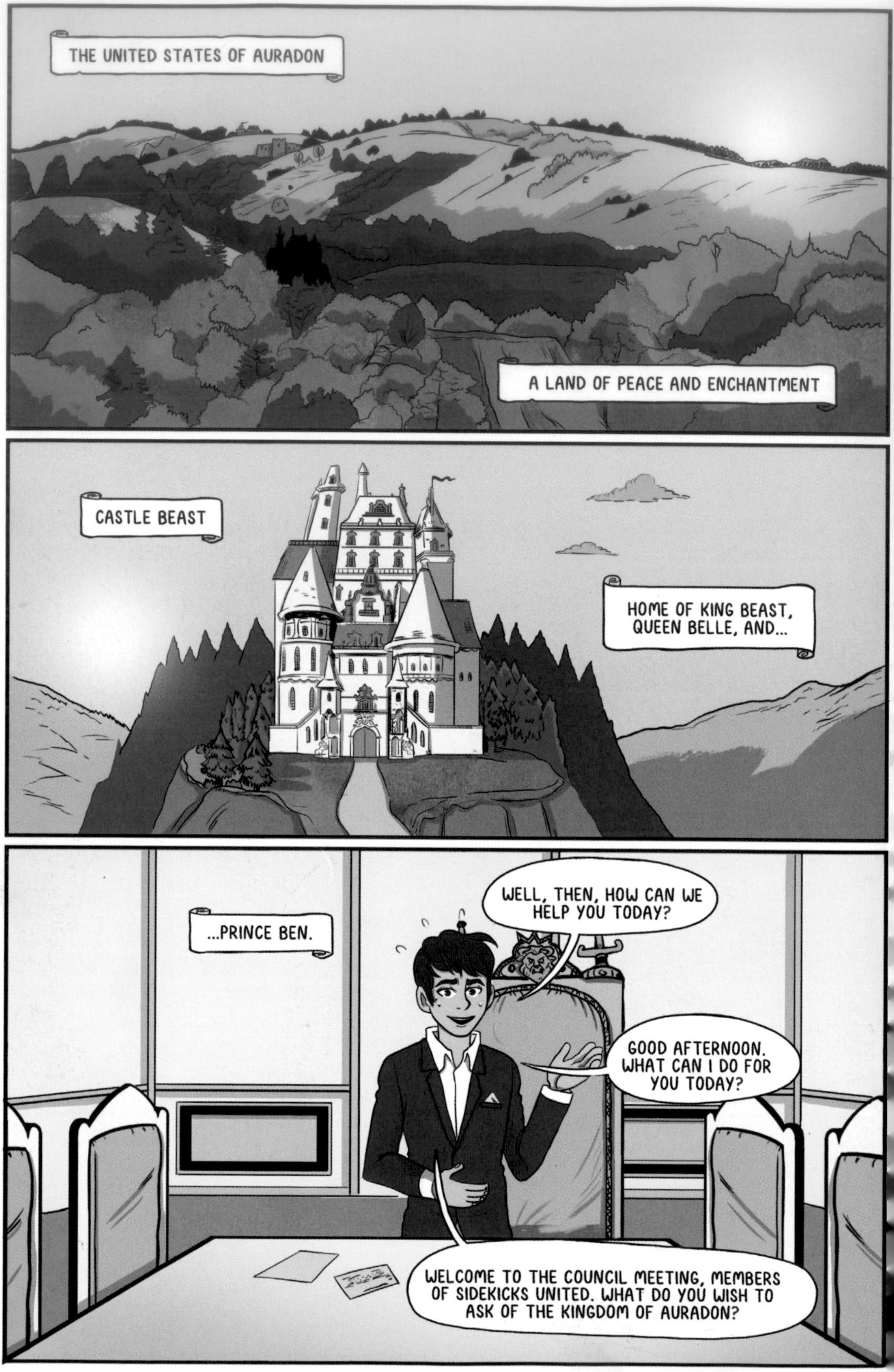
THE UNITED STATES OF AURADON
A LAND OF PEACE AND ENCHANTMENT
CASTLE BEAST
HOME OF KING BEAST, QUEEN BELLE, AND...
...PRINCE BEN.
WELL, THEN, HOW CAN WE HELP YOU TODAY?
GOOD AFTERNOON. WHAT CAN I DO FOR YOU TODAY?
WELCOME TO THE COUNCIL MEETING, MEMBERS OF SIDEKICKS UNITED. WHAT DO YOU WISH TO ASK OF THE KINGDOM OF AURADON?

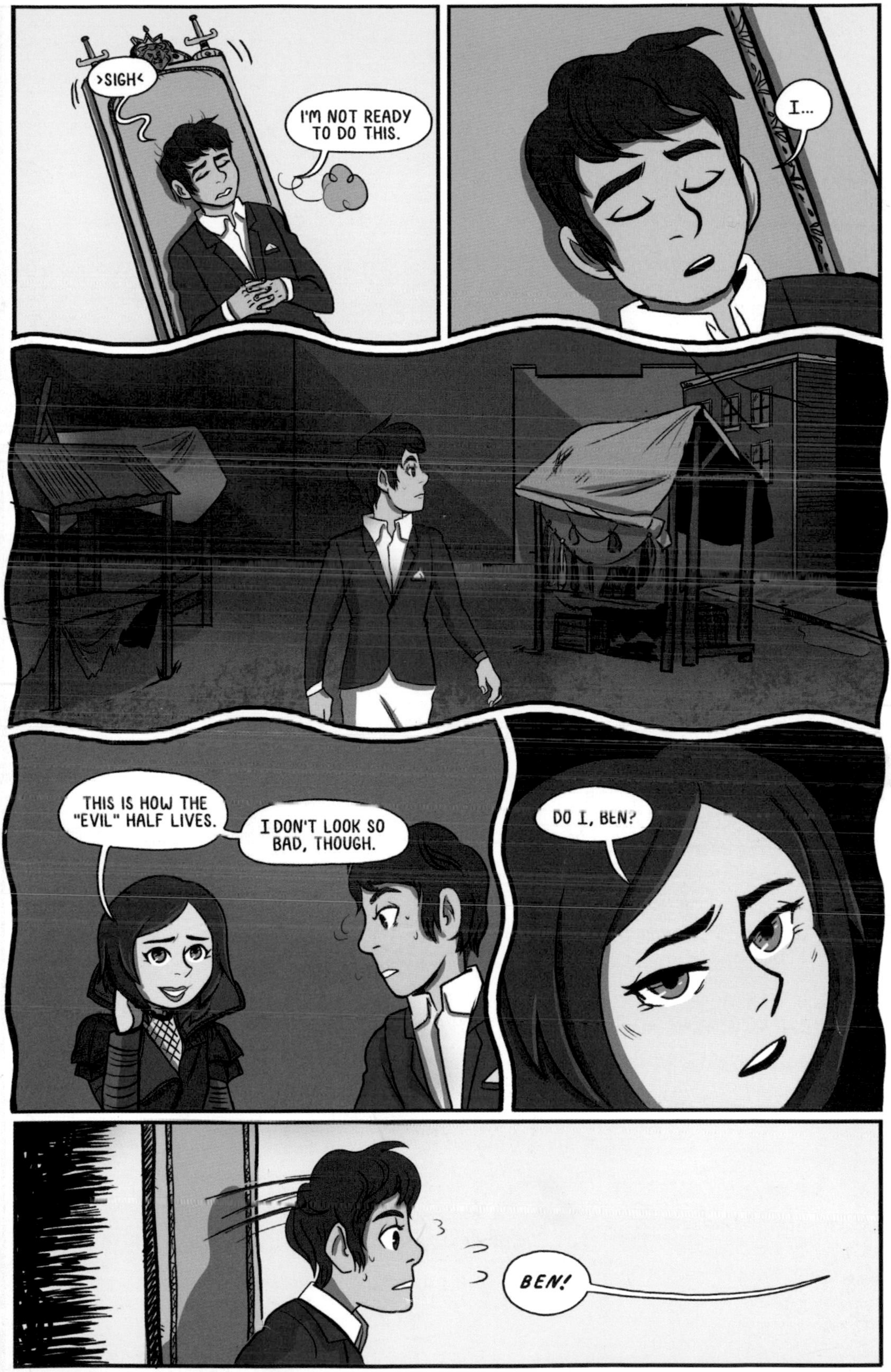
>SIGH<
I'M NOT READY TO DO THIS.
I...
THIS IS HOW THE "EVIL" HALF LIVES.
I DON'T LOOK SO BAD, THOUGH.
DO I, BEN?
BEN!

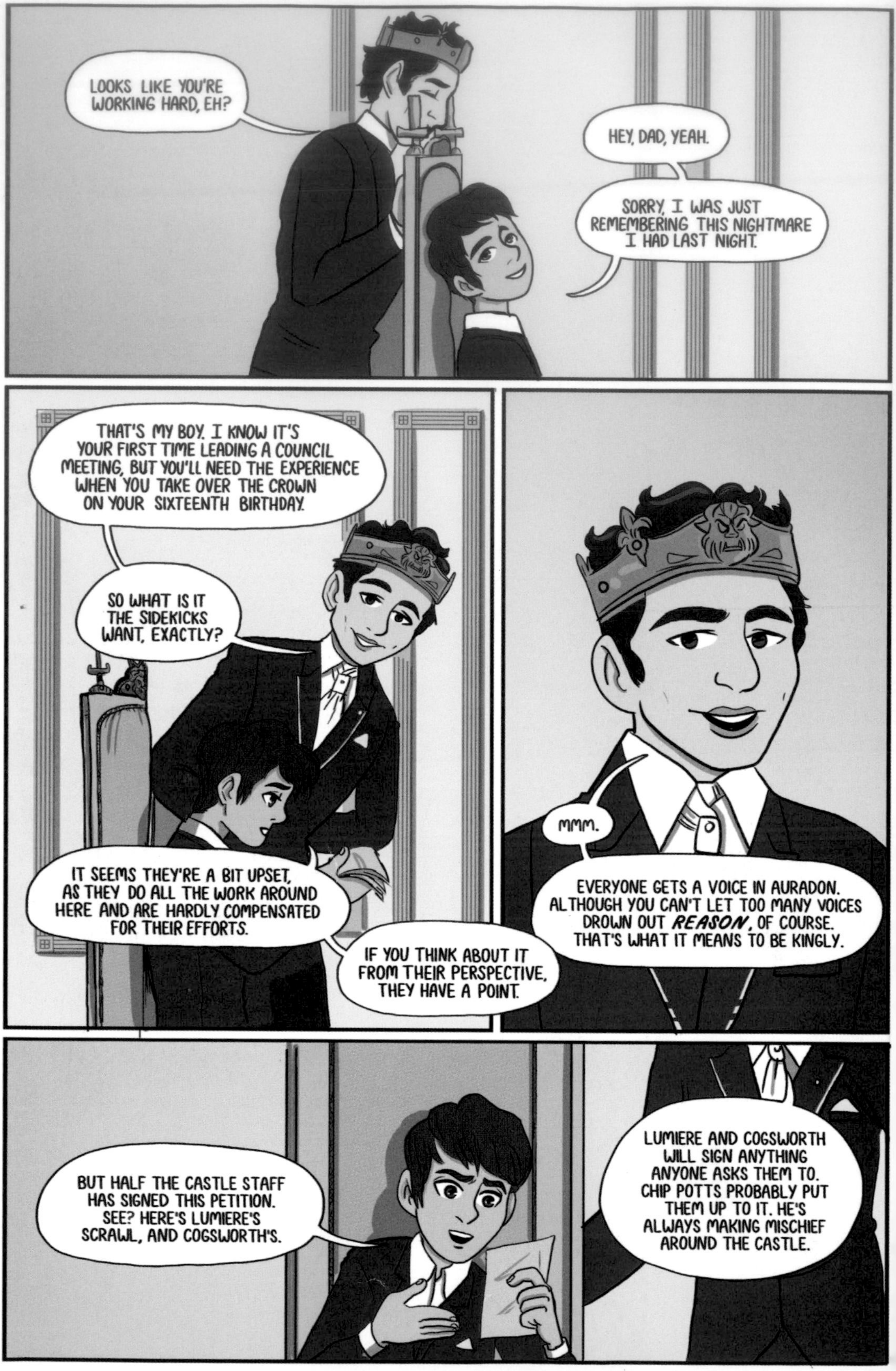
LOOKS LIKE YOU'RE WORKING HARD, EH?
HEY, DAD, YEAH.
SORRY, I WAS JUST REMEMBERING THIS NIGHTMARE I HAD LAST NIGHT.
THAT'S MY BOY. I KNOW IT'S YOUR FIRST TIME LEADING A COUNCIL MEETING, BUT YOU'LL NEED THE EXPERIENCE WHEN YOU TAKE OVER THE CROWN ON YOUR SIXTEENTH BIRTHDAY.
SO WHAT IS IT THE SIDEKICKS WANT, EXACTLY?
IT SEEMS THEY'RE A BIT UPSET, AS THEY DO ALL THE WORK AROUND HERE AND ARE HARDLY COMPENSATED FOR THEIR EFFORTS.
IF YOU THINK ABOUT IT FROM THEIR PERSPECTIVE, THEY HAVE A POINT.
MMM.
EVERYONE GETS A VOICE IN AURADON. ALTHOUGH YOU CAN'T LET TOO MANY VOICES DROWN OUT *REASON*, OF COURSE. THAT'S WHAT IT MEANS TO BE KINGLY.
BUT HALF THE CASTLE STAFF HAS SIGNED THIS PETITION. SEE? HERE'S LUMIERE'S SCRAWL, AND COGSWORTH'S.
LUMIERE AND COGSWORTH WILL SIGN ANYTHING ANYONE ASKS THEM TO. CHIP POTTS PROBABLY PUT THEM UP TO IT. HE'S ALWAYS MAKING MISCHIEF AROUND THE CASTLE.

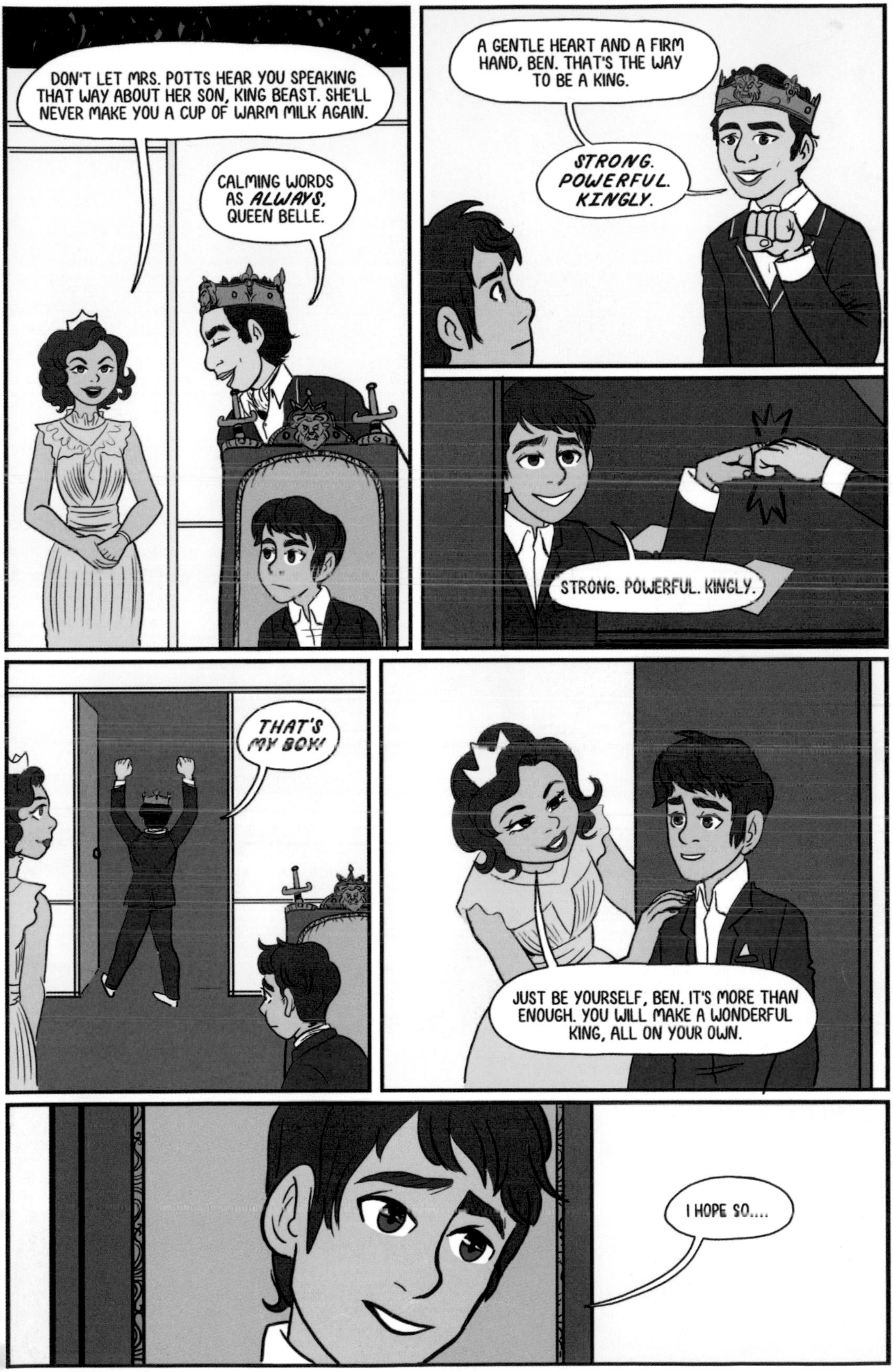
DON'T LET MRS. POTTS HEAR YOU SPEAKING THAT WAY ABOUT HER SON, KING BEAST. SHE'LL NEVER MAKE YOU A CUP OF WARM MILK AGAIN.
CALMING WORDS AS *ALWAYS*, QUEEN BELLE.
A GENTLE HEART AND A FIRM HAND, BEN. THAT'S THE WAY TO BE A KING.
STRONG. POWERFUL. KINGLY.
STRONG. POWERFUL. KINGLY.
THAT'S MY BOY!
JUST BE YOURSELF, BEN. IT'S MORE THAN ENOUGH. YOU WILL MAKE A WONDERFUL KING, ALL ON YOUR OWN.
I HOPE SO....

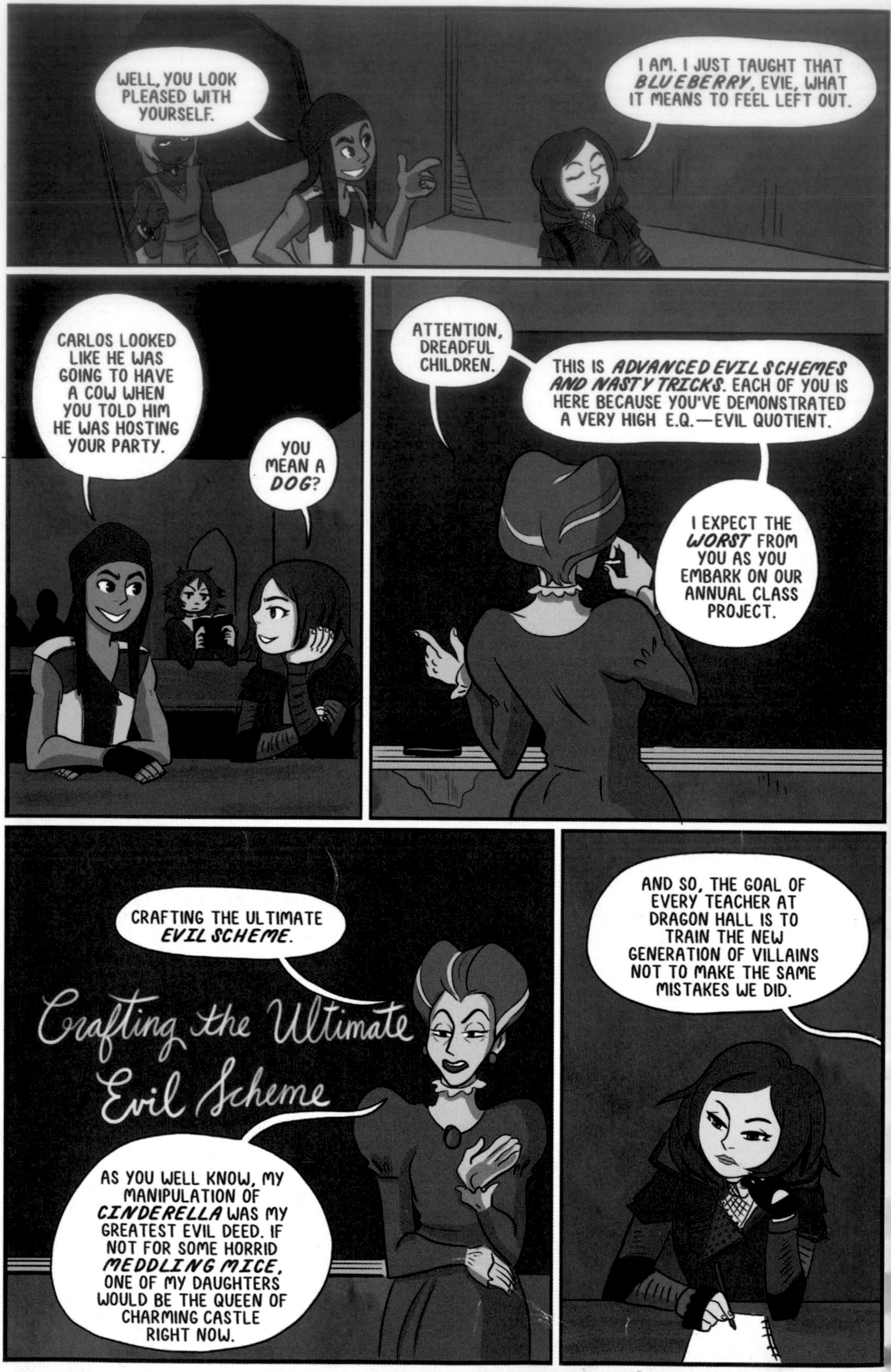
WELL, YOU LOOK PLEASED WITH YOURSELF.
I AM. I JUST TAUGHT THAT BLUEBERRY, EVIE, WHAT IT MEANS TO FEEL LEFT OUT.
CARLOS LOOKED LIKE HE WAS GOING TO HAVE A COW WHEN YOU TOLD HIM HE WAS HOSTING YOUR PARTY.
YOU MEAN A DOG?
ATTENTION, DREADFUL CHILDREN.
THIS IS ADVANCED EVIL SCHEMES AND NASTY TRICKS. EACH OF YOU IS HERE BECAUSE YOU'VE DEMONSTRATED A VERY HIGH E.Q.—EVIL QUOTIENT.
I EXPECT THE WORST FROM YOU AS YOU EMBARK ON OUR ANNUAL CLASS PROJECT.
CRAFTING THE ULTIMATE EVIL SCHEME.
Crafting the Ultimate Evil Scheme
AS YOU WELL KNOW, MY MANIPULATION OF CINDERELLA WAS MY GREATEST EVIL DEED. IF NOT FOR SOME HORRID MEDDLING MICE, ONE OF MY DAUGHTERS WOULD BE THE QUEEN OF CHARMING CASTLE RIGHT NOW.
AND SO, THE GOAL OF EVERY TEACHER AT DRAGON HALL IS TO TRAIN THE NEW GENERATION OF VILLAINS NOT TO MAKE THE SAME MISTAKES WE DID.

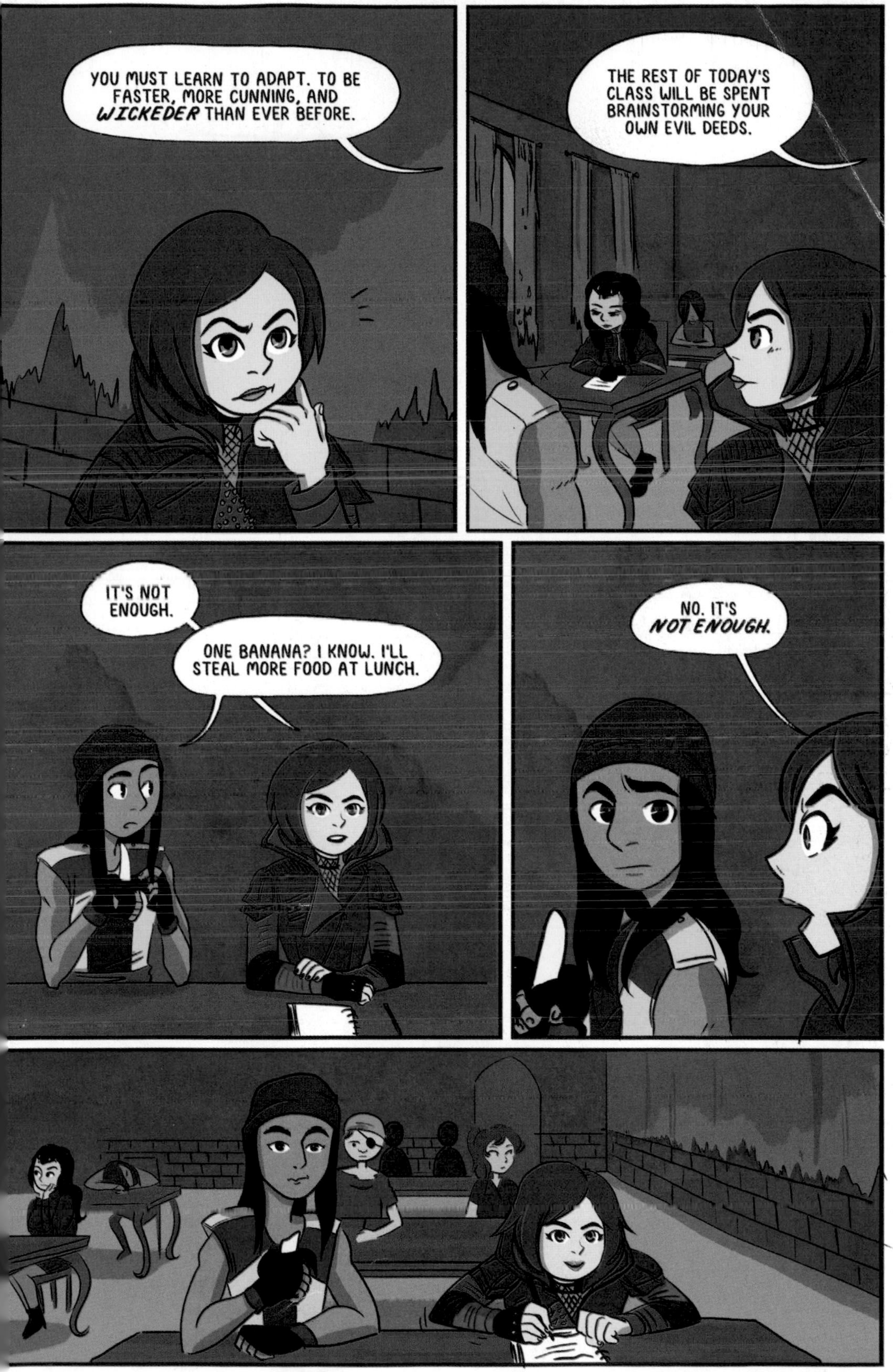
YOU MUST LEARN TO ADAPT. TO BE FASTER, MORE CUNNING, AND *WICKEDER* THAN EVER BEFORE.
THE REST OF TODAY'S CLASS WILL BE SPENT BRAINSTORMING YOUR OWN EVIL DEEDS.
IT'S NOT ENOUGH.
ONE BANANA? I KNOW. I'LL STEAL MORE FOOD AT LUNCH.
NO. IT'S *NOT ENOUGH.*

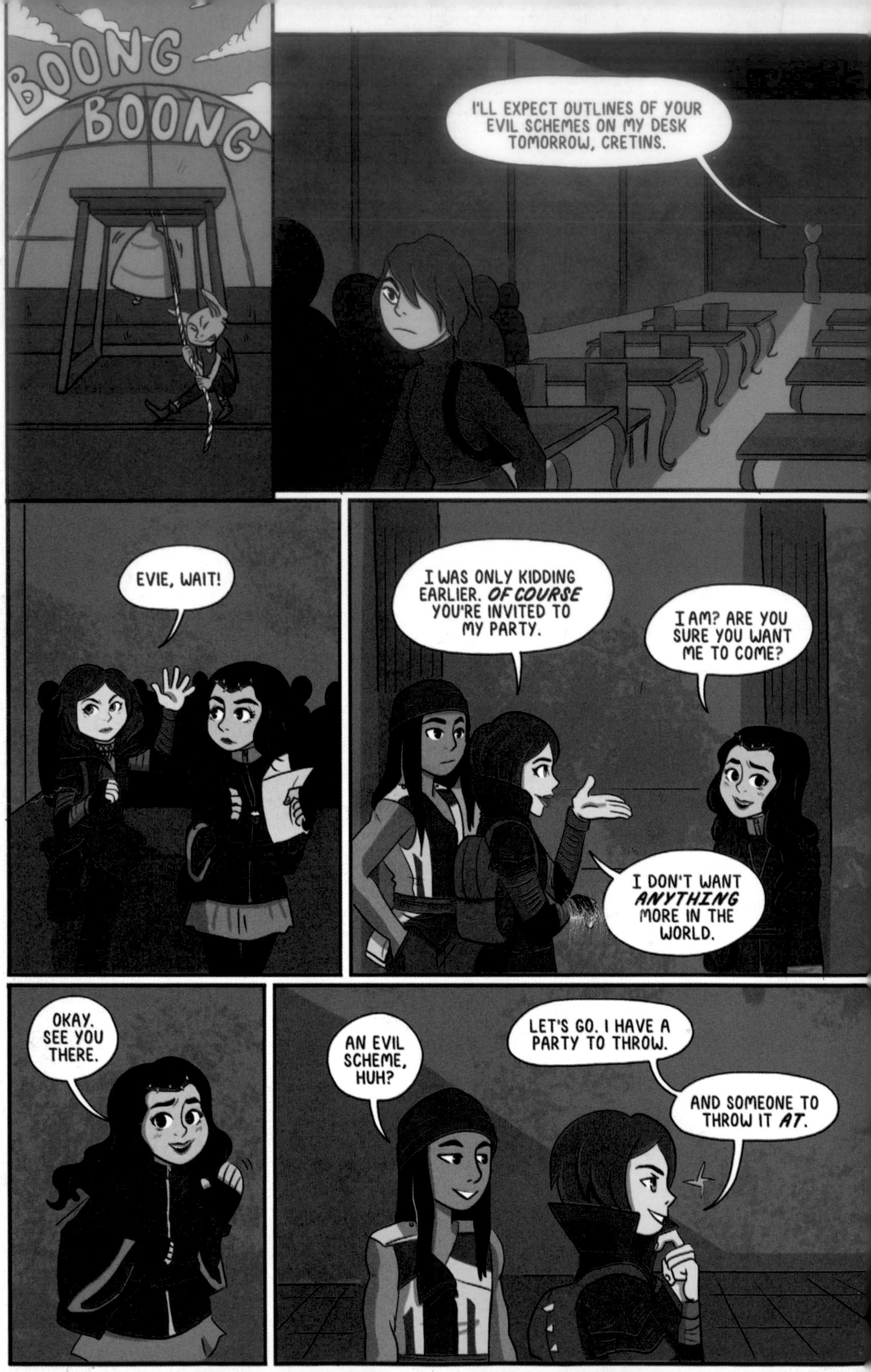
BOONG
BOONG
I'LL EXPECT OUTLINES OF YOUR EVIL SCHEMES ON MY DESK TOMORROW, CRETINS.
EVIE, WAIT!
I WAS ONLY KIDDING EARLIER. OF COURSE YOU'RE INVITED TO MY PARTY.
I AM? ARE YOU SURE YOU WANT ME TO COME?
I DON'T WANT ANYTHING MORE IN THE WORLD.
OKAY. SEE YOU THERE.
AN EVIL SCHEME, HUH?
LET'S GO. I HAVE A PARTY TO THROW.
AND SOMEONE TO THROW IT AT.

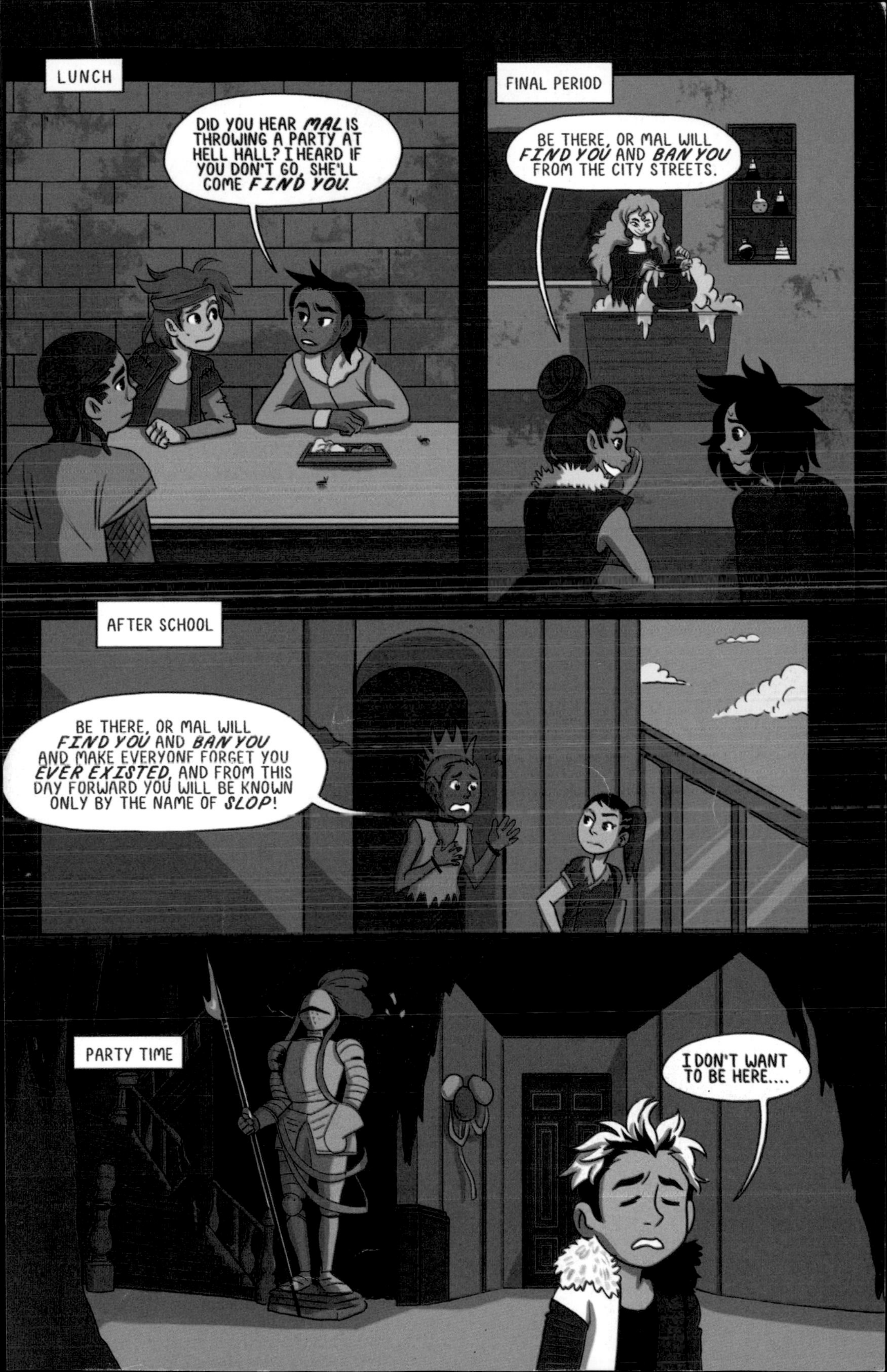
LUNCH
DID YOU HEAR MAL IS THROWING A PARTY AT HELL HALL? I HEARD IF YOU DON'T GO, SHE'LL COME FIND YOU.
FINAL PERIOD
BE THERE, OR MAL WILL FIND YOU AND BAN YOU FROM THE CITY STREETS.
AFTER SCHOOL
BE THERE, OR MAL WILL FIND YOU AND BAN YOU AND MAKE EVERYONE FORGET YOU EVER EXISTED, AND FROM THIS DAY FORWARD YOU WILL BE KNOWN ONLY BY THE NAME OF SLOP!
PARTY TIME
I DON'T WANT TO BE HERE....

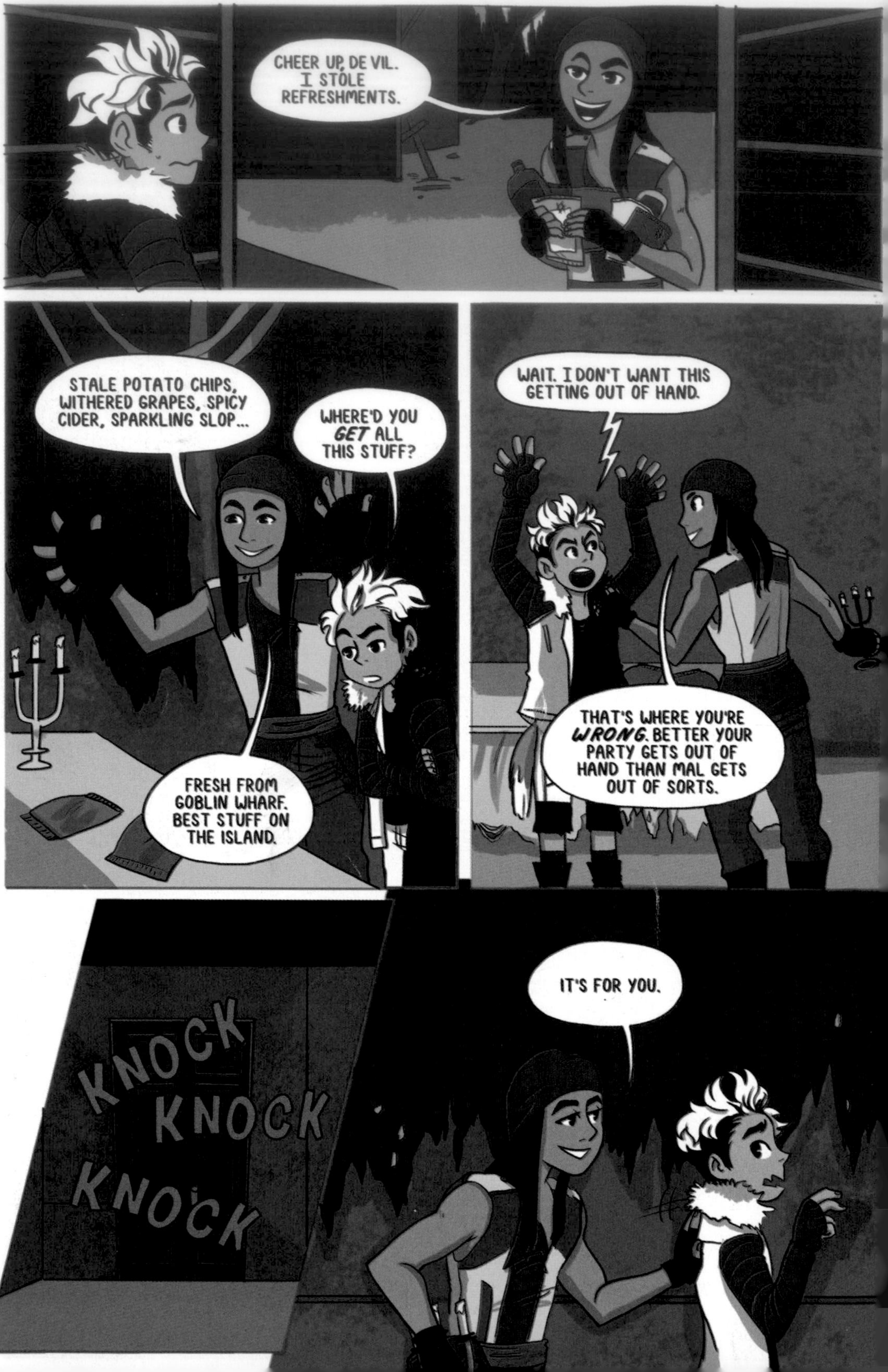
CHEER UP, DE VIL. I STOLE REFRESHMENTS.
STALE POTATO CHIPS, WITHERED GRAPES, SPICY CIDER, SPARKLING SLOP...
WHERE'D YOU GET ALL THIS STUFF?
FRESH FROM GOBLIN WHARF. BEST STUFF ON THE ISLAND.
WAIT. I DON'T WANT THIS GETTING OUT OF HAND.
THAT'S WHERE YOU'RE WRONG. BETTER YOUR PARTY GETS OUT OF HAND THAN MAL GETS OUT OF SORTS.
KNOCK KNOCK KNOCK
IT'S FOR YOU.

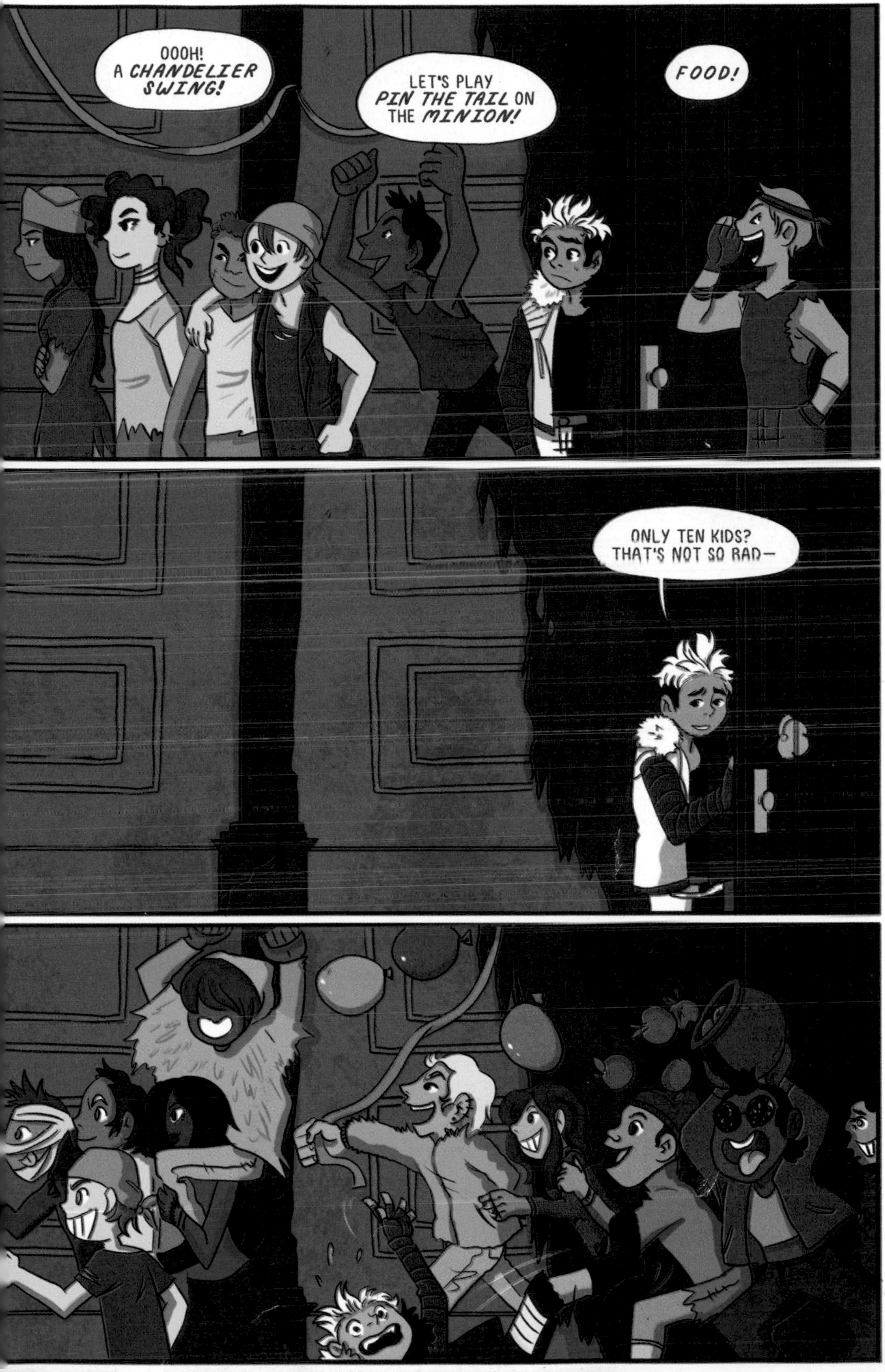
OOOH! A CHANDELIER SWING!
LET'S PLAY PIN THE TAIL ON THE MINION!
FOOD!
ONLY TEN KIDS? THAT'S NOT SO BAD—

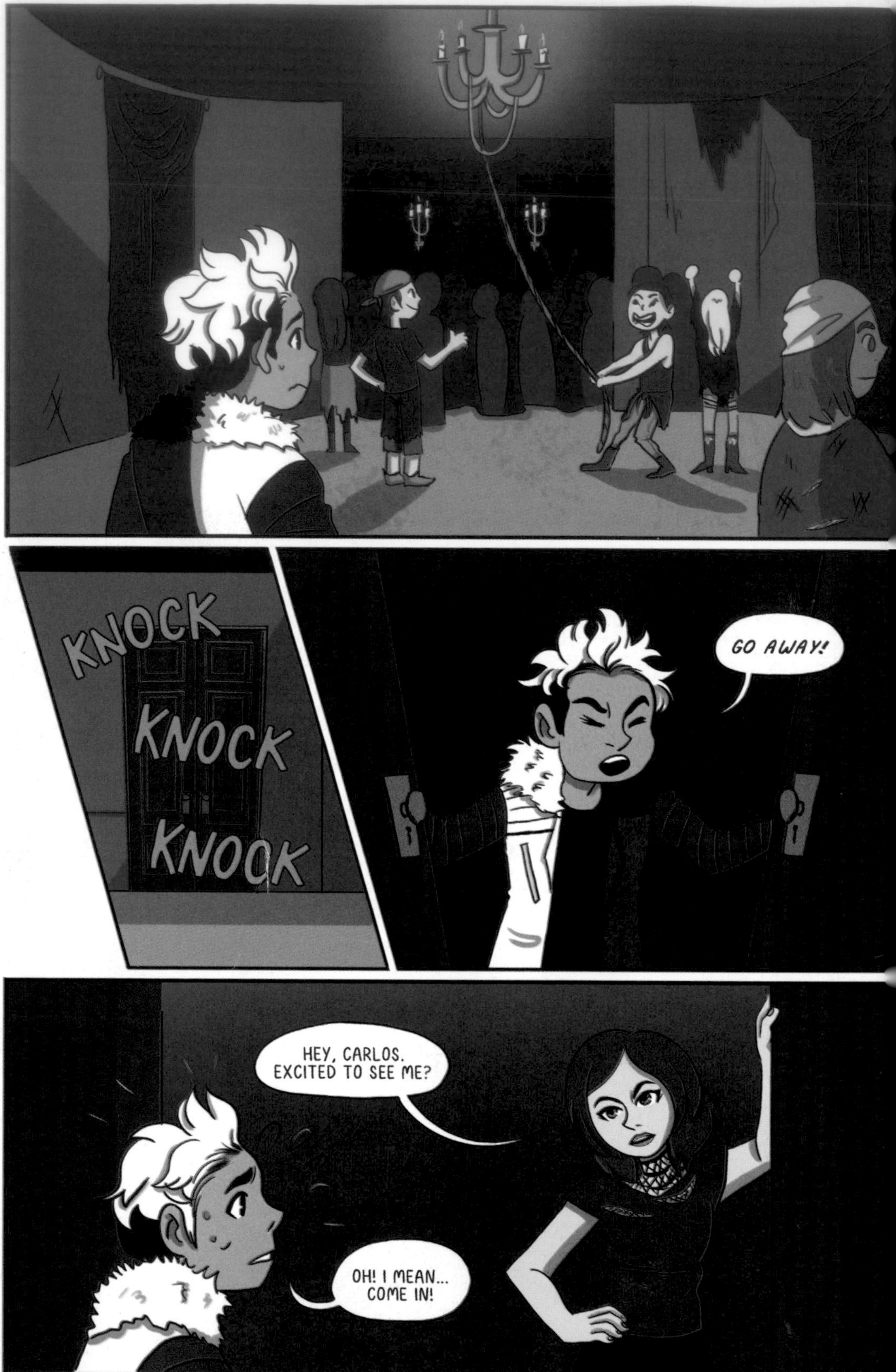
KNOCK
KNOCK
KNOCK
GO AWAY!
HEY, CARLOS. EXCITED TO SEE ME?
OH! I MEAN... COME IN!

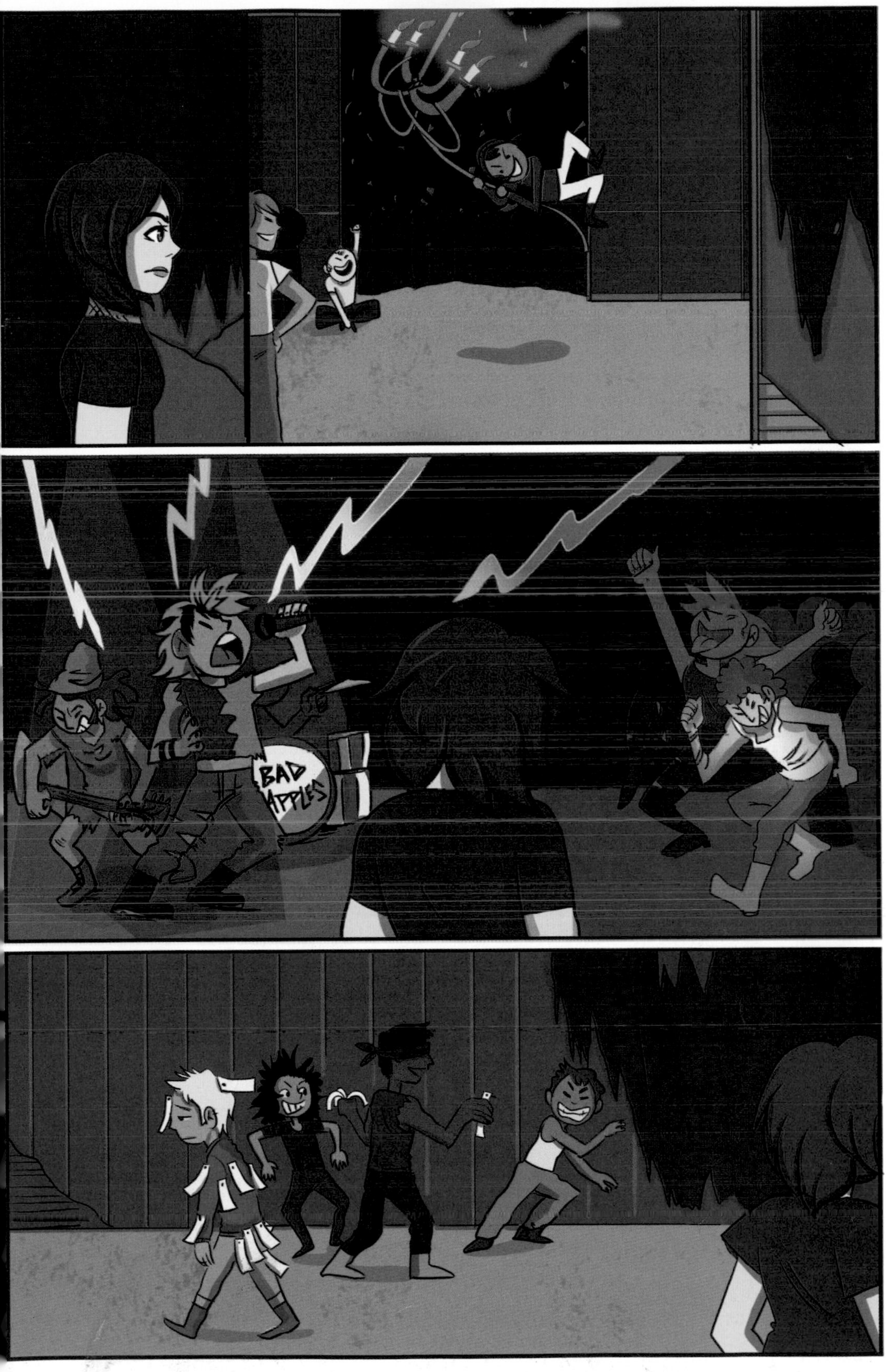
BAD APPLES

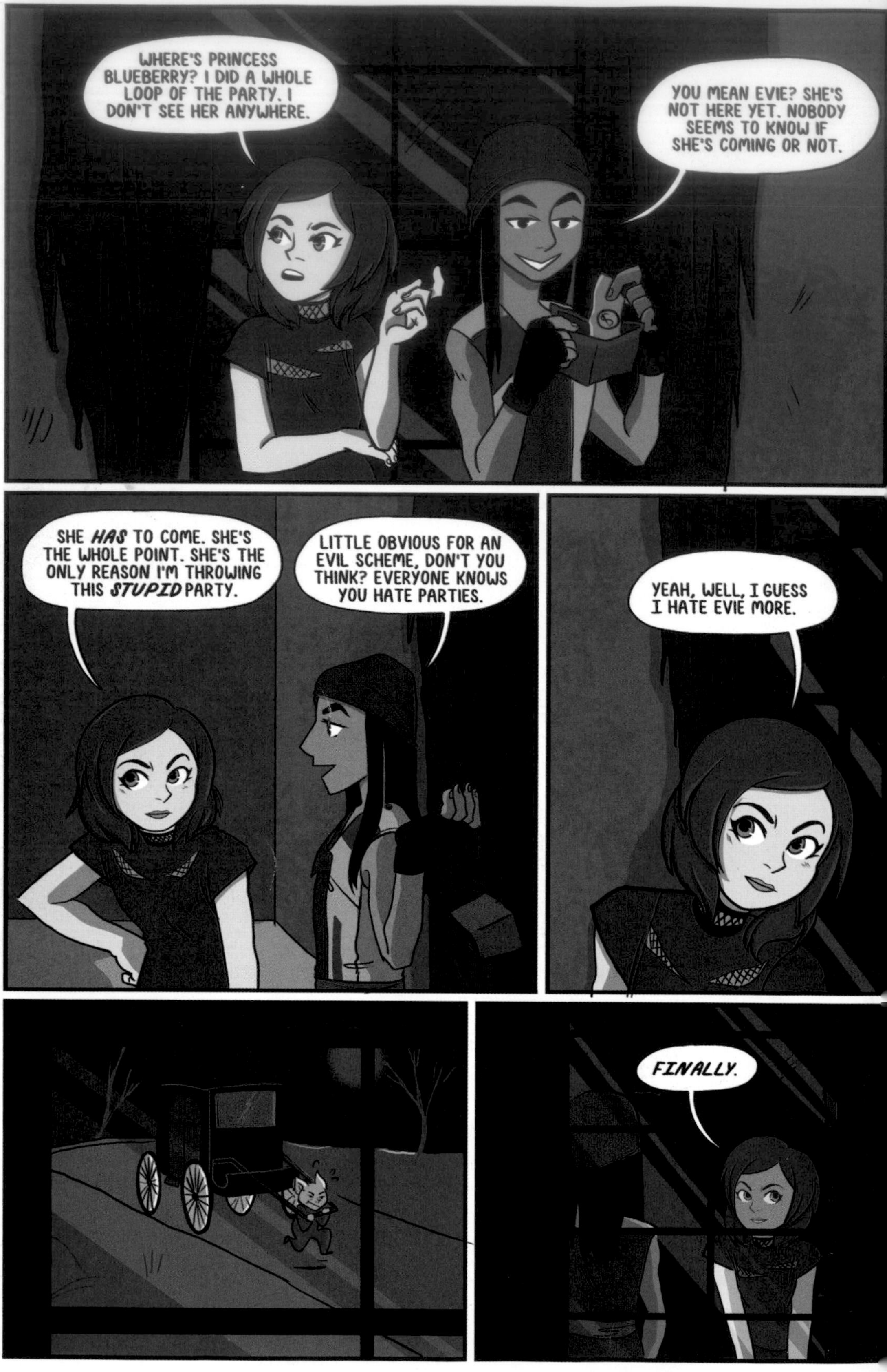
WHERE'S PRINCESS BLUEBERRY? I DID A WHOLE LOOP OF THE PARTY. I DON'T SEE HER ANYWHERE.
YOU MEAN EVIE? SHE'S NOT HERE YET. NOBODY SEEMS TO KNOW IF SHE'S COMING OR NOT.
SHE *HAS* TO COME. SHE'S THE WHOLE POINT. SHE'S THE ONLY REASON I'M THROWING THIS *STUPID* PARTY.
LITTLE OBVIOUS FOR AN EVIL SCHEME, DON'T YOU THINK? EVERYONE KNOWS YOU HATE PARTIES.
YEAH, WELL, I GUESS I HATE EVIE MORE.
FINALLY.

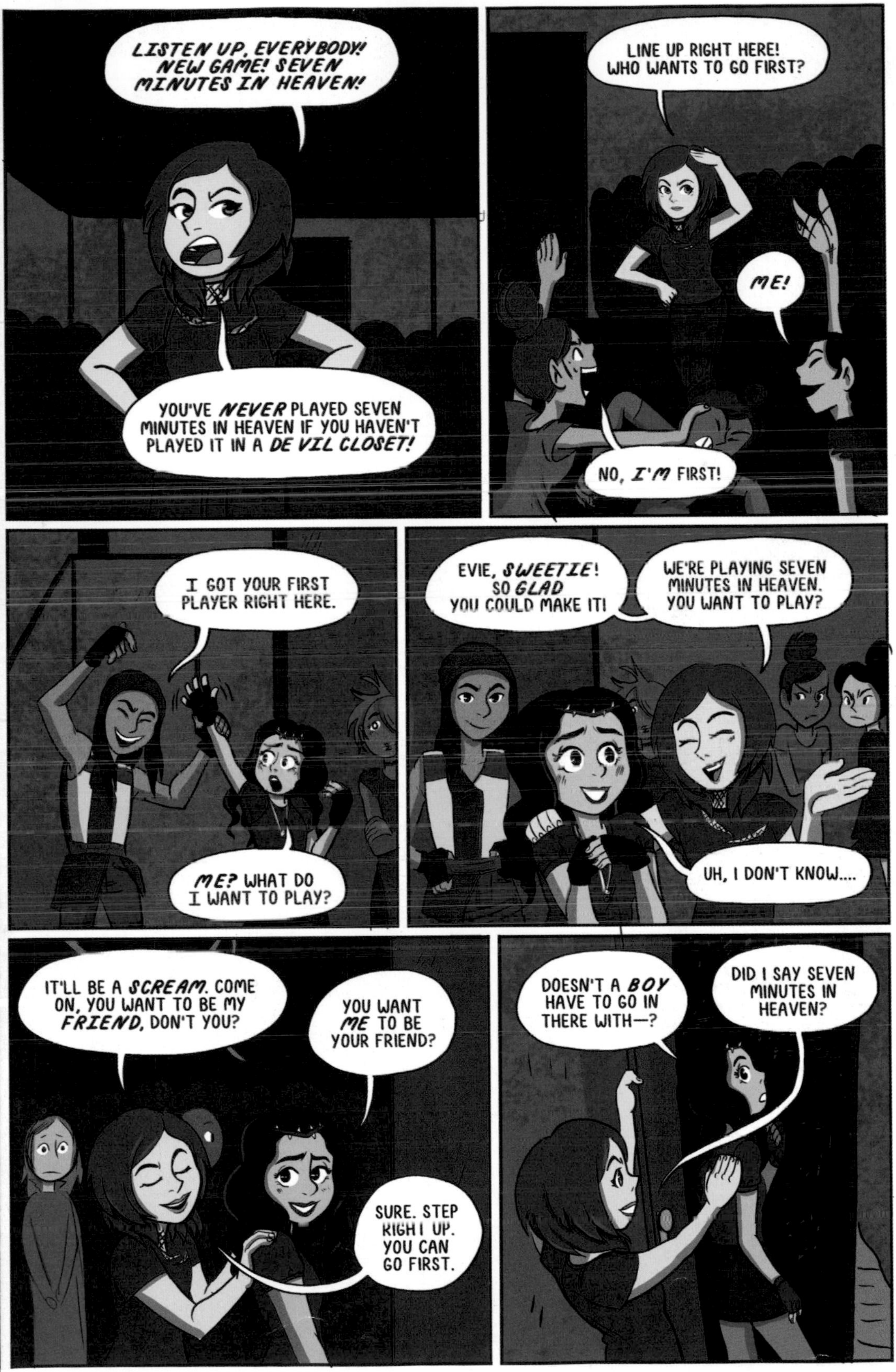
LISTEN UP, EVERYBODY! NEW GAME! SEVEN MINUTES IN HEAVEN!
YOU'VE NEVER PLAYED SEVEN MINUTES IN HEAVEN IF YOU HAVEN'T PLAYED IT IN A DE VIL CLOSET!
LINE UP RIGHT HERE! WHO WANTS TO GO FIRST?
ME!
NO, I'M FIRST!
I GOT YOUR FIRST PLAYER RIGHT HERE.
ME? WHAT DO I WANT TO PLAY?
EVIE, SWEETIE! SO GLAD YOU COULD MAKE IT!
WE'RE PLAYING SEVEN MINUTES IN HEAVEN. YOU WANT TO PLAY?
UH, I DON'T KNOW....
IT'LL BE A SCREAM. COME ON, YOU WANT TO BE MY FRIEND, DON'T YOU?
YOU WANT ME TO BE YOUR FRIEND?
SURE. STEP RIGHT UP. YOU CAN GO FIRST.
DOESN'T A BOY HAVE TO GO IN THERE WITH—?
DID I SAY SEVEN MINUTES IN HEAVEN?

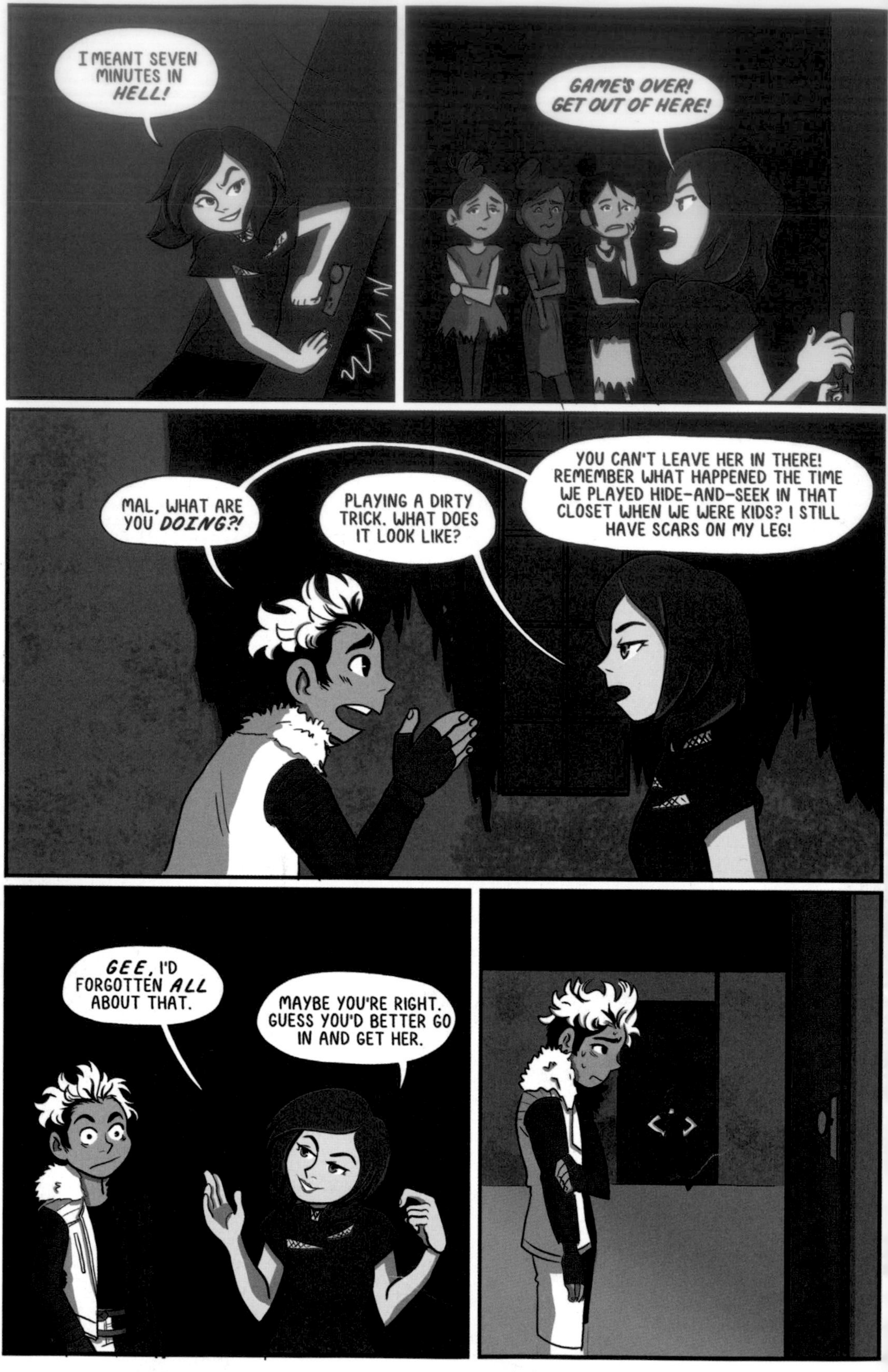
I MEANT SEVEN MINUTES IN *HELL!*
GAME'S OVER! GET OUT OF HERE!
MAL, WHAT ARE YOU *DOING?!*
PLAYING A DIRTY TRICK. WHAT DOES IT LOOK LIKE?
YOU CAN'T LEAVE HER IN THERE! REMEMBER WHAT HAPPENED THE TIME WE PLAYED HIDE-AND-SEEK IN THAT CLOSET WHEN WE WERE KIDS? I STILL HAVE SCARS ON MY LEG!
GEE, I'D FORGOTTEN *ALL* ABOUT THAT.
MAYBE YOU'RE RIGHT. GUESS YOU'D BETTER GO IN AND GET HER.

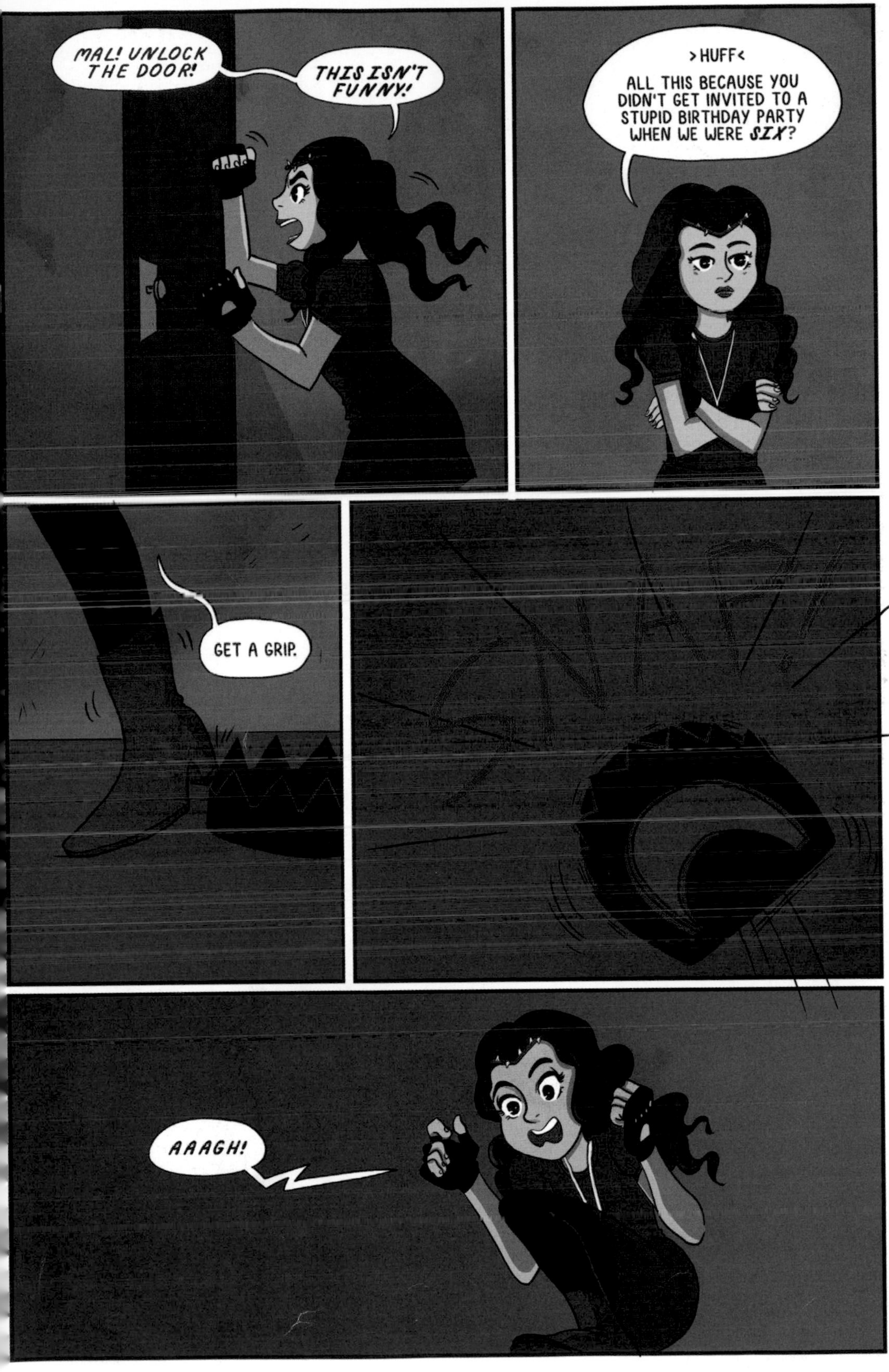
MAL! UNLOCK THE DOOR!
THIS ISN'T FUNNY!
>HUFF<
ALL THIS BECAUSE YOU DIDN'T GET INVITED TO A STUPID BIRTHDAY PARTY WHEN WE WERE *SIX*?
GET A GRIP.
SNAP!
AAAGH!

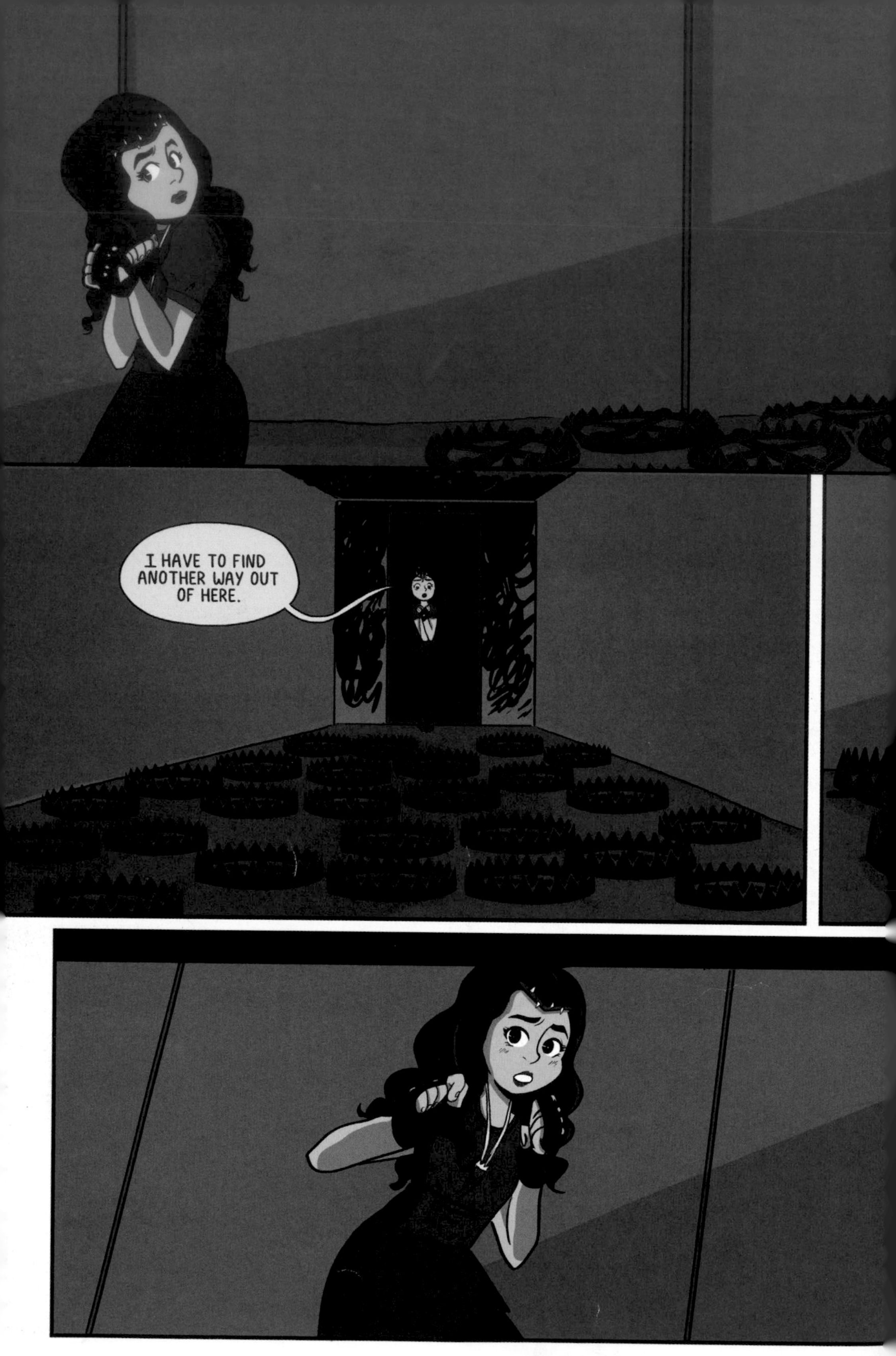
I HAVE TO FIND ANOTHER WAY OUT OF HERE.

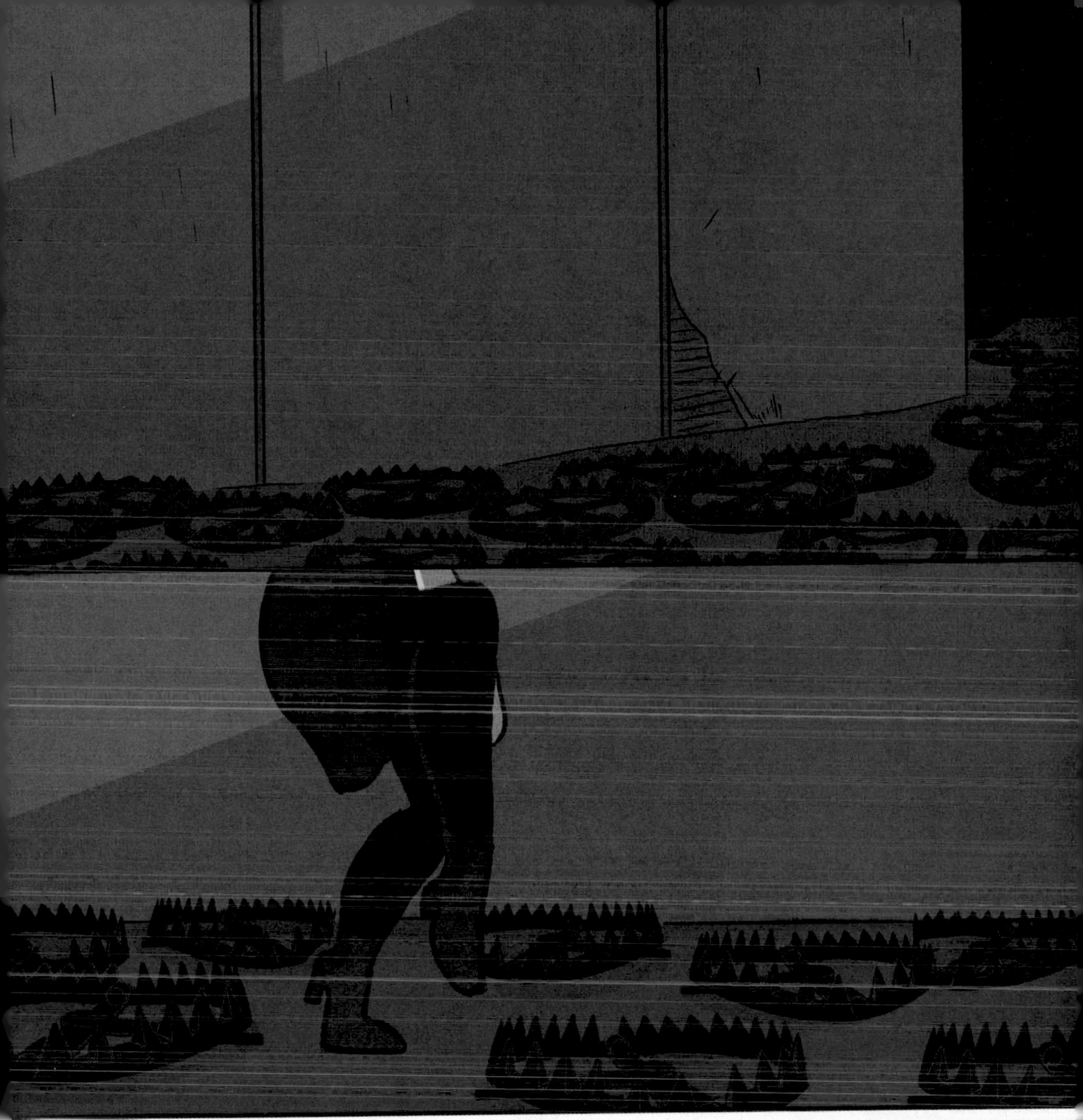
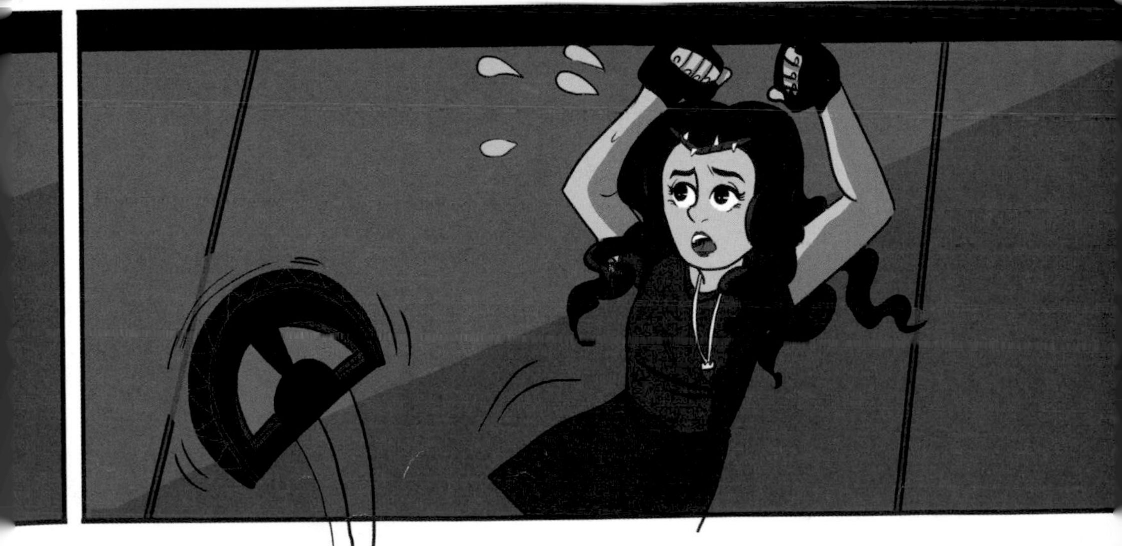

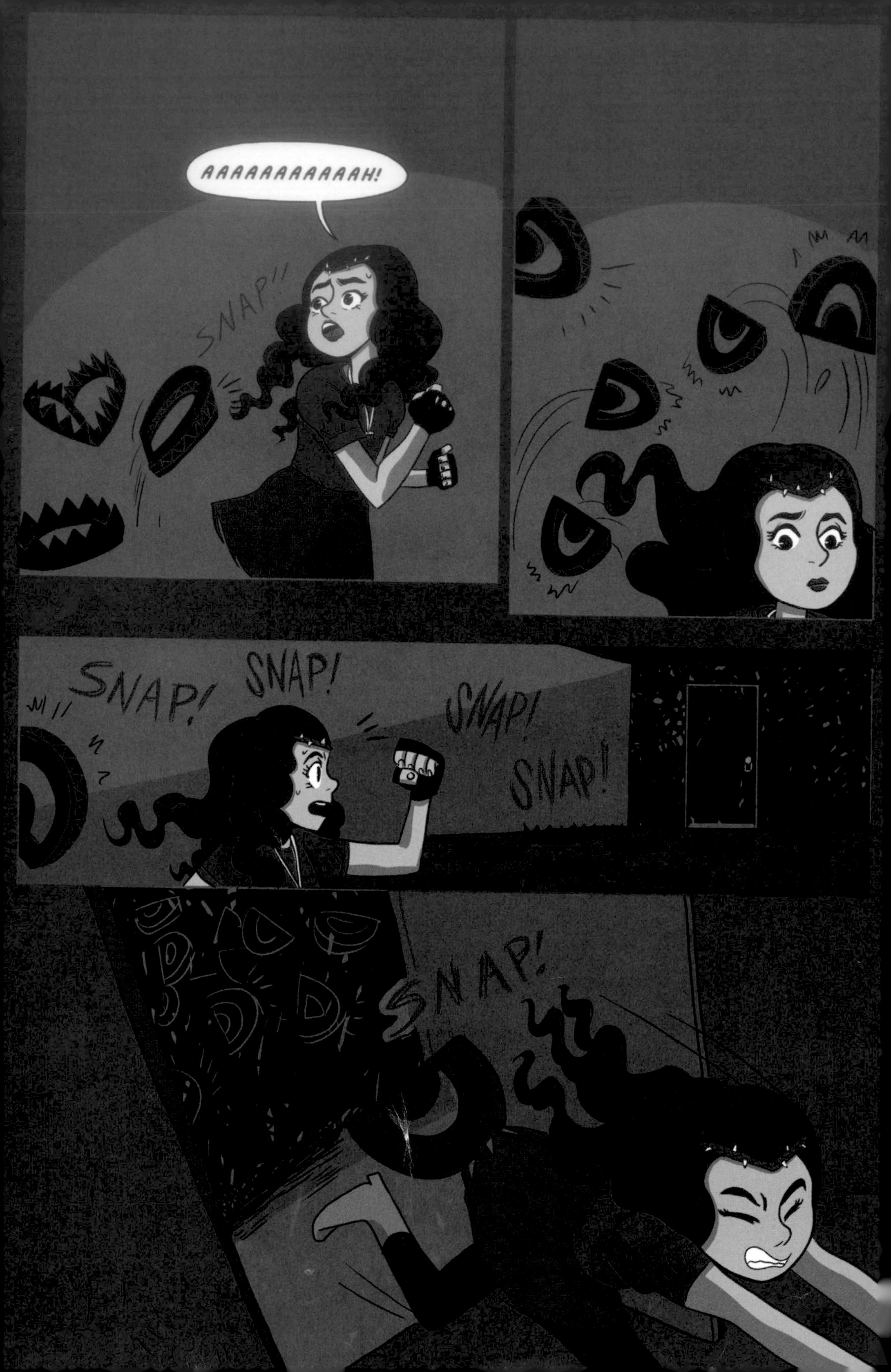
AAAAAAAAAAAAH!
SNAP!!
SNAP!
SNAP!
SNAP!
SNAP!
SNAP!

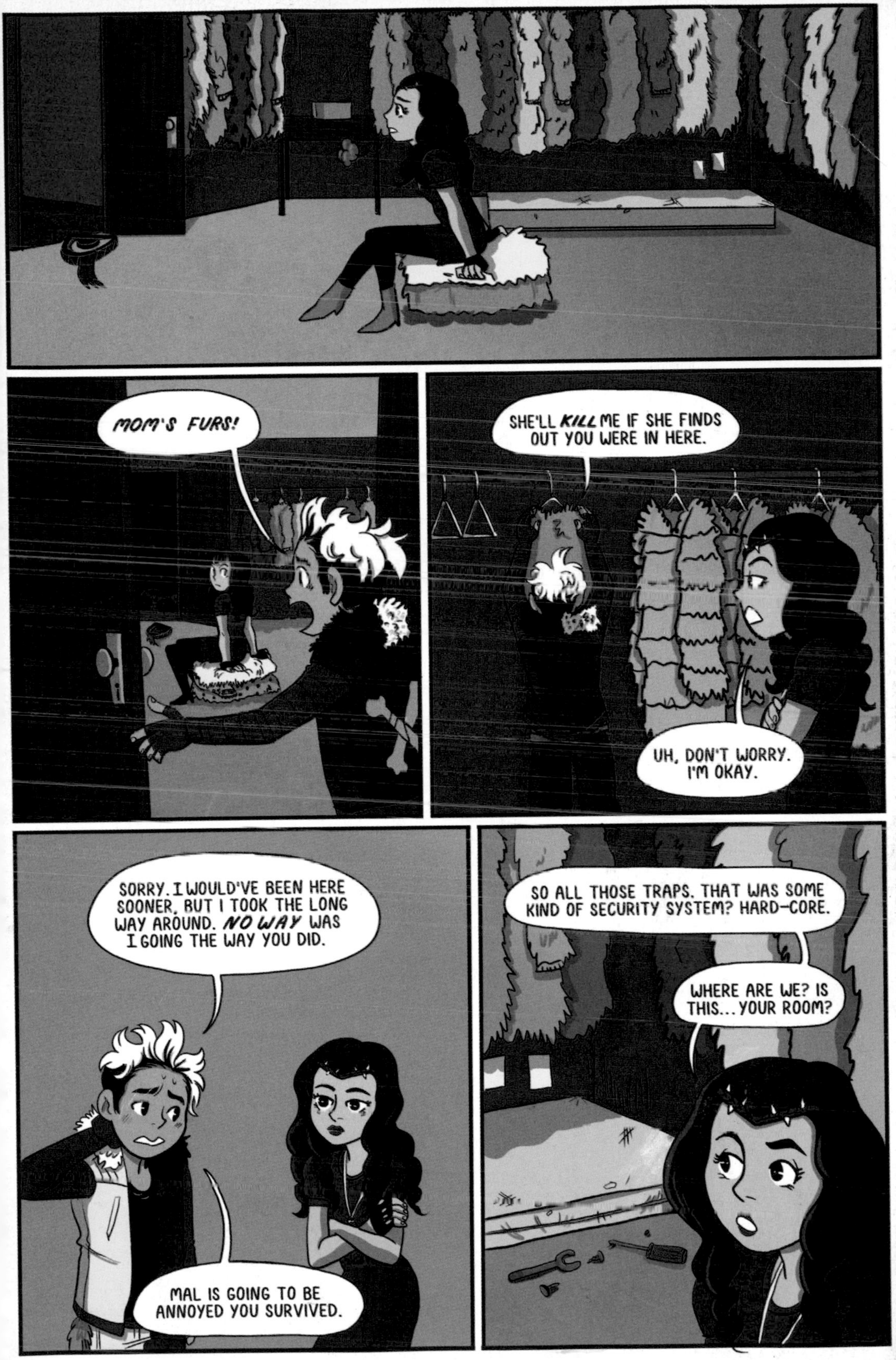
MOM'S FURS!
SHE'LL KILL ME IF SHE FINDS OUT YOU WERE IN HERE.
UH, DON'T WORRY. I'M OKAY.
SORRY. I WOULD'VE BEEN HERE SOONER, BUT I TOOK THE LONG WAY AROUND. NO WAY WAS I GOING THE WAY YOU DID.
MAL IS GOING TO BE ANNOYED YOU SURVIVED.
SO ALL THOSE TRAPS. THAT WAS SOME KIND OF SECURITY SYSTEM? HARD-CORE.
WHERE ARE WE? IS THIS... YOUR ROOM?

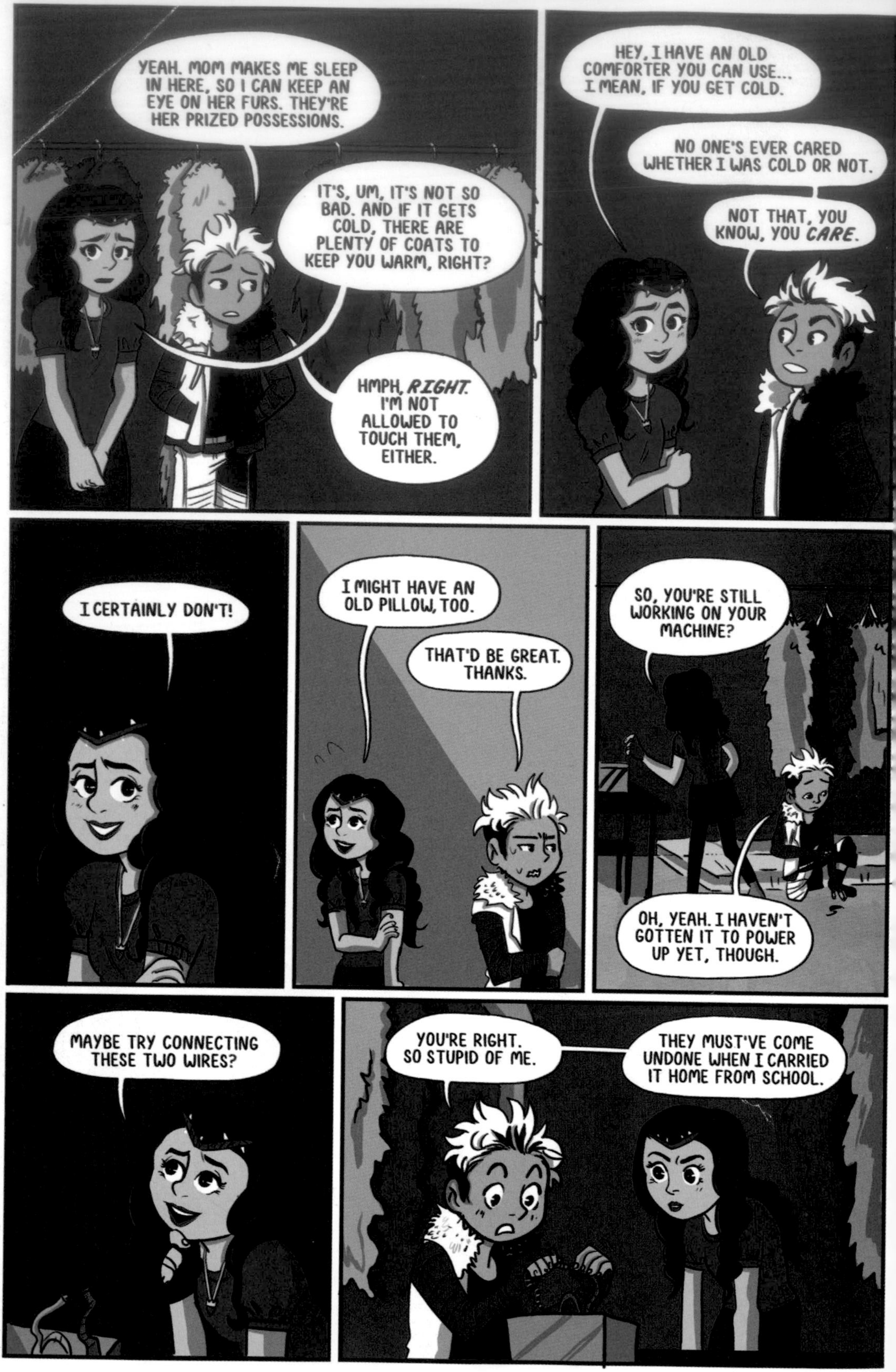
YEAH. MOM MAKES ME SLEEP IN HERE, SO I CAN KEEP AN EYE ON HER FURS. THEY'RE HER PRIZED POSSESSIONS.
IT'S, UM, IT'S NOT SO BAD. AND IF IT GETS COLD, THERE ARE PLENTY OF COATS TO KEEP YOU WARM, RIGHT?
HMPH, *RIGHT.* I'M NOT ALLOWED TO TOUCH THEM, EITHER.
HEY, I HAVE AN OLD COMFORTER YOU CAN USE... I MEAN, IF YOU GET COLD.
NO ONE'S EVER CARED WHETHER I WAS COLD OR NOT.
NOT THAT, YOU KNOW, YOU *CARE.*
I CERTAINLY DON'T!
I MIGHT HAVE AN OLD PILLOW, TOO.
THAT'D BE GREAT. THANKS.
SO, YOU'RE STILL WORKING ON YOUR MACHINE?
OH, YEAH. I HAVEN'T GOTTEN IT TO POWER UP YET, THOUGH.
MAYBE TRY CONNECTING THESE TWO WIRES?
YOU'RE RIGHT. SO STUPID OF ME.
THEY MUST'VE COME UNDONE WHEN I CARRIED IT HOME FROM SCHOOL.

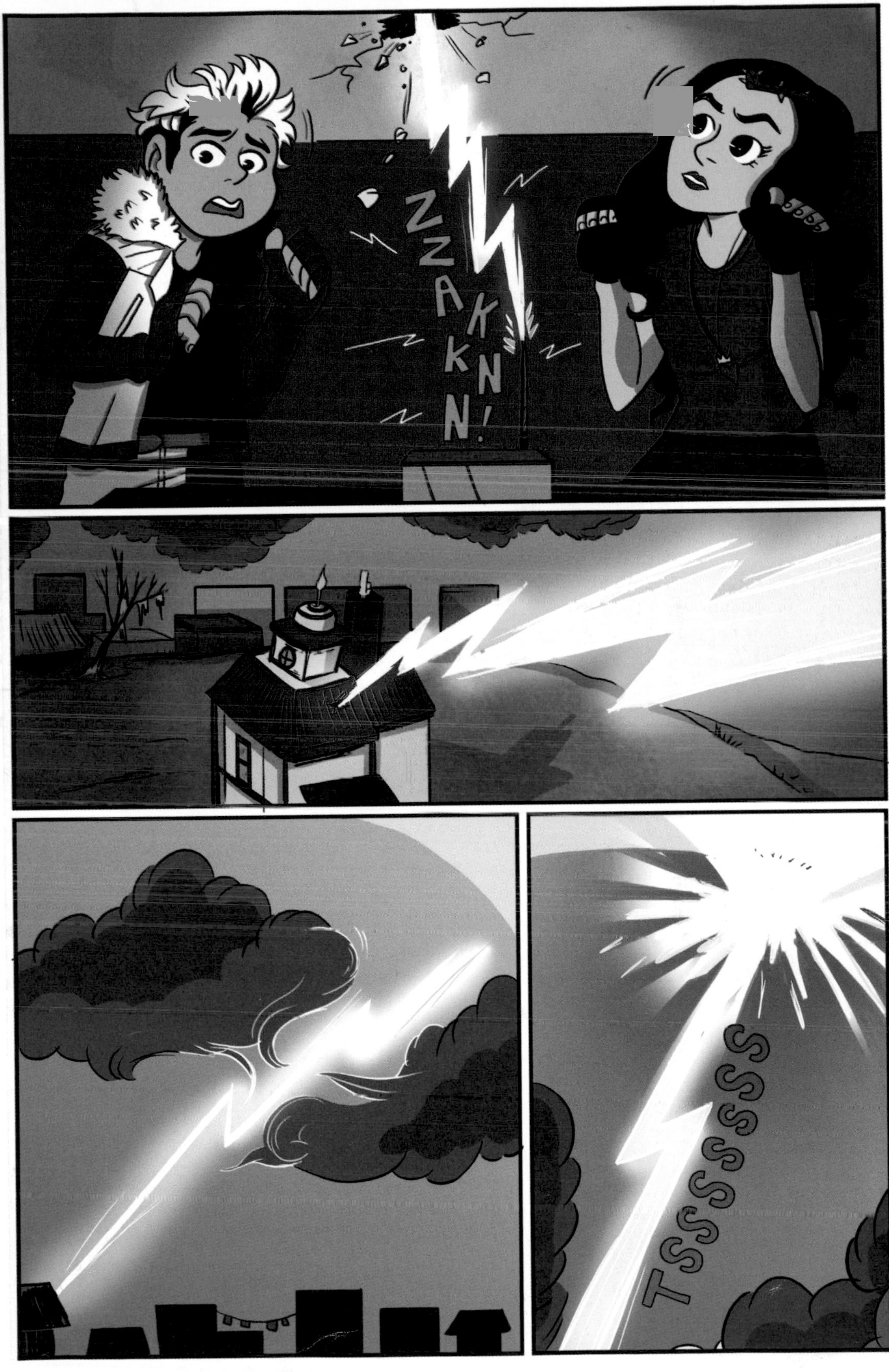

ZZAKKNN!
TSSSSSS

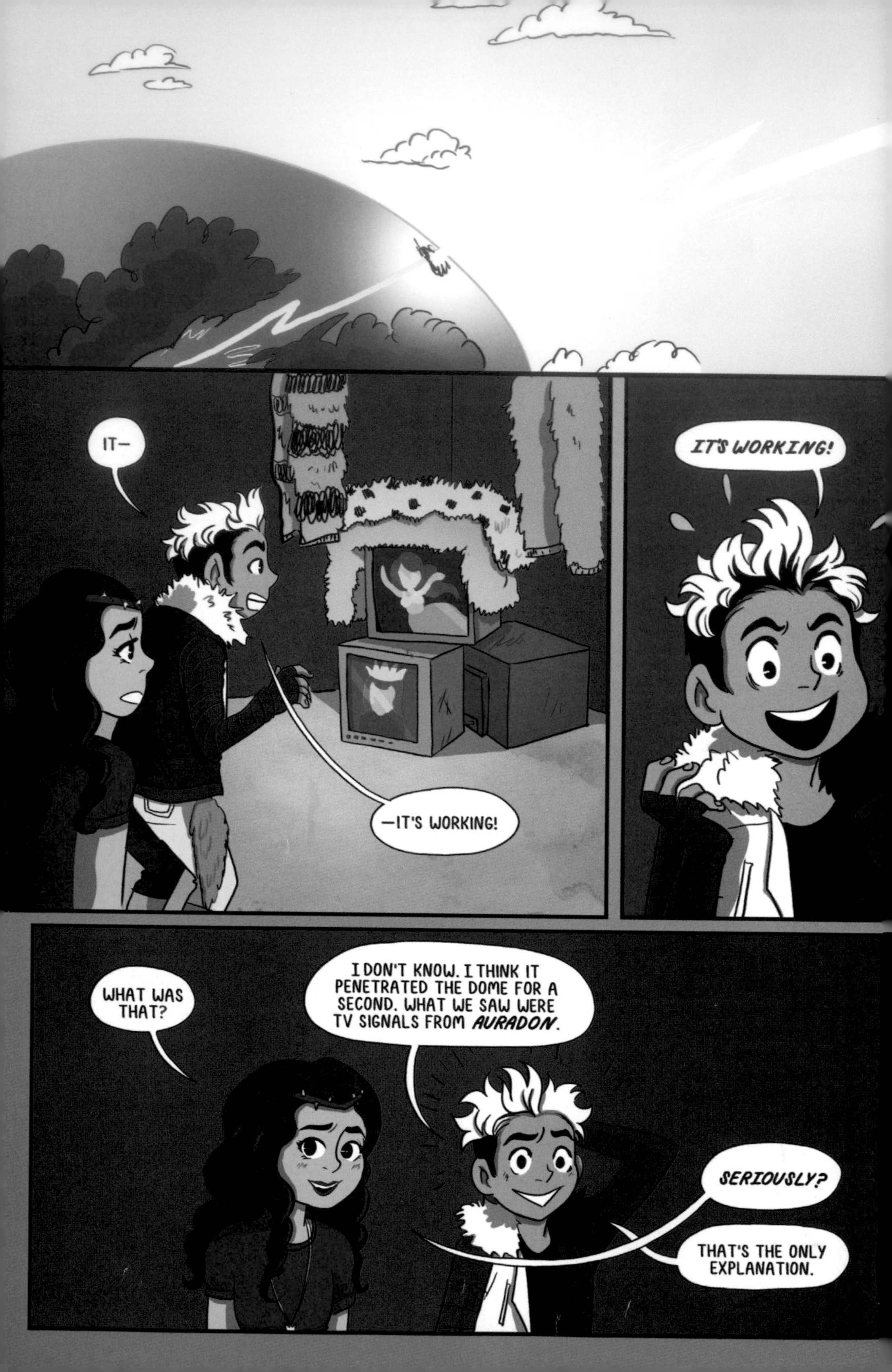
IT—
—IT'S WORKING!
IT'S WORKING!
WHAT WAS THAT?
I DON'T KNOW. I THINK IT PENETRATED THE DOME FOR A SECOND. WHAT WE SAW WERE TV SIGNALS FROM *AURADON*.
SERIOUSLY?
THAT'S THE ONLY EXPLANATION.

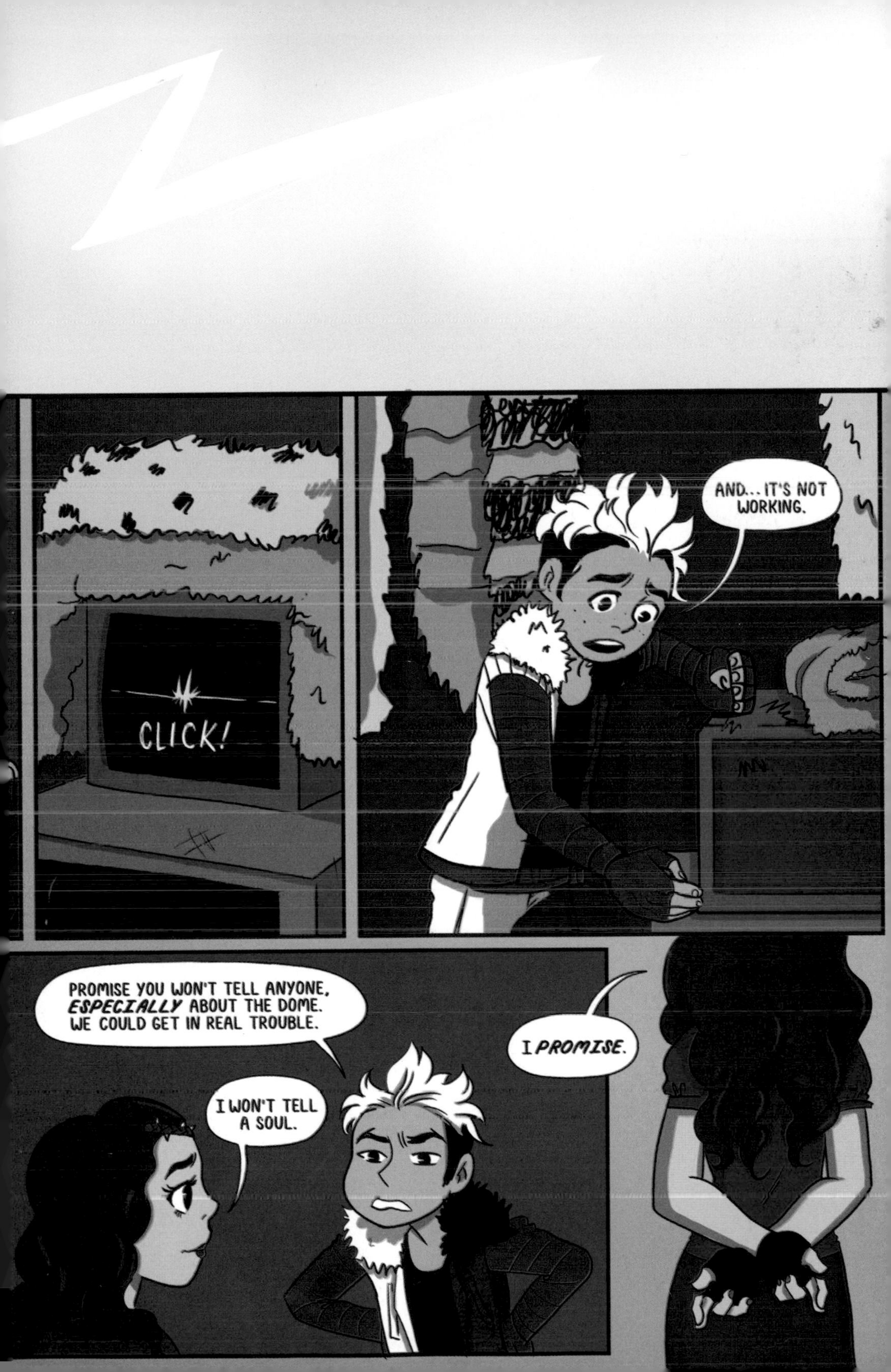
CLICK!
AND... IT'S NOT WORKING.
PROMISE YOU WON'T TELL ANYONE, ESPECIALLY ABOUT THE DOME. WE COULD GET IN REAL TROUBLE.
I WON'T TELL A SOUL.
I PROMISE.

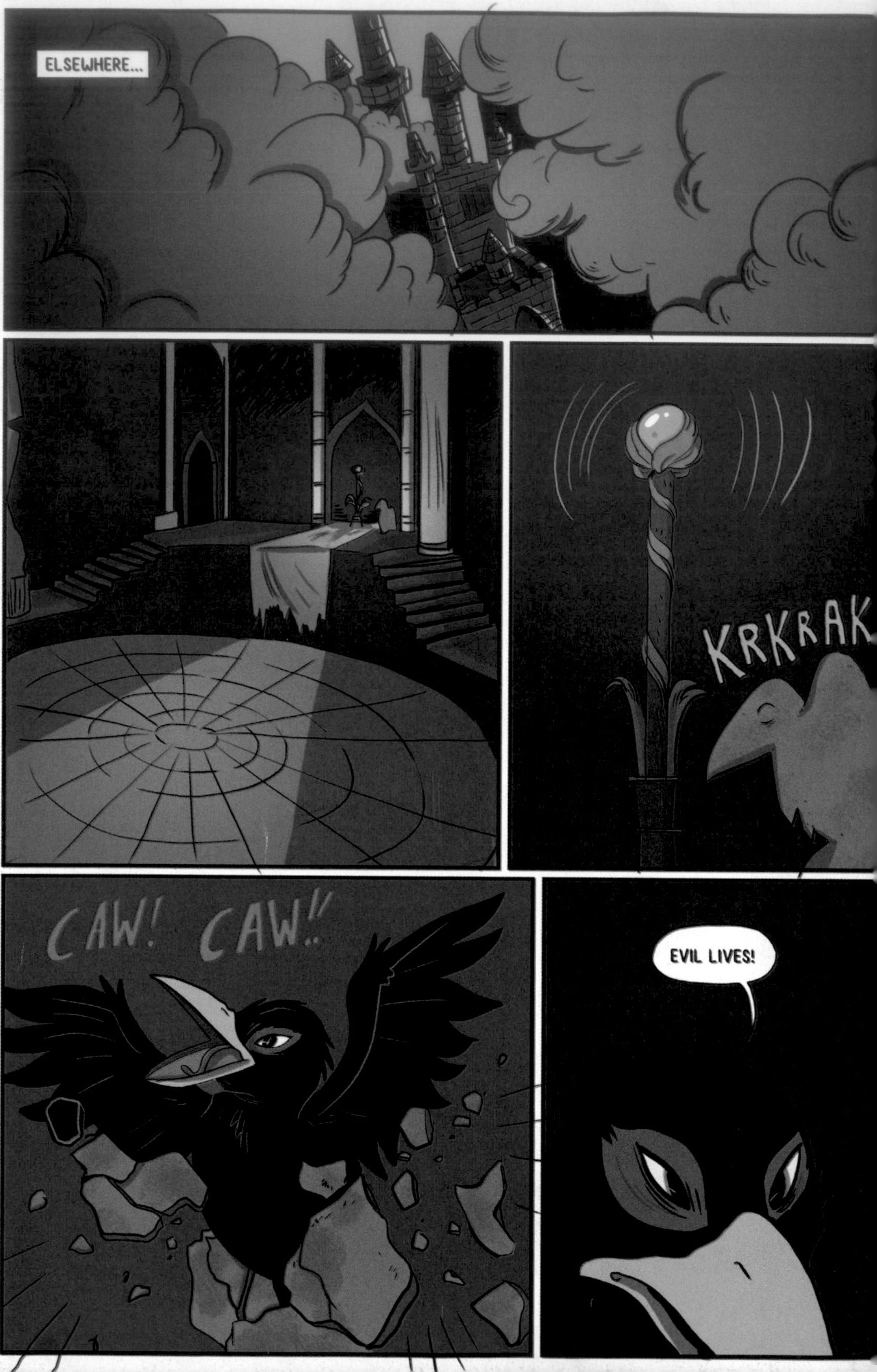
ELSEWHERE...
KRKRAK
CAW! CAW!!
EVIL LIVES!

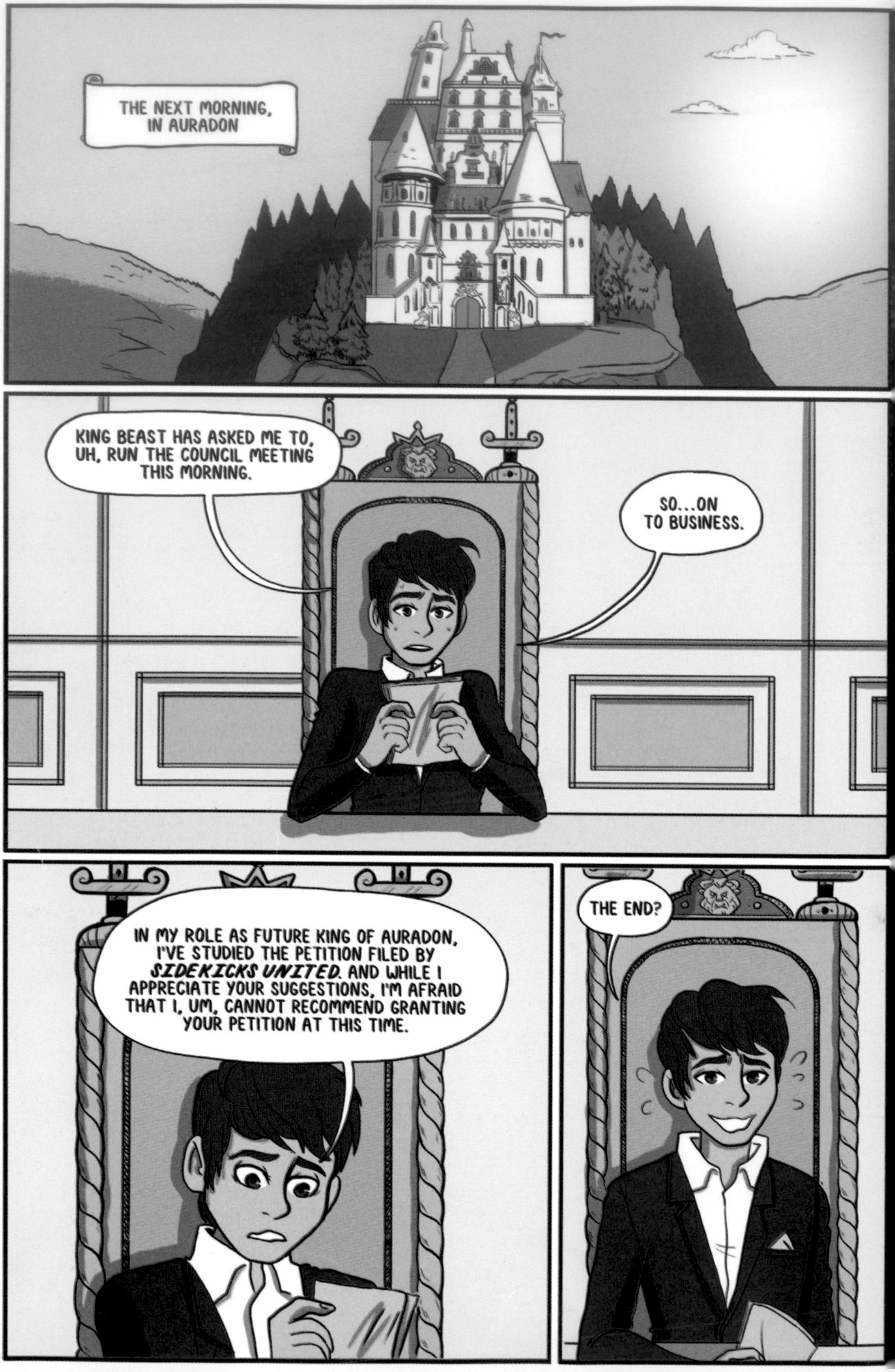
THE NEXT MORNING, IN AURADON
KING BEAST HAS ASKED ME TO, UH, RUN THE COUNCIL MEETING THIS MORNING.
SO...ON TO BUSINESS.
IN MY ROLE AS FUTURE KING OF AURADON, I'VE STUDIED THE PETITION FILED BY SIDEKICKS UNITED. AND WHILE I APPRECIATE YOUR SUGGESTIONS, I'M AFRAID THAT I, UM, CANNOT RECOMMEND GRANTING YOUR PETITION AT THIS TIME.
THE END?

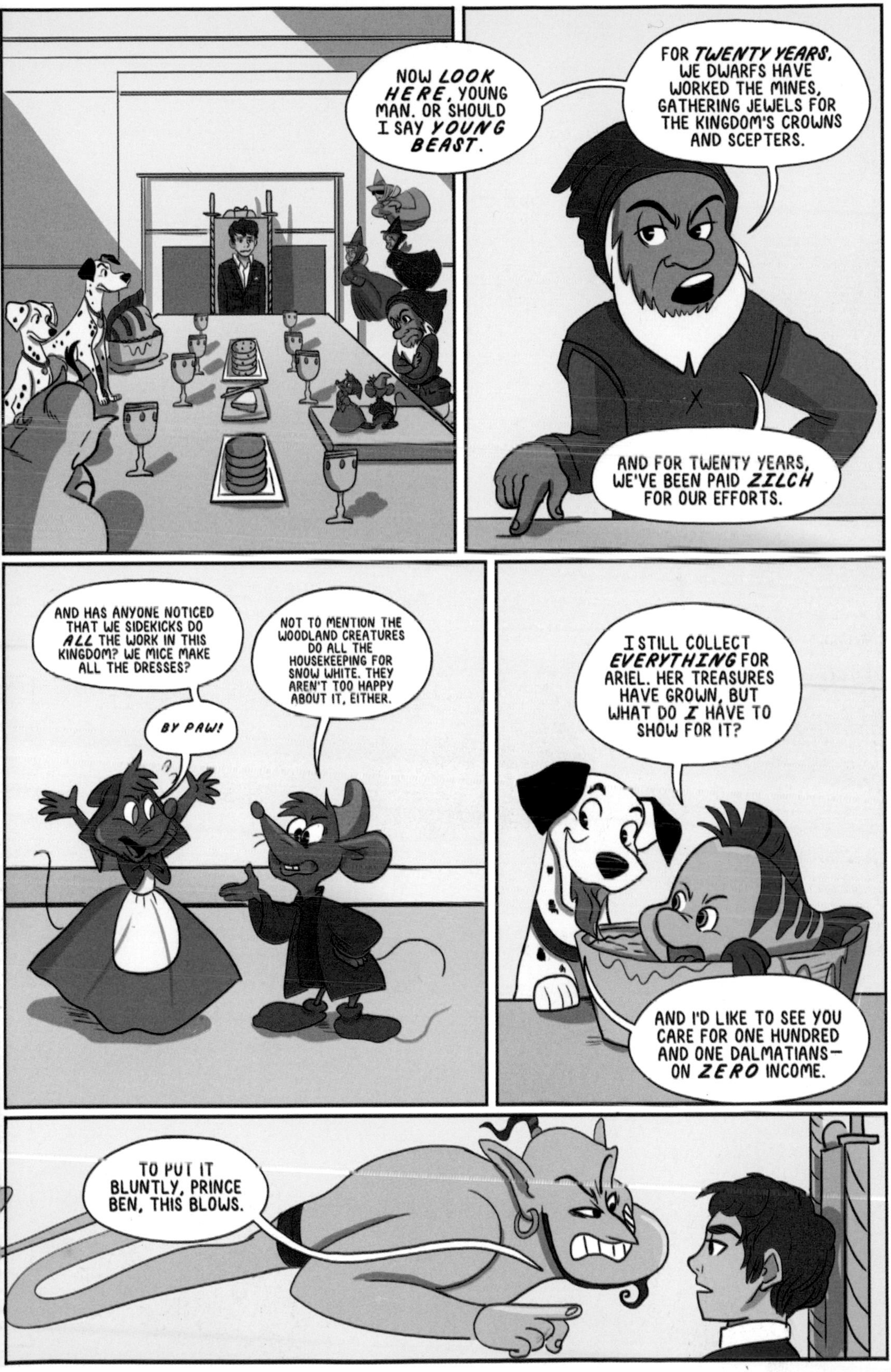
NOW LOOK HERE, YOUNG MAN. OR SHOULD I SAY YOUNG BEAST.
FOR TWENTY YEARS, WE DWARFS HAVE WORKED THE MINES, GATHERING JEWELS FOR THE KINGDOM'S CROWNS AND SCEPTERS.
AND FOR TWENTY YEARS, WE'VE BEEN PAID ZILCH FOR OUR EFFORTS.
AND HAS ANYONE NOTICED THAT WE SIDEKICKS DO ALL THE WORK IN THIS KINGDOM? WE MICE MAKE ALL THE DRESSES?
BY PAW!
NOT TO MENTION THE WOODLAND CREATURES DO ALL THE HOUSEKEEPING FOR SNOW WHITE. THEY AREN'T TOO HAPPY ABOUT IT, EITHER.
I STILL COLLECT EVERYTHING FOR ARIEL. HER TREASURES HAVE GROWN, BUT WHAT DO I HAVE TO SHOW FOR IT?
AND I'D LIKE TO SEE YOU CARE FOR ONE HUNDRED AND ONE DALMATIANS—ON ZERO INCOME.
TO PUT IT BLUNTLY, PRINCE BEN, THIS BLOWS.

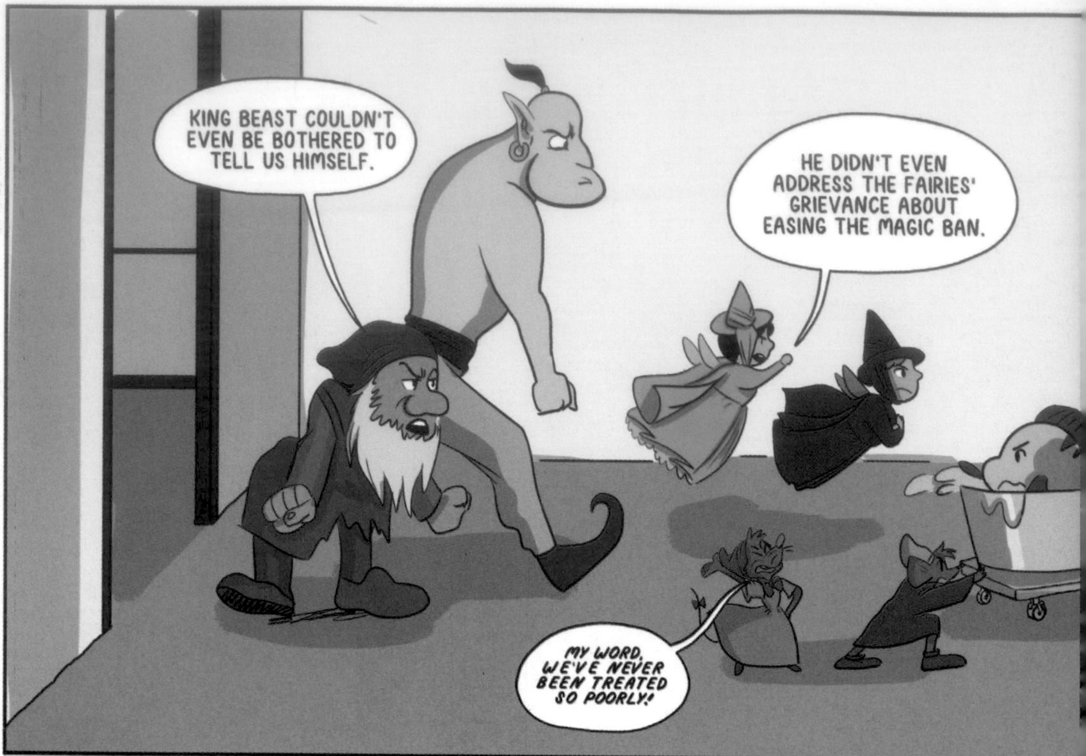
KING BEAST COULDN'T EVEN BE BOTHERED TO TELL US HIMSELF.
HE DIDN'T EVEN ADDRESS THE FAIRIES' GRIEVANCE ABOUT EASING THE MAGIC BAN.
MY WORD, WE'VE NEVER BEEN TREATED SO POORLY!

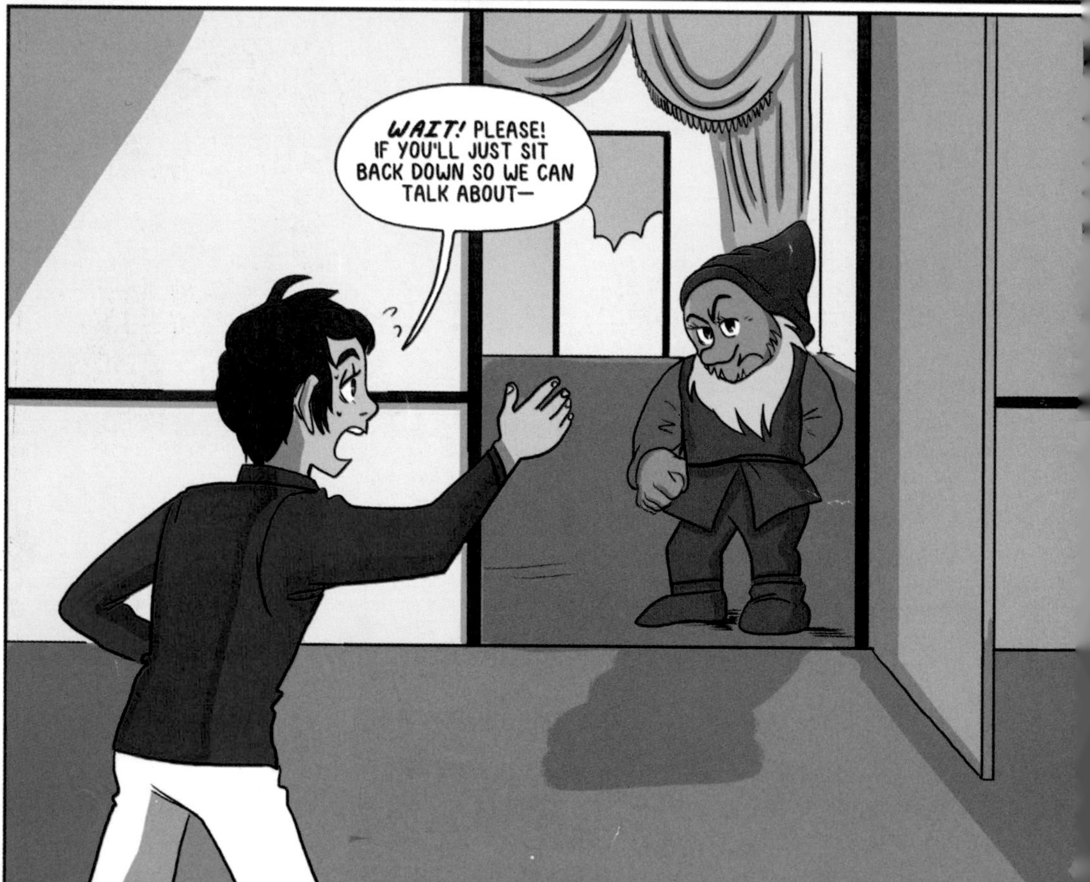
WAIT! PLEASE! IF YOU'LL JUST SIT BACK DOWN SO WE CAN TALK ABOUT—

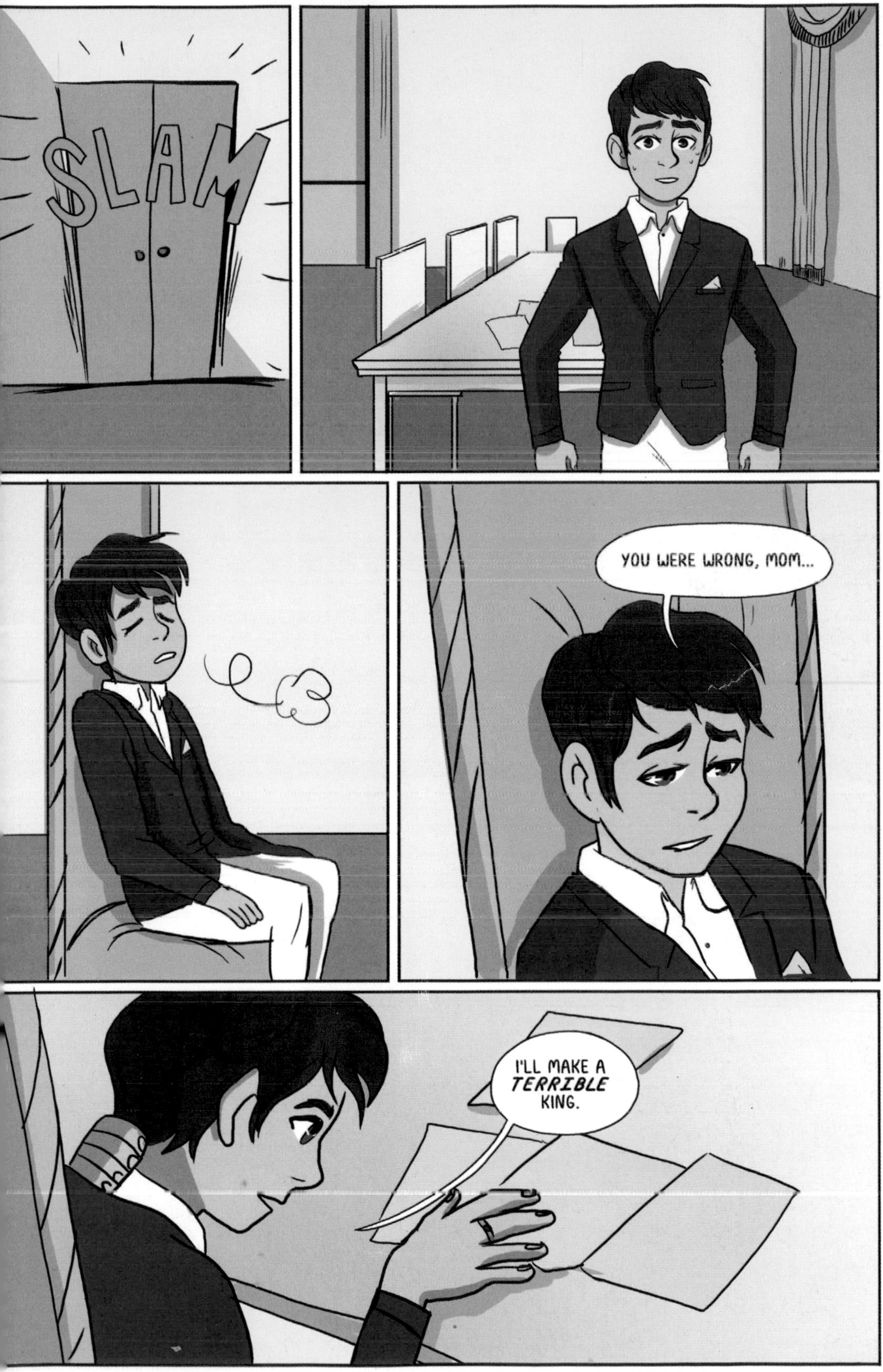
SLAM
YOU WERE WRONG, MOM...
I'LL MAKE A *TERRIBLE* KING.

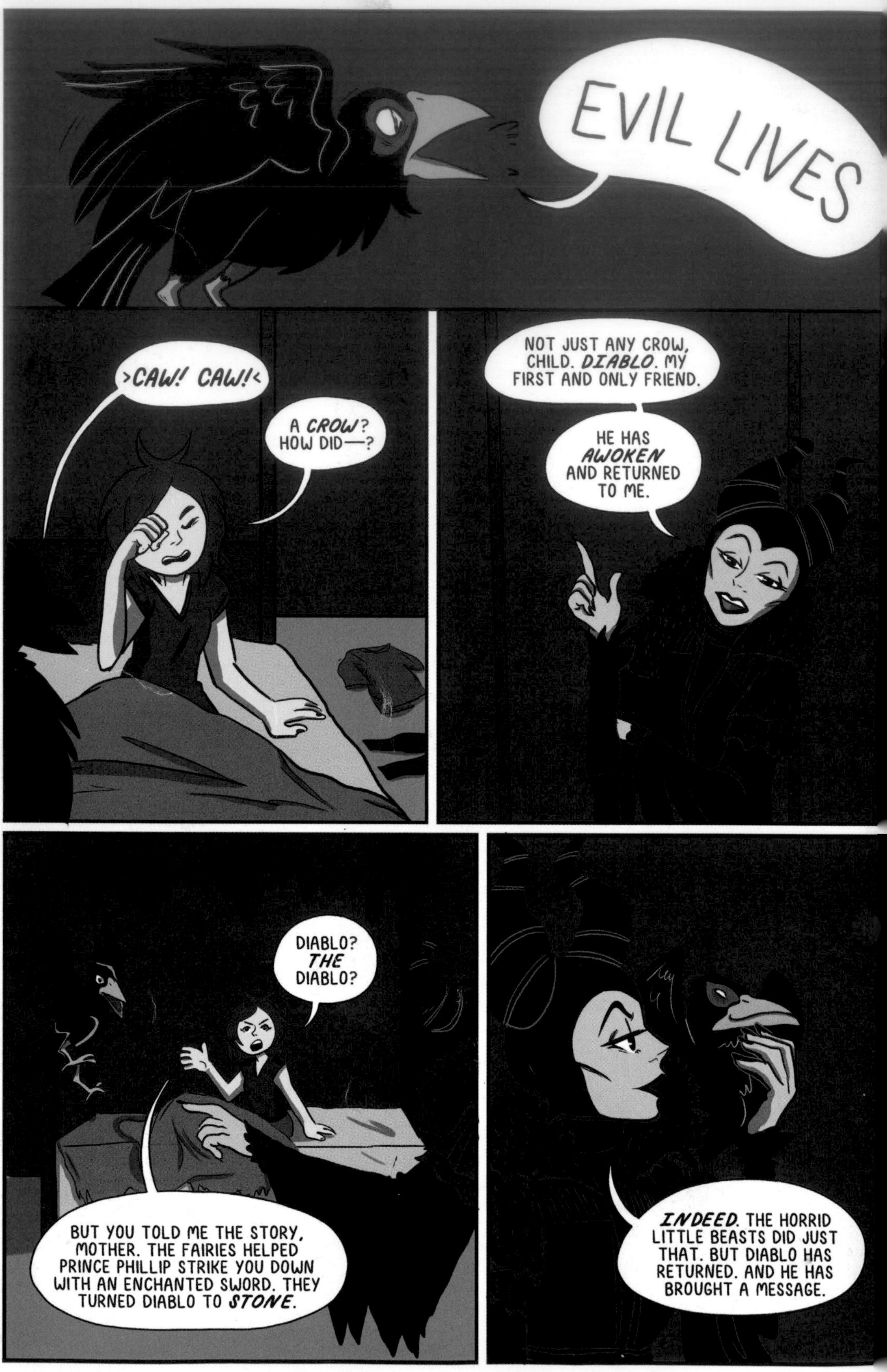
EVIL LIVES
>CAW! CAW!<
A CROW? HOW DID—?
NOT JUST ANY CROW, CHILD. DIABLO. MY FIRST AND ONLY FRIEND.
HE HAS AWOKEN AND RETURNED TO ME.
DIABLO? THE DIABLO?
BUT YOU TOLD ME THE STORY, MOTHER. THE FAIRIES HELPED PRINCE PHILLIP STRIKE YOU DOWN WITH AN ENCHANTED SWORD. THEY TURNED DIABLO TO STONE.
INDEED. THE HORRID LITTLE BEASTS DID JUST THAT. BUT DIABLO HAS RETURNED. AND HE HAS BROUGHT A MESSAGE.

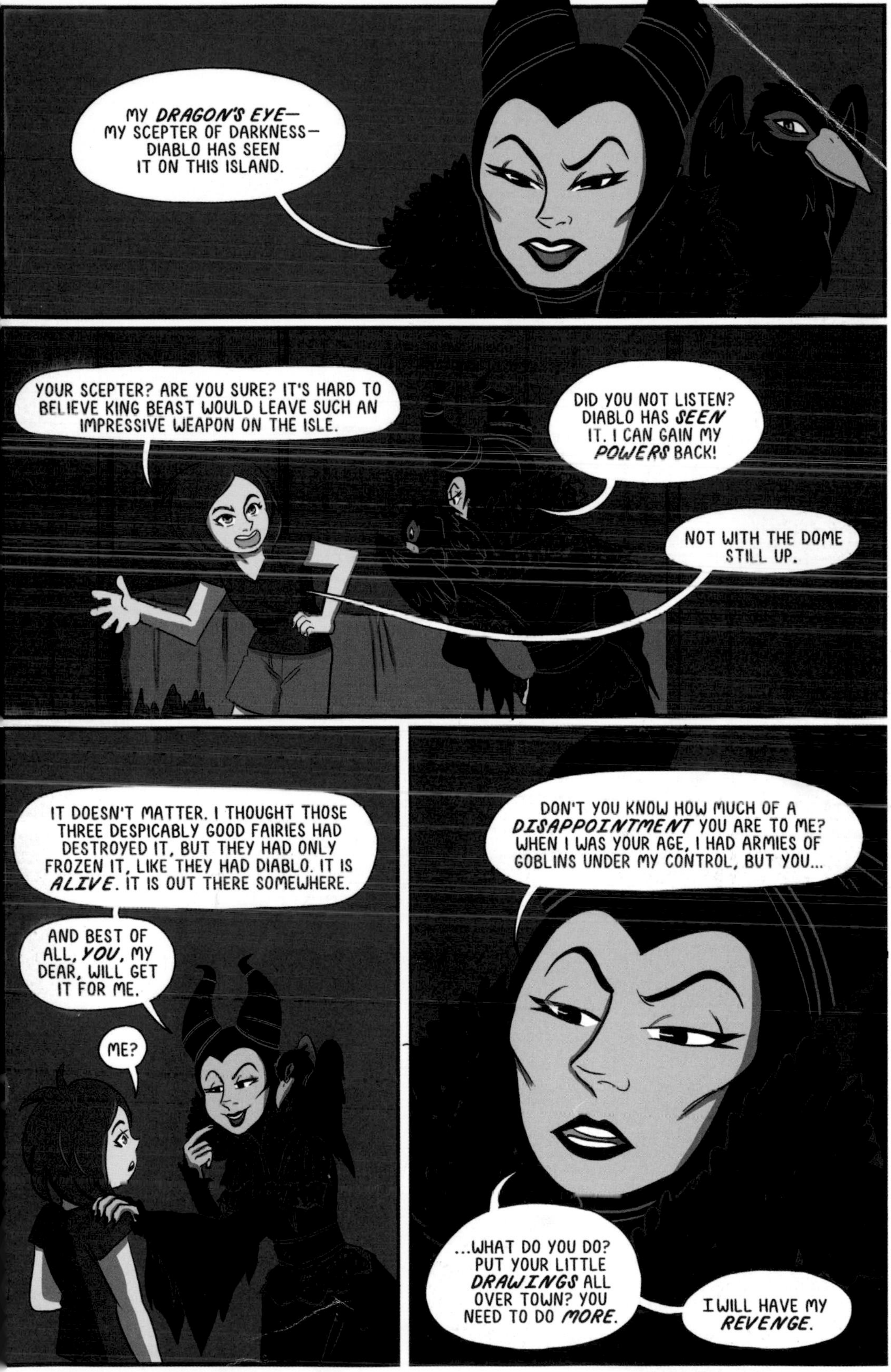
MY DRAGON'S EYE— MY SCEPTER OF DARKNESS— DIABLO HAS SEEN IT ON THIS ISLAND.
YOUR SCEPTER? ARE YOU SURE? IT'S HARD TO BELIEVE KING BEAST WOULD LEAVE SUCH AN IMPRESSIVE WEAPON ON THE ISLE.
DID YOU NOT LISTEN? DIABLO HAS SEEN IT. I CAN GAIN MY POWERS BACK!
NOT WITH THE DOME STILL UP.
IT DOESN'T MATTER. I THOUGHT THOSE THREE DESPICABLY GOOD FAIRIES HAD DESTROYED IT, BUT THEY HAD ONLY FROZEN IT, LIKE THEY HAD DIABLO. IT IS ALIVE. IT IS OUT THERE SOMEWHERE.
AND BEST OF ALL, YOU, MY DEAR, WILL GET IT FOR ME.
ME?
DON'T YOU KNOW HOW MUCH OF A DISAPPOINTMENT YOU ARE TO ME? WHEN I WAS YOUR AGE, I HAD ARMIES OF GOBLINS UNDER MY CONTROL, BUT YOU...
...WHAT DO YOU DO? PUT YOUR LITTLE DRAWINGS ALL OVER TOWN? YOU NEED TO DO MORE.
I WILL HAVE MY REVENGE.

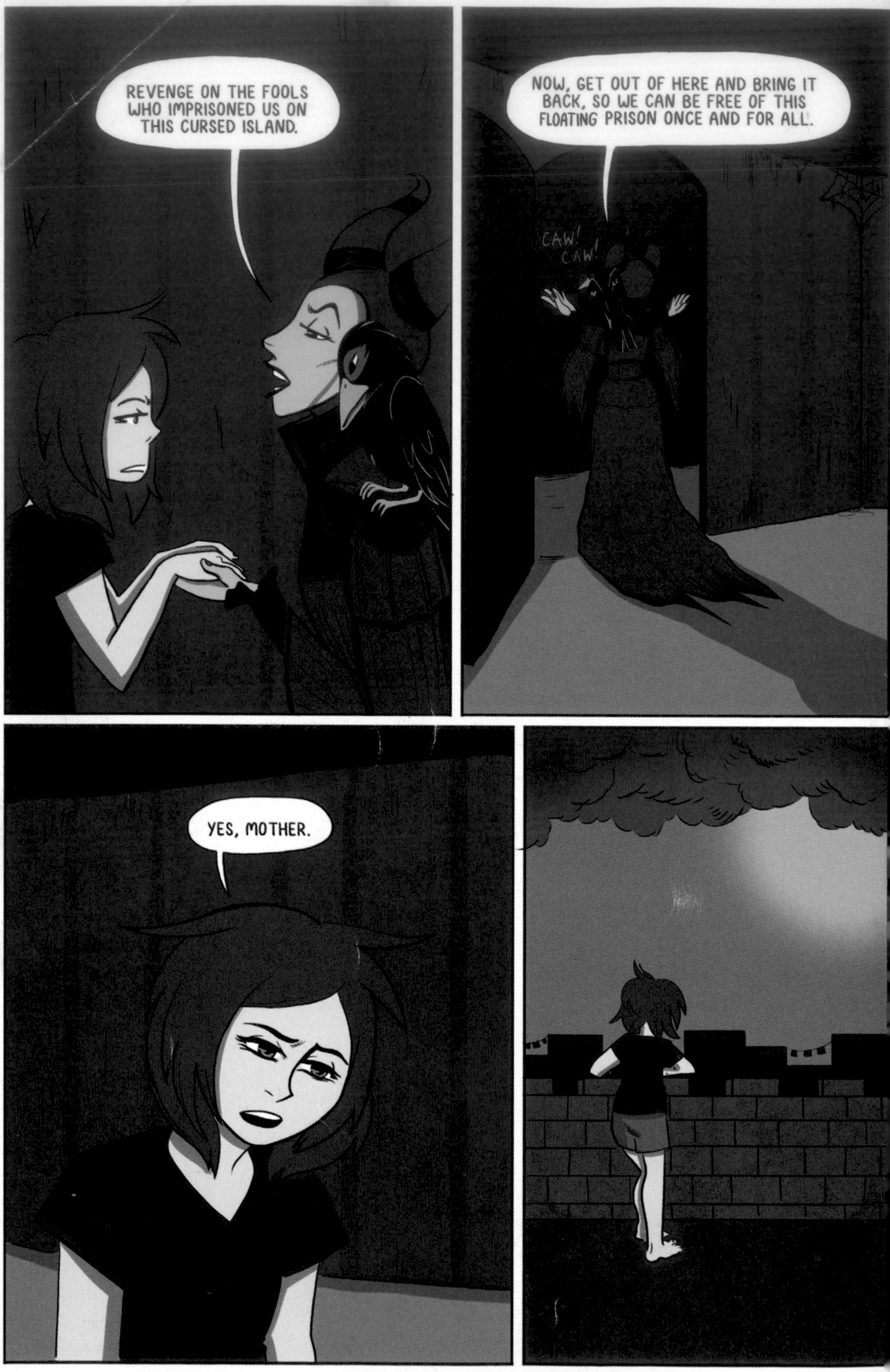
REVENGE ON THE FOOLS WHO IMPRISONED US ON THIS CURSED ISLAND.
NOW, GET OUT OF HERE AND BRING IT BACK, SO WE CAN BE FREE OF THIS FLOATING PRISON ONCE AND FOR ALL.
CAW! CAW!
YES, MOTHER.

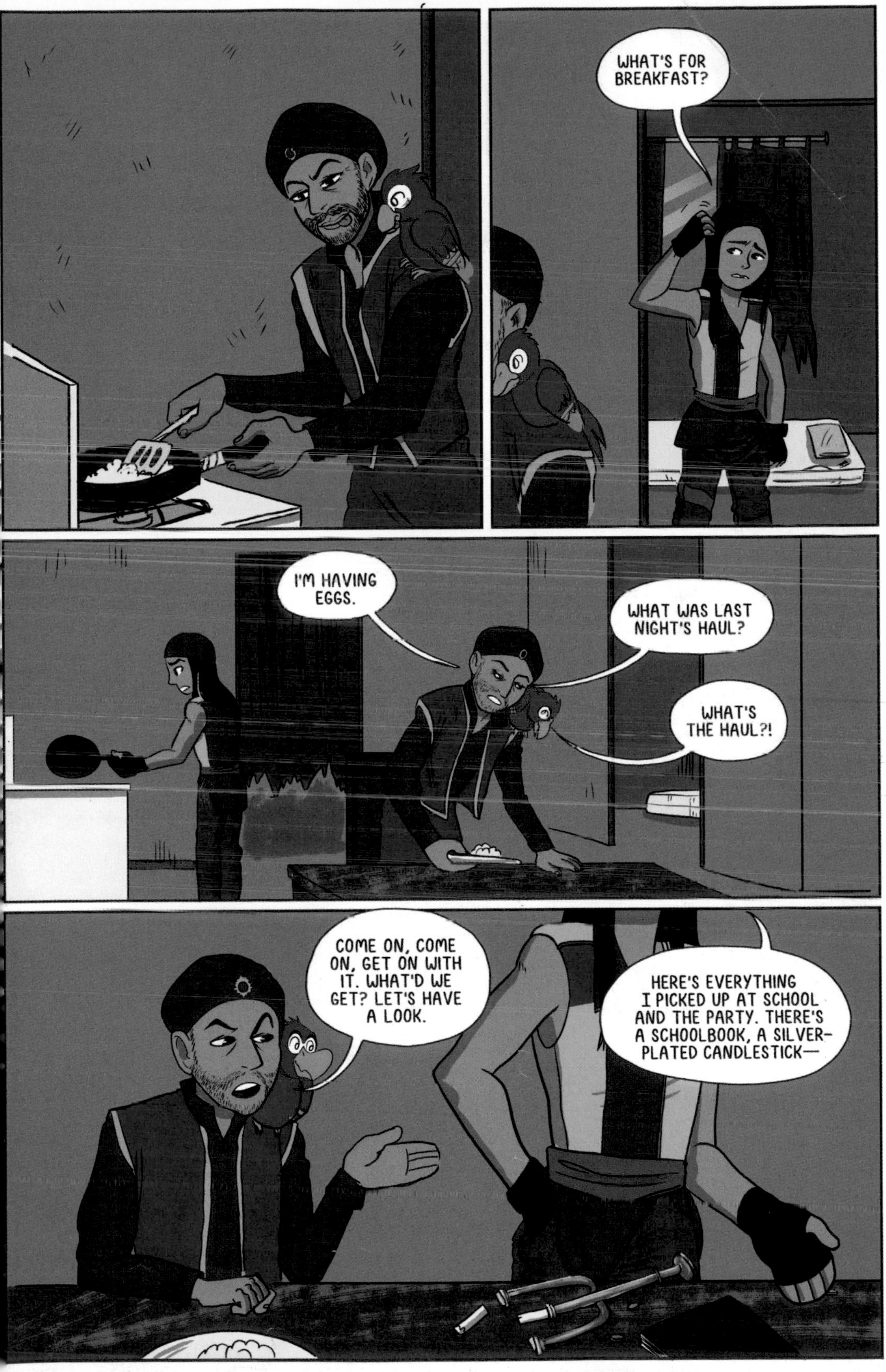
WHAT'S FOR BREAKFAST?
I'M HAVING EGGS.
WHAT WAS LAST NIGHT'S HAUL?
WHAT'S THE HAUL?!
COME ON, COME ON, GET ON WITH IT. WHAT'D WE GET? LET'S HAVE A LOOK.
HERE'S EVERYTHING I PICKED UP AT SCHOOL AND THE PARTY. THERE'S A SCHOOLBOOK, A SILVER-PLATED CANDLESTICK—

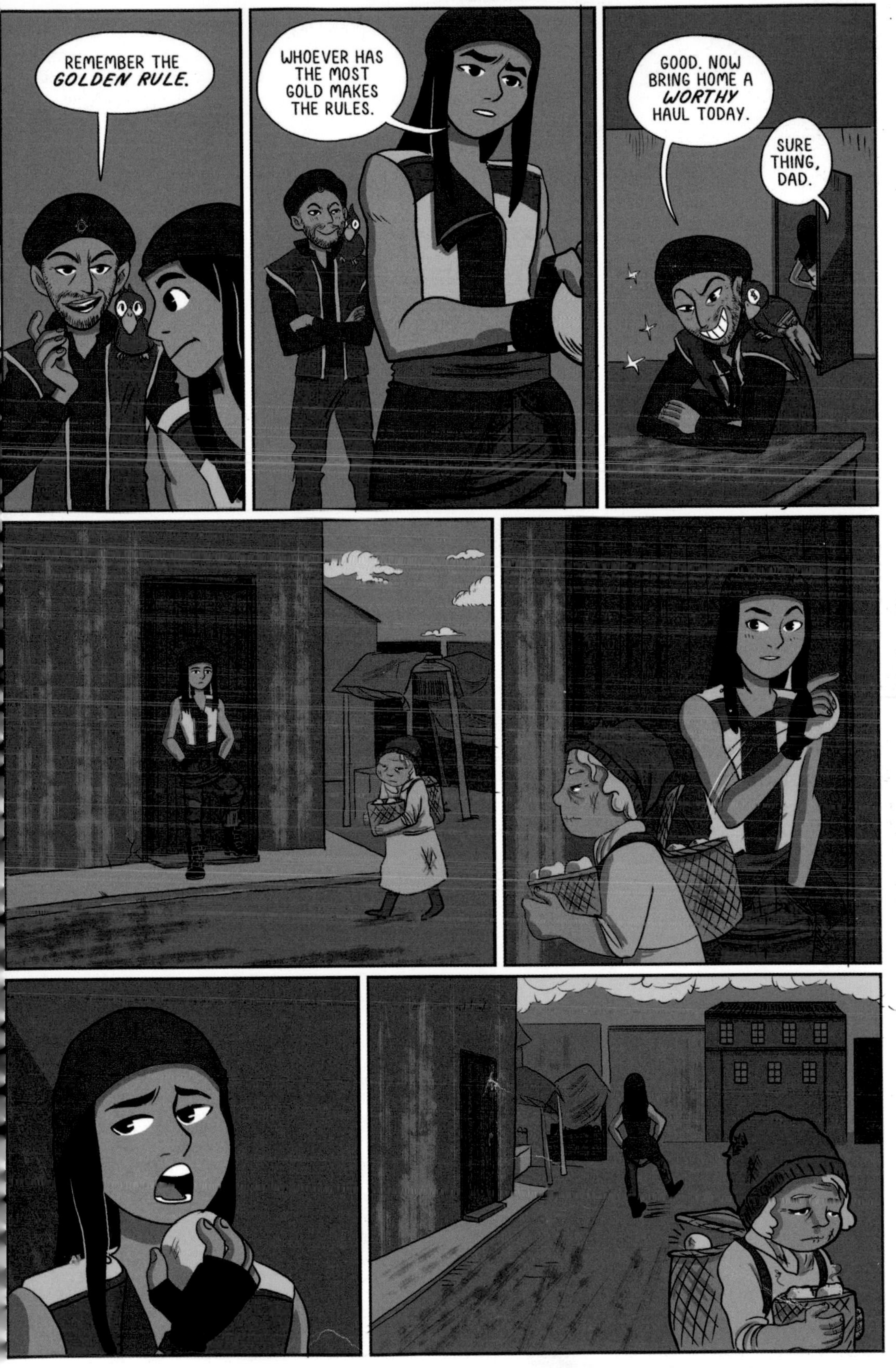
REMEMBER THE *GOLDEN RULE.*
WHOEVER HAS THE MOST GOLD MAKES THE RULES.
GOOD. NOW BRING HOME A *WORTHY* HAUL TODAY.
SURE THING, DAD.

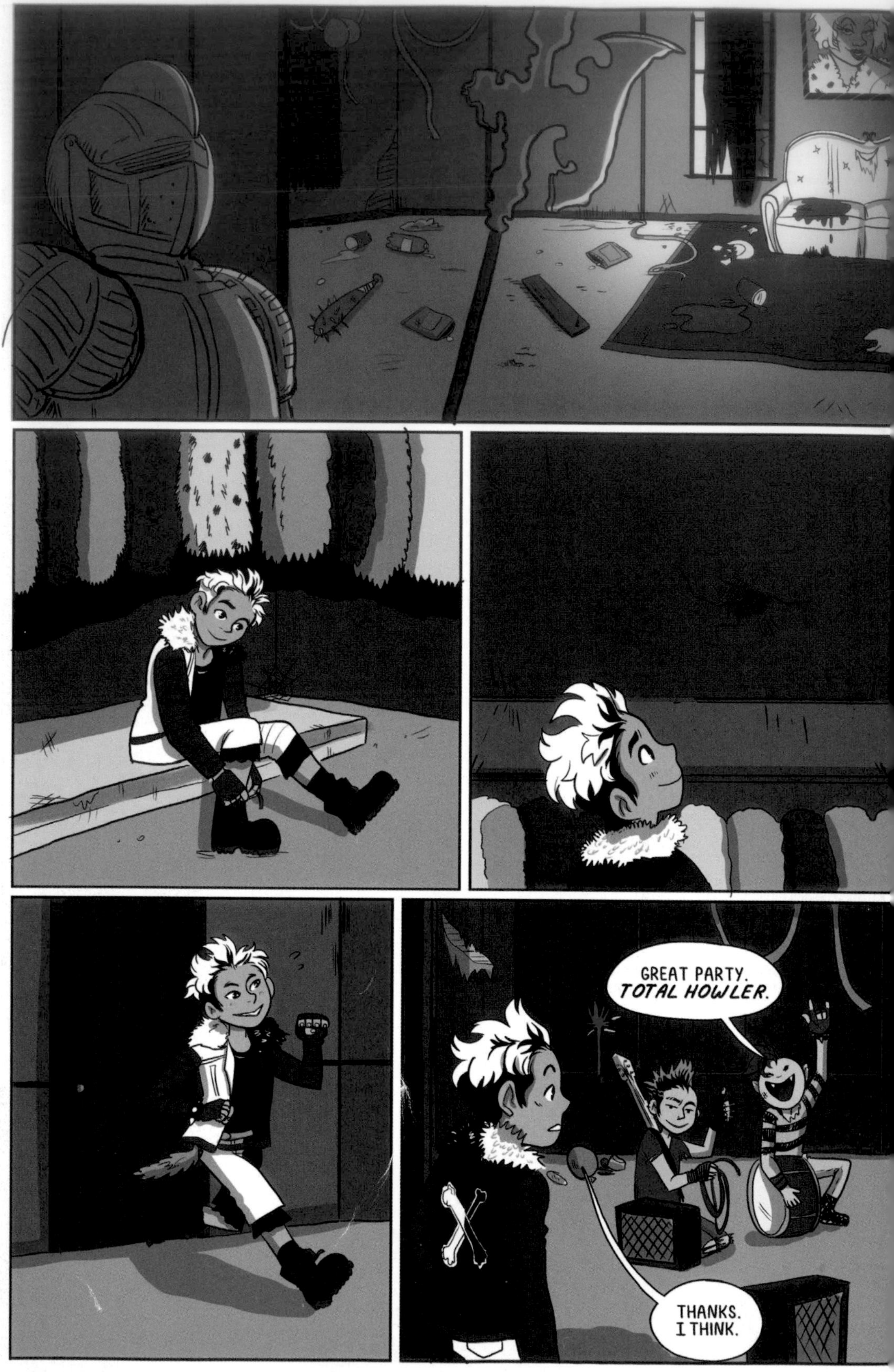
GREAT PARTY. TOTAL HOWLER.
THANKS. I THINK.

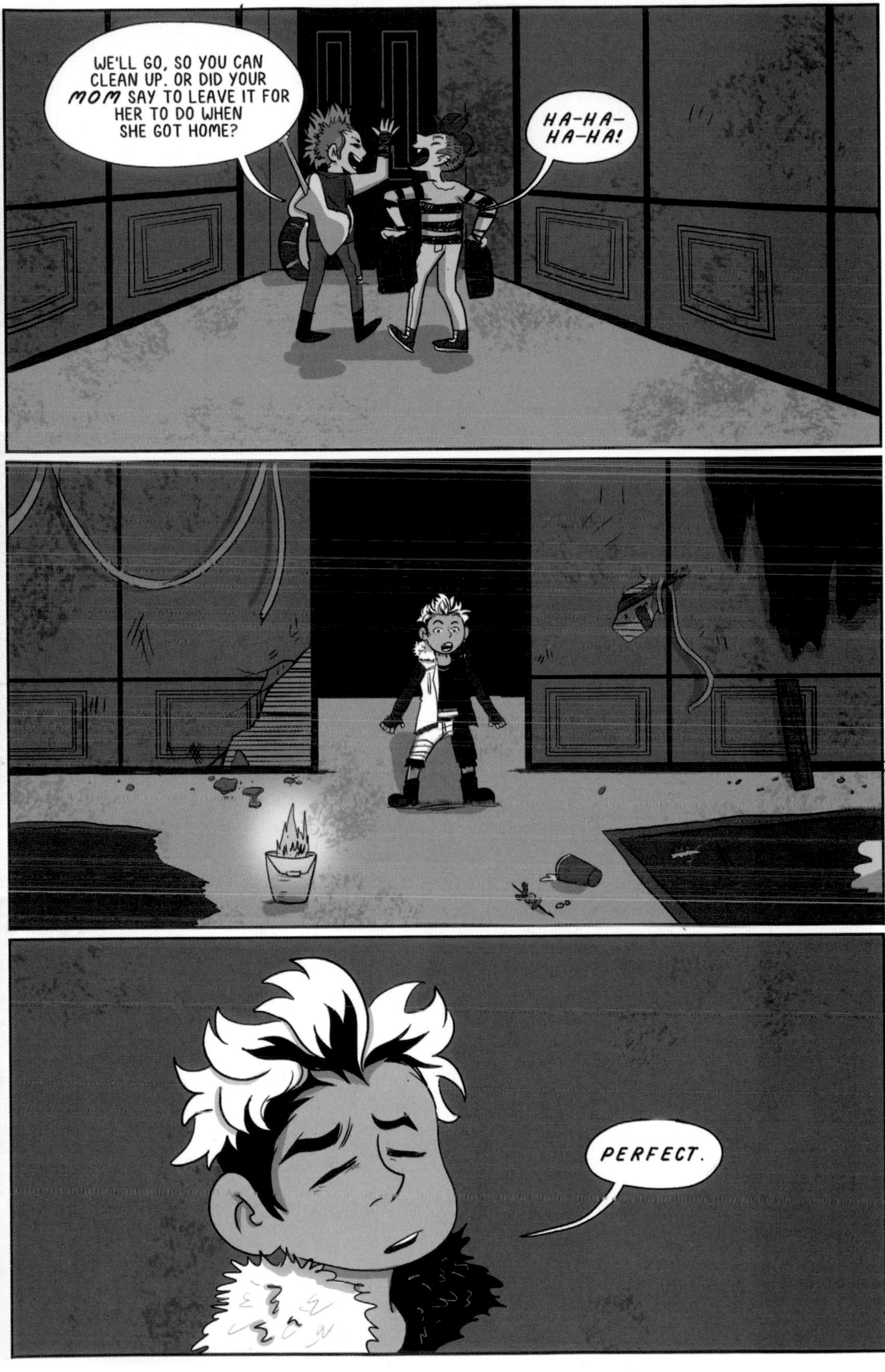
WE'LL GO, SO YOU CAN CLEAN UP. OR DID YOUR MOM SAY TO LEAVE IT FOR HER TO DO WHEN SHE GOT HOME?
HA-HA-HA-HA!
PERFECT.

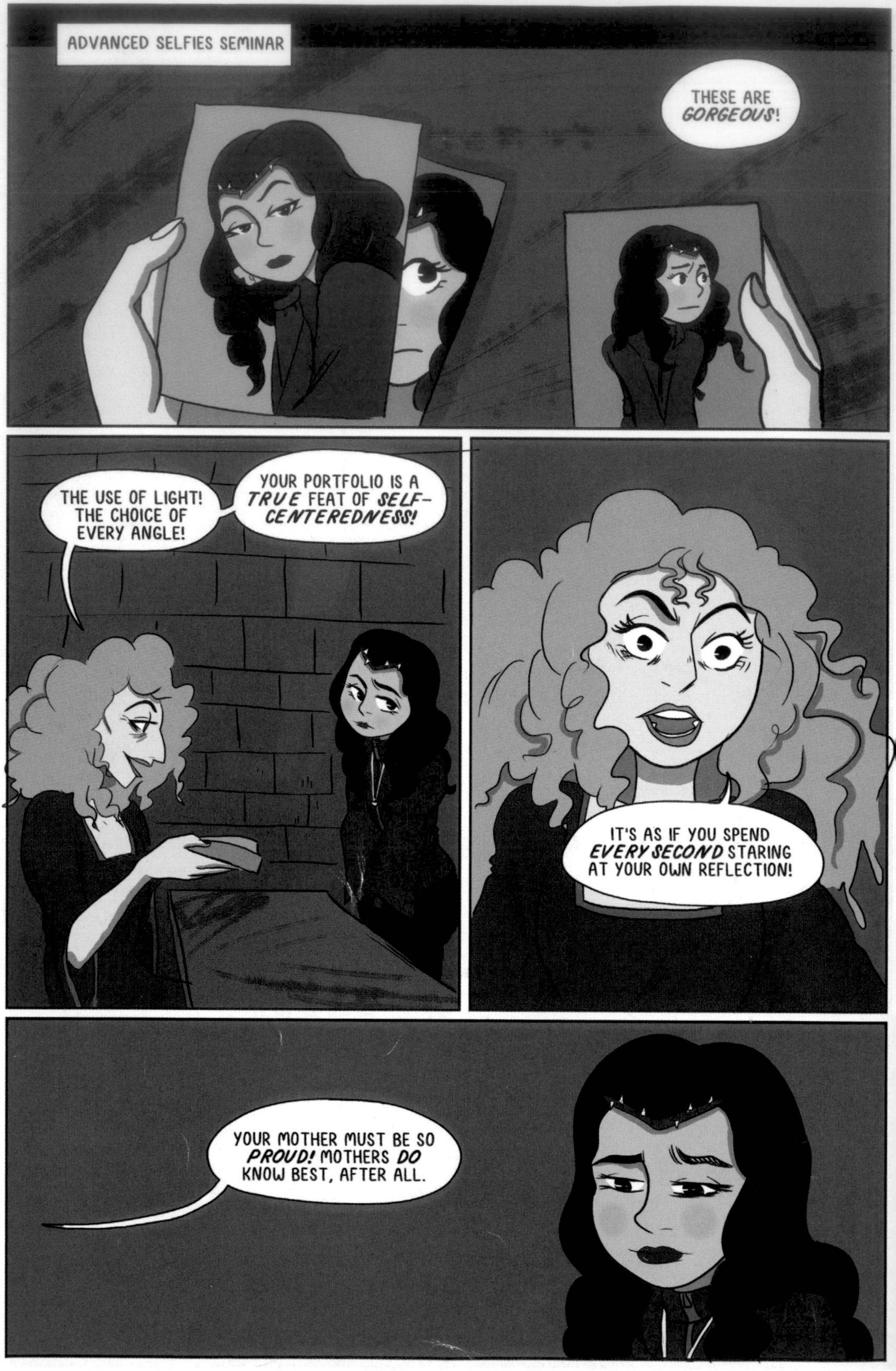
ADVANCED SELFIES SEMINAR
THESE ARE GORGEOUS!
THE USE OF LIGHT! THE CHOICE OF EVERY ANGLE!
YOUR PORTFOLIO IS A TRUE FEAT OF SELF-CENTEREDNESS!
IT'S AS IF YOU SPEND EVERY SECOND STARING AT YOUR OWN REFLECTION!
YOUR MOTHER MUST BE SO PROUD! MOTHERS DO KNOW BEST, AFTER ALL.

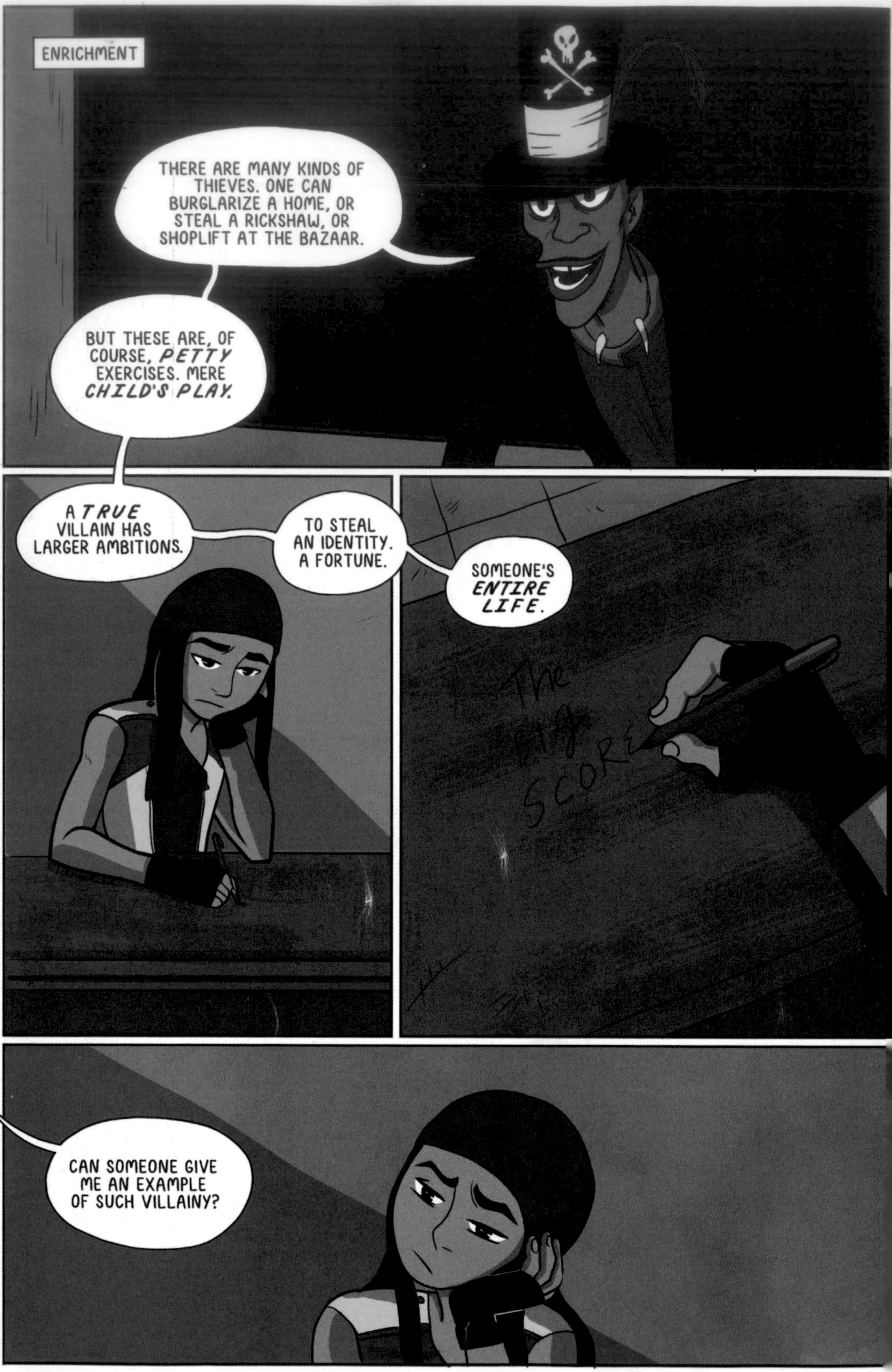
ENRICHMENT
THERE ARE MANY KINDS OF THIEVES. ONE CAN BURGLARIZE A HOME, OR STEAL A RICKSHAW, OR SHOPLIFT AT THE BAZAAR.
BUT THESE ARE, OF COURSE, *PETTY* EXERCISES. MERE *CHILD'S PLAY.*
A *TRUE* VILLAIN HAS LARGER AMBITIONS.
TO STEAL AN IDENTITY. A FORTUNE.
SOMEONE'S *ENTIRE LIFE.*
The Big SCORE
CAN SOMEONE GIVE ME AN EXAMPLE OF SUCH VILLAINY?

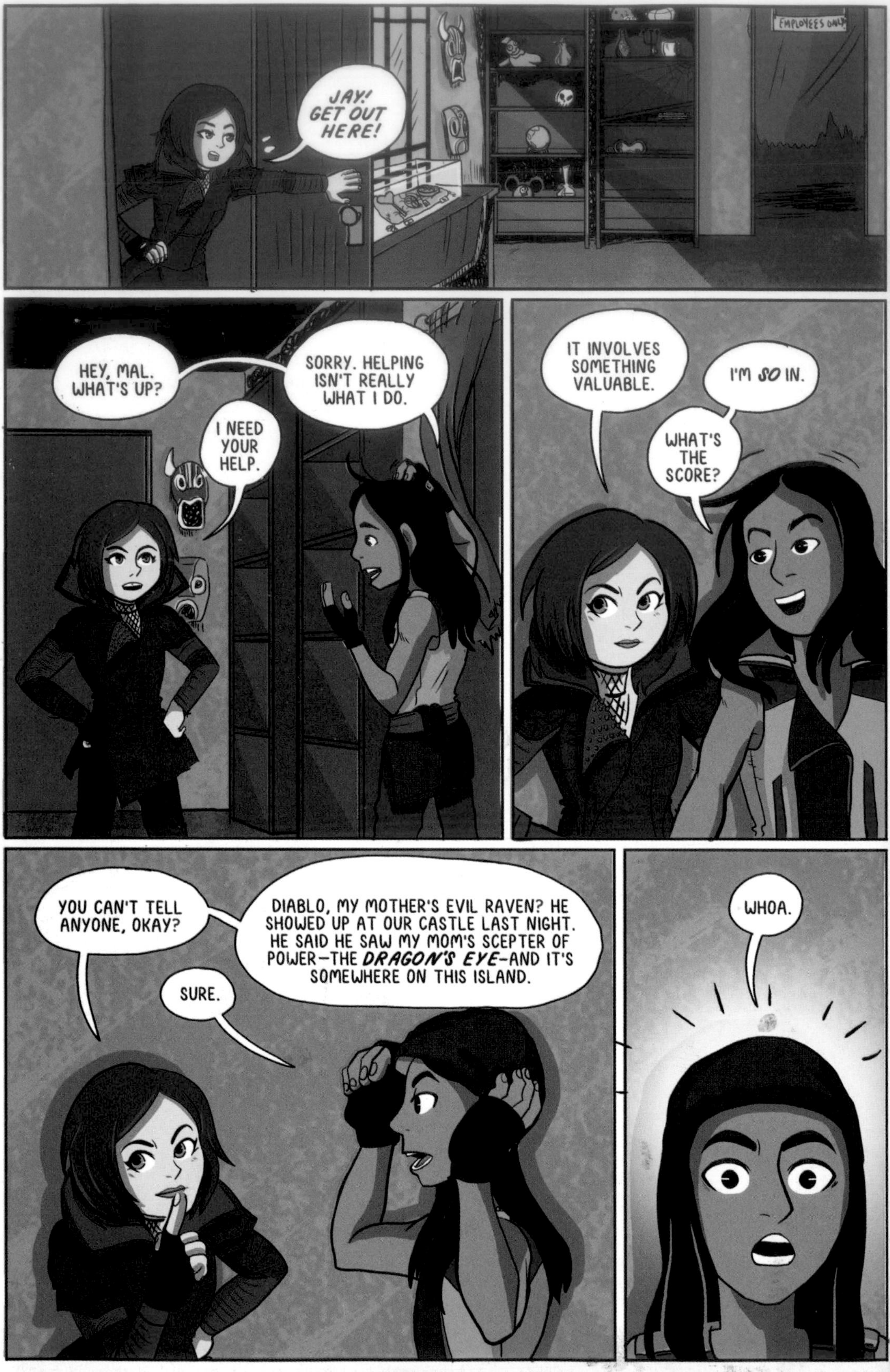
JAY! GET OUT HERE!
EMPLOYEES ONLY
HEY, MAL. WHAT'S UP?
SORRY. HELPING ISN'T REALLY WHAT I DO.
I NEED YOUR HELP.
IT INVOLVES SOMETHING VALUABLE.
I'M SO IN.
WHAT'S THE SCORE?
YOU CAN'T TELL ANYONE, OKAY?
DIABLO, MY MOTHER'S EVIL RAVEN? HE SHOWED UP AT OUR CASTLE LAST NIGHT. HE SAID HE SAW MY MOM'S SCEPTER OF POWER—THE DRAGON'S EYE—AND IT'S SOMEWHERE ON THIS ISLAND.
SURE.
WHOA.

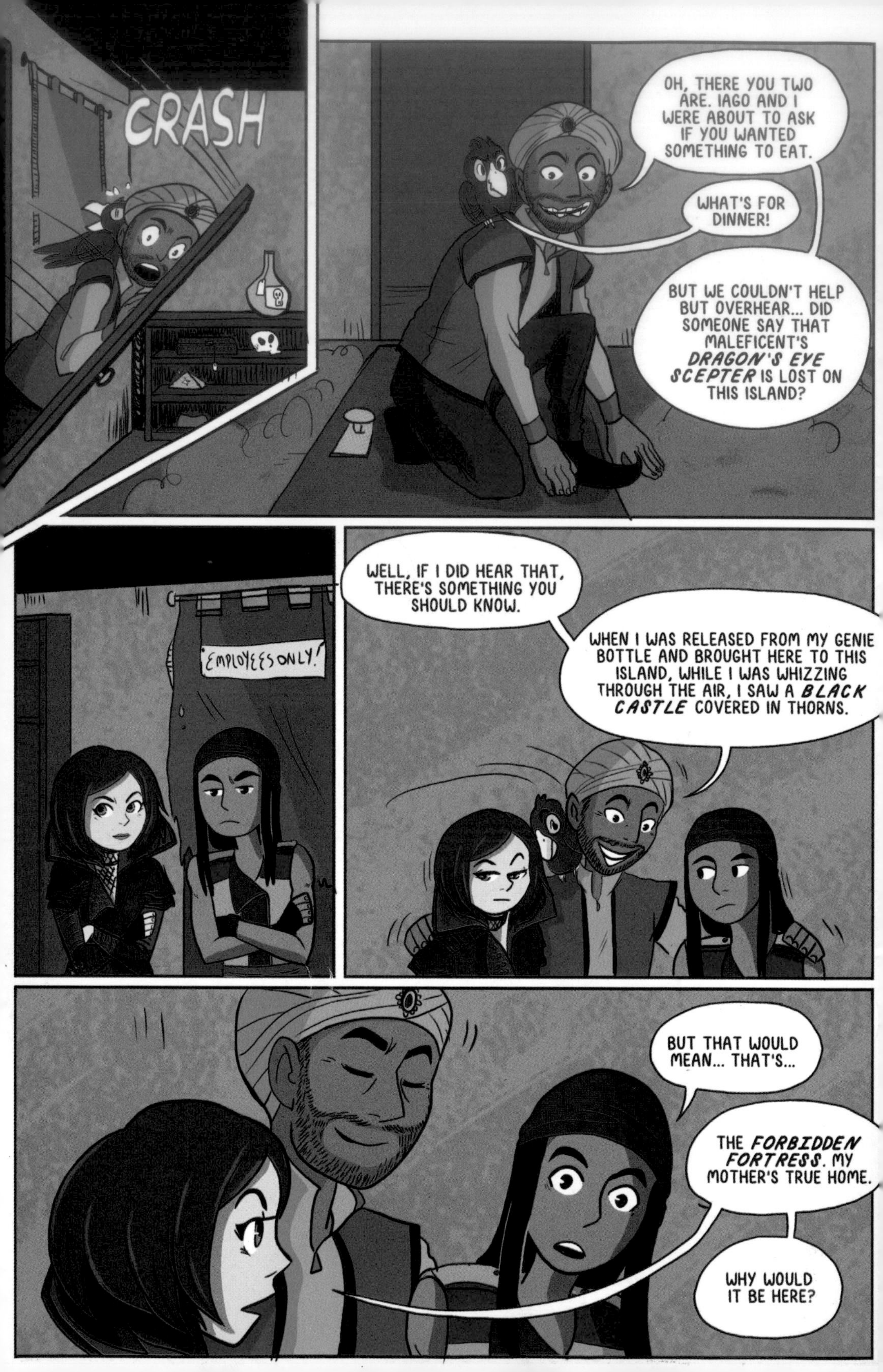
CRASH
OH, THERE YOU TWO ARE. IAGO AND I WERE ABOUT TO ASK IF YOU WANTED SOMETHING TO EAT.
WHAT'S FOR DINNER!
BUT WE COULDN'T HELP BUT OVERHEAR... DID SOMEONE SAY THAT MALEFICENT'S *DRAGON'S EYE SCEPTER* IS LOST ON THIS ISLAND?
EMPLOYEES ONLY!
WELL, IF I DID HEAR THAT, THERE'S SOMETHING YOU SHOULD KNOW.
WHEN I WAS RELEASED FROM MY GENIE BOTTLE AND BROUGHT HERE TO THIS ISLAND, WHILE I WAS WHIZZING THROUGH THE AIR, I SAW A *BLACK CASTLE* COVERED IN THORNS.
BUT THAT WOULD MEAN... THAT'S...
THE *FORBIDDEN FORTRESS*. MY MOTHER'S TRUE HOME.
WHY WOULD IT BE HERE?

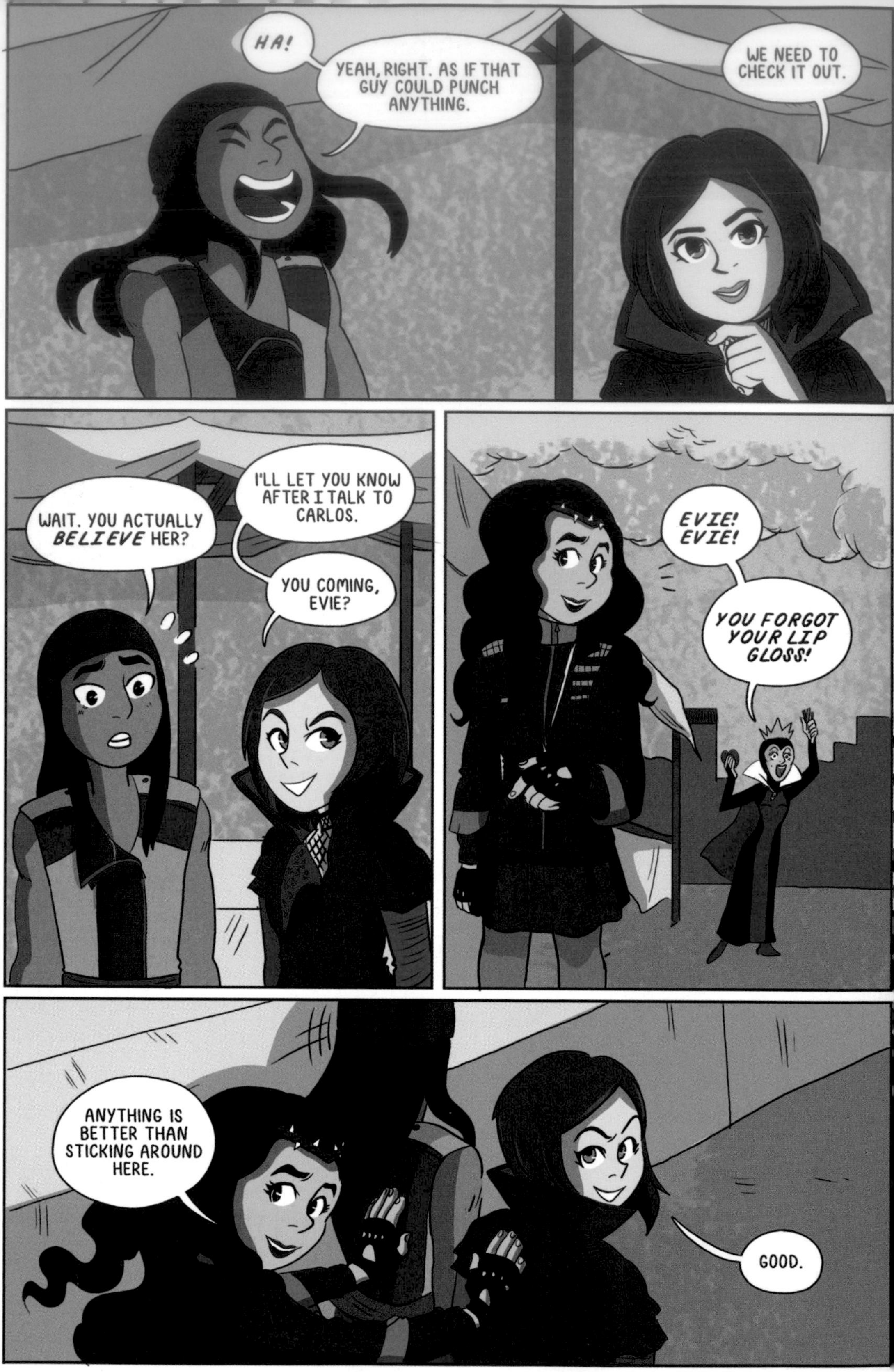
HA!
YEAH, RIGHT. AS IF THAT GUY COULD PUNCH ANYTHING.
WE NEED TO CHECK IT OUT.
WAIT. YOU ACTUALLY *BELIEVE* HER?
I'LL LET YOU KNOW AFTER I TALK TO CARLOS.
YOU COMING, EVIE?
EVIE! EVIE!
YOU FORGOT YOUR LIP GLOSS!
ANYTHING IS BETTER THAN STICKING AROUND HERE.
GOOD.

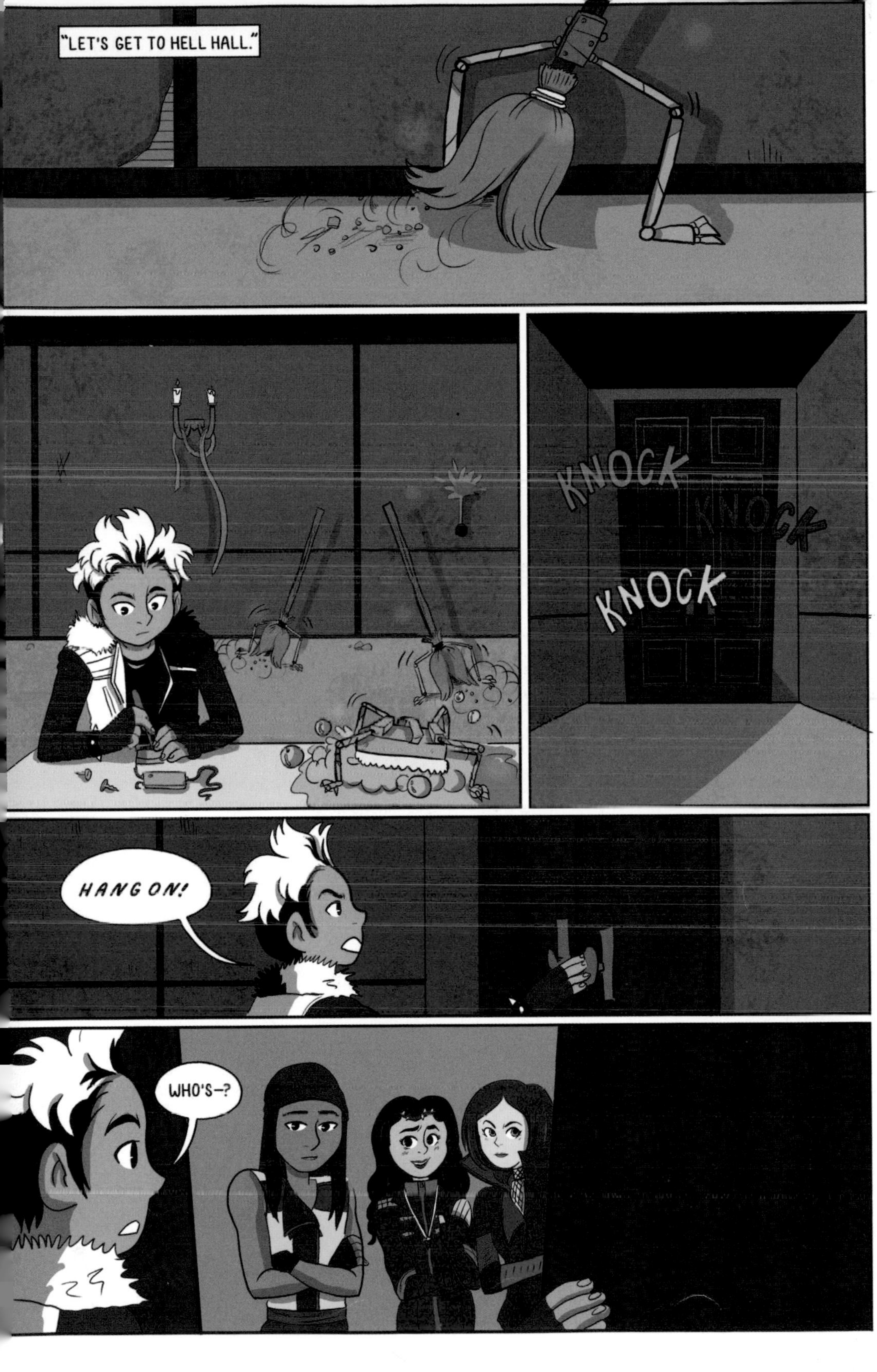
"LET'S GET TO HELL HALL."
KNOCK
KNOCK
KNOCK
HANG ON!
WHO'S—?

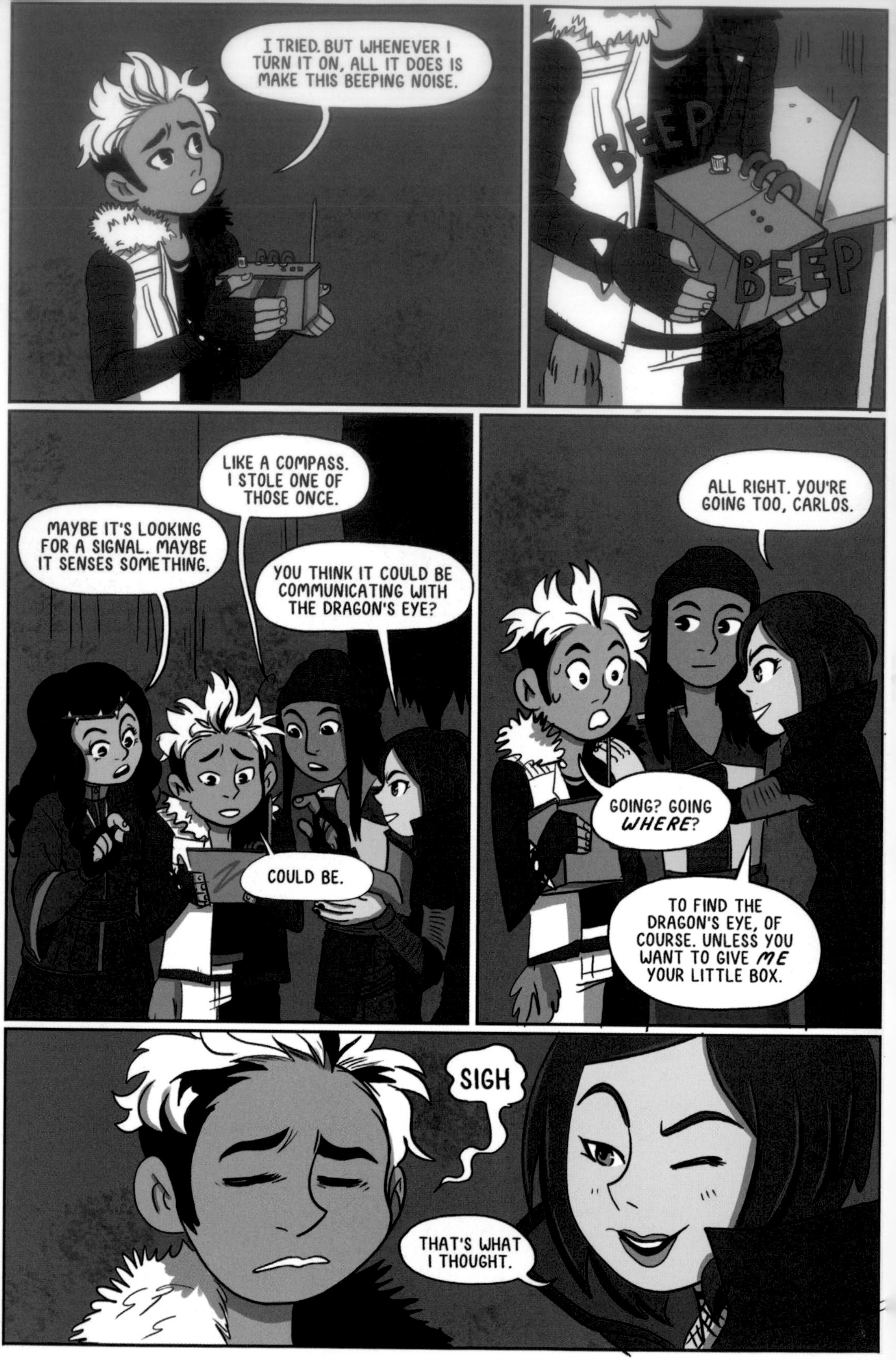
I TRIED. BUT WHENEVER I TURN IT ON, ALL IT DOES IS MAKE THIS BEEPING NOISE.
BEEP
BEEP
MAYBE IT'S LOOKING FOR A SIGNAL. MAYBE IT SENSES SOMETHING.
LIKE A COMPASS. I STOLE ONE OF THOSE ONCE.
YOU THINK IT COULD BE COMMUNICATING WITH THE DRAGON'S EYE?
COULD BE.
ALL RIGHT. YOU'RE GOING TOO, CARLOS.
GOING? GOING *WHERE*?
TO FIND THE DRAGON'S EYE, OF COURSE. UNLESS YOU WANT TO GIVE *ME* YOUR LITTLE BOX.
SIGH
THAT'S WHAT I THOUGHT.

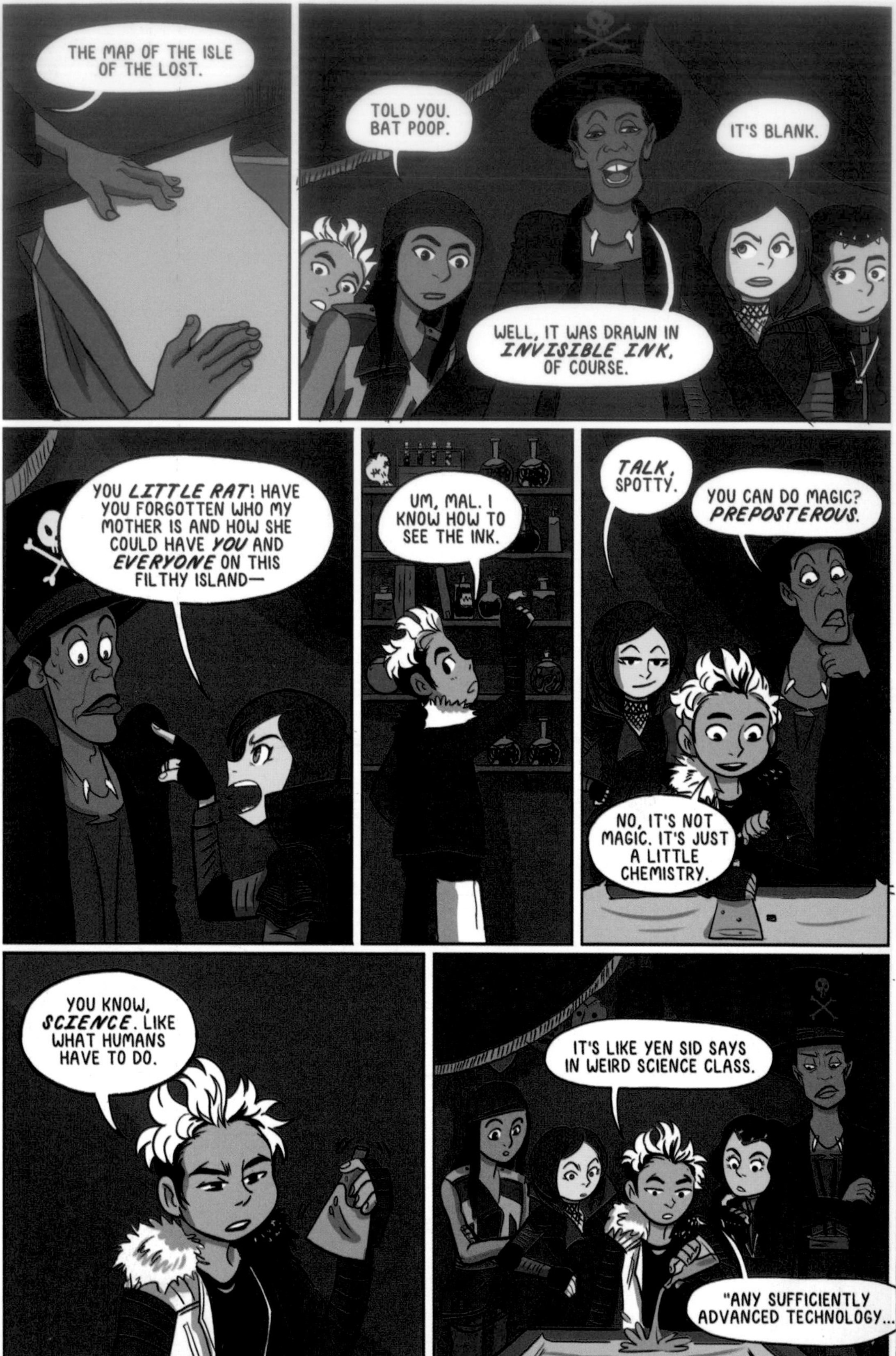
THE MAP OF THE ISLE OF THE LOST.
TOLD YOU. BAT POOP.
IT'S BLANK.
WELL, IT WAS DRAWN IN *INVISIBLE INK*, OF COURSE.
YOU *LITTLE RAT*! HAVE YOU FORGOTTEN WHO MY MOTHER IS AND HOW SHE COULD HAVE *YOU* AND *EVERYONE* ON THIS FILTHY ISLAND—
UM, MAL. I KNOW HOW TO SEE THE INK.
TALK, SPOTTY.
YOU CAN DO MAGIC? *PREPOSTEROUS*.
NO, IT'S NOT MAGIC. IT'S JUST A LITTLE CHEMISTRY.
YOU KNOW, *SCIENCE*. LIKE WHAT HUMANS HAVE TO DO.
IT'S LIKE YEN SID SAYS IN WEIRD SCIENCE CLASS.
"ANY SUFFICIENTLY ADVANCED TECHNOLOGY...

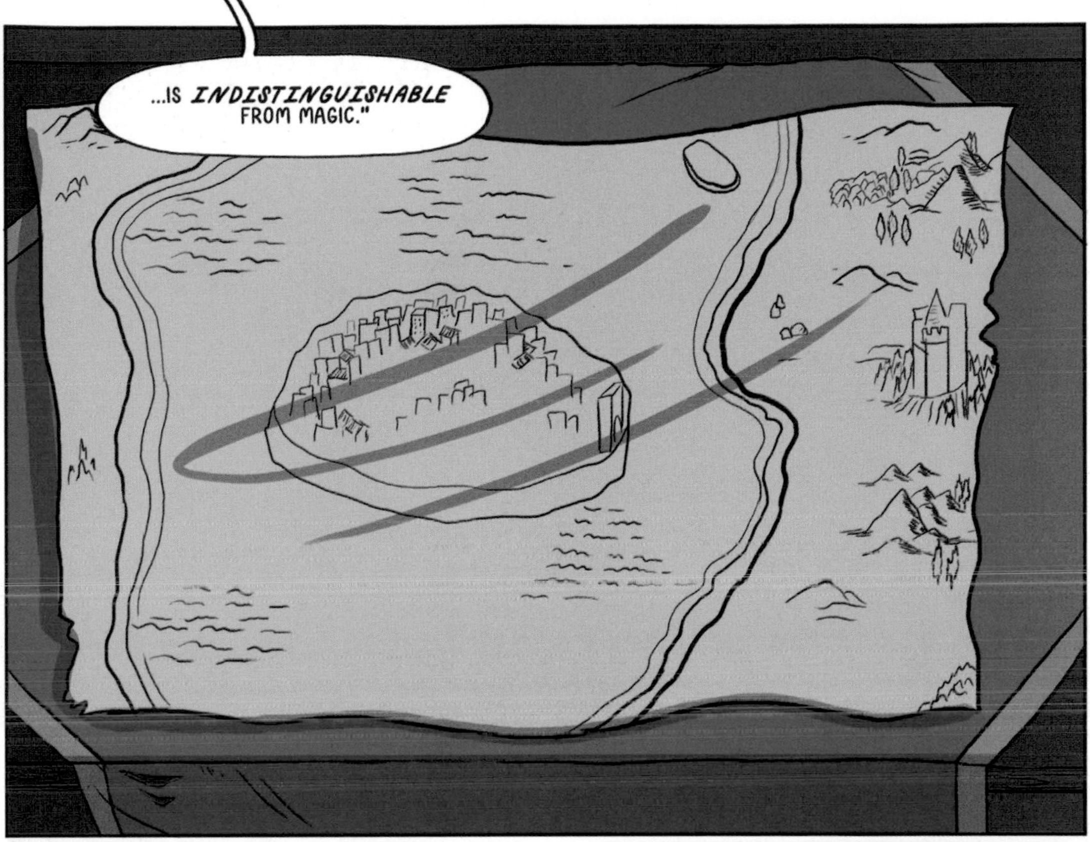
...IS *INDISTINGUISHABLE* FROM MAGIC."

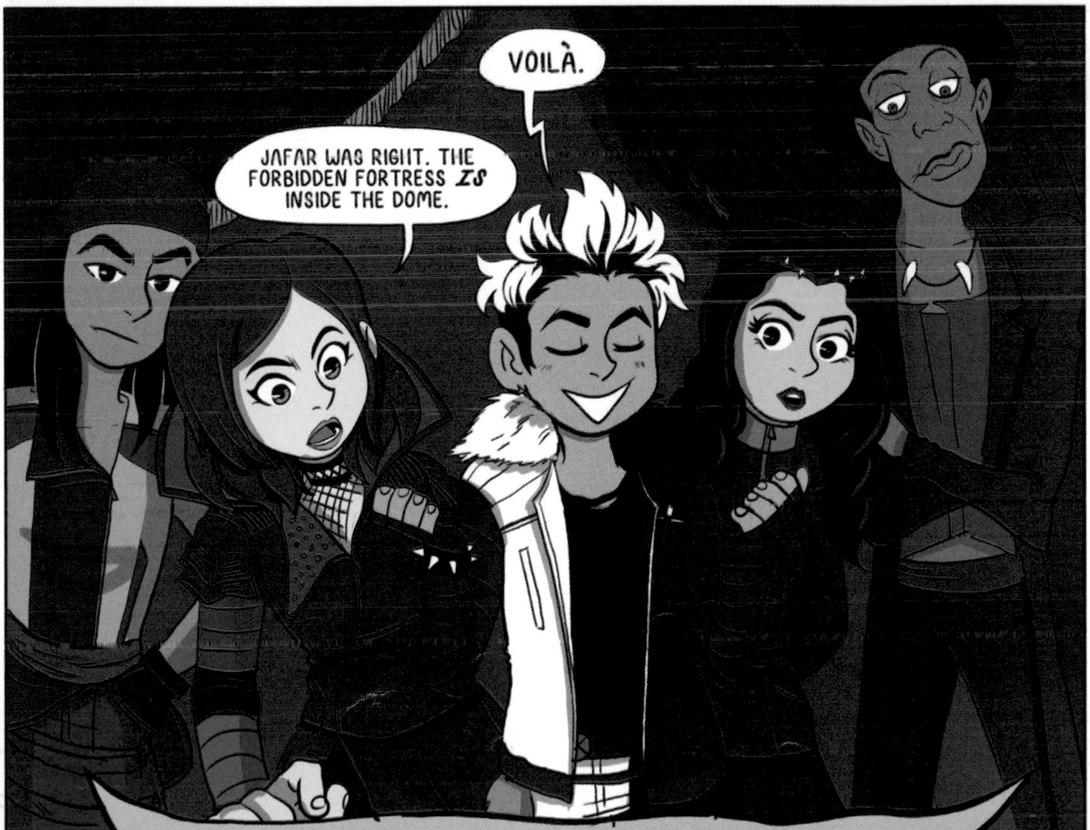
VOILÀ.
JAFAR WAS RIGHT. THE FORBIDDEN FORTRESS *IS* INSIDE THE DOME.

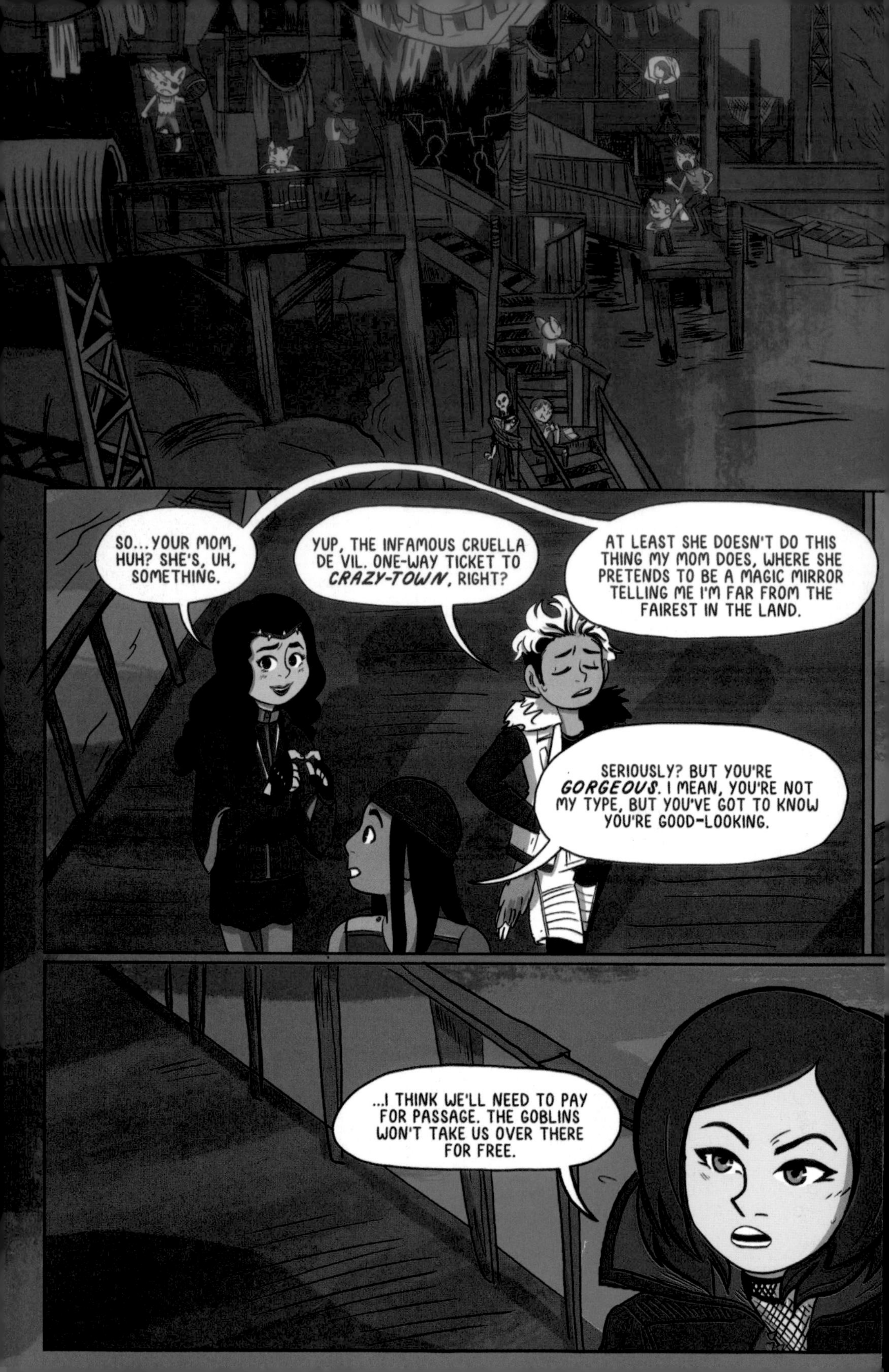
SO...YOUR MOM, HUH? SHE'S, UH, SOMETHING.
YUP, THE INFAMOUS CRUELLA DE VIL. ONE-WAY TICKET TO *CRAZY-TOWN*, RIGHT?
AT LEAST SHE DOESN'T DO THIS THING MY MOM DOES, WHERE SHE PRETENDS TO BE A MAGIC MIRROR TELLING ME I'M FAR FROM THE FAIREST IN THE LAND.
SERIOUSLY? BUT YOU'RE *GORGEOUS*. I MEAN, YOU'RE NOT MY TYPE, BUT YOU'VE GOT TO KNOW YOU'RE GOOD-LOOKING.
...I THINK WE'LL NEED TO PAY FOR PASSAGE. THE GOBLINS WON'T TAKE US OVER THERE FOR FREE.

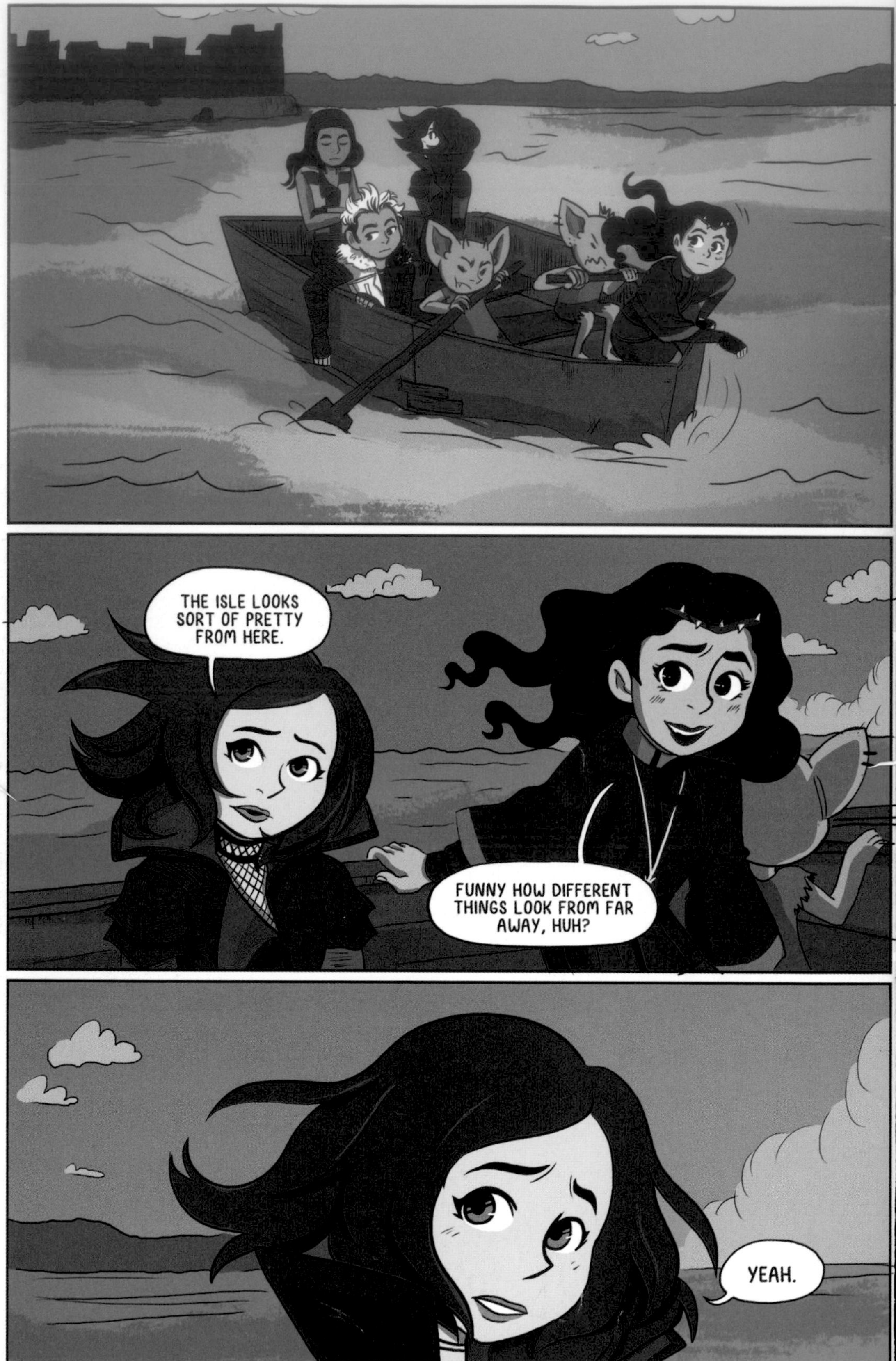
THE ISLE LOOKS SORT OF PRETTY FROM HERE.
FUNNY HOW DIFFERENT THINGS LOOK FROM FAR AWAY, HUH?
YEAH.

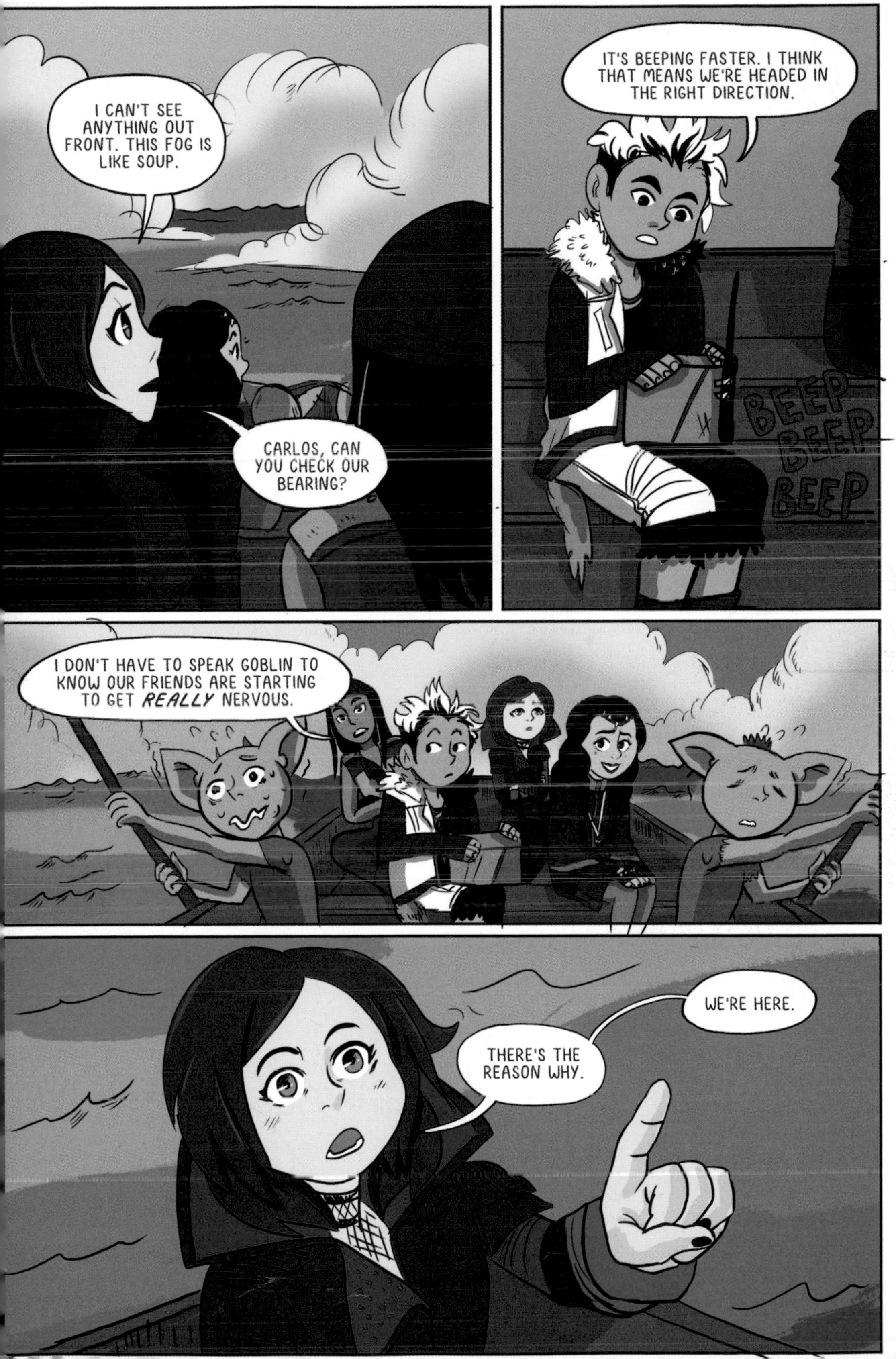
I CAN'T SEE ANYTHING OUT FRONT. THIS FOG IS LIKE SOUP.
CARLOS, CAN YOU CHECK OUR BEARING?
IT'S BEEPING FASTER. I THINK THAT MEANS WE'RE HEADED IN THE RIGHT DIRECTION.
BEEP BEEP BEEP
I DON'T HAVE TO SPEAK GOBLIN TO KNOW OUR FRIENDS ARE STARTING TO GET *REALLY* NERVOUS.
THERE'S THE REASON WHY.
WE'RE HERE.

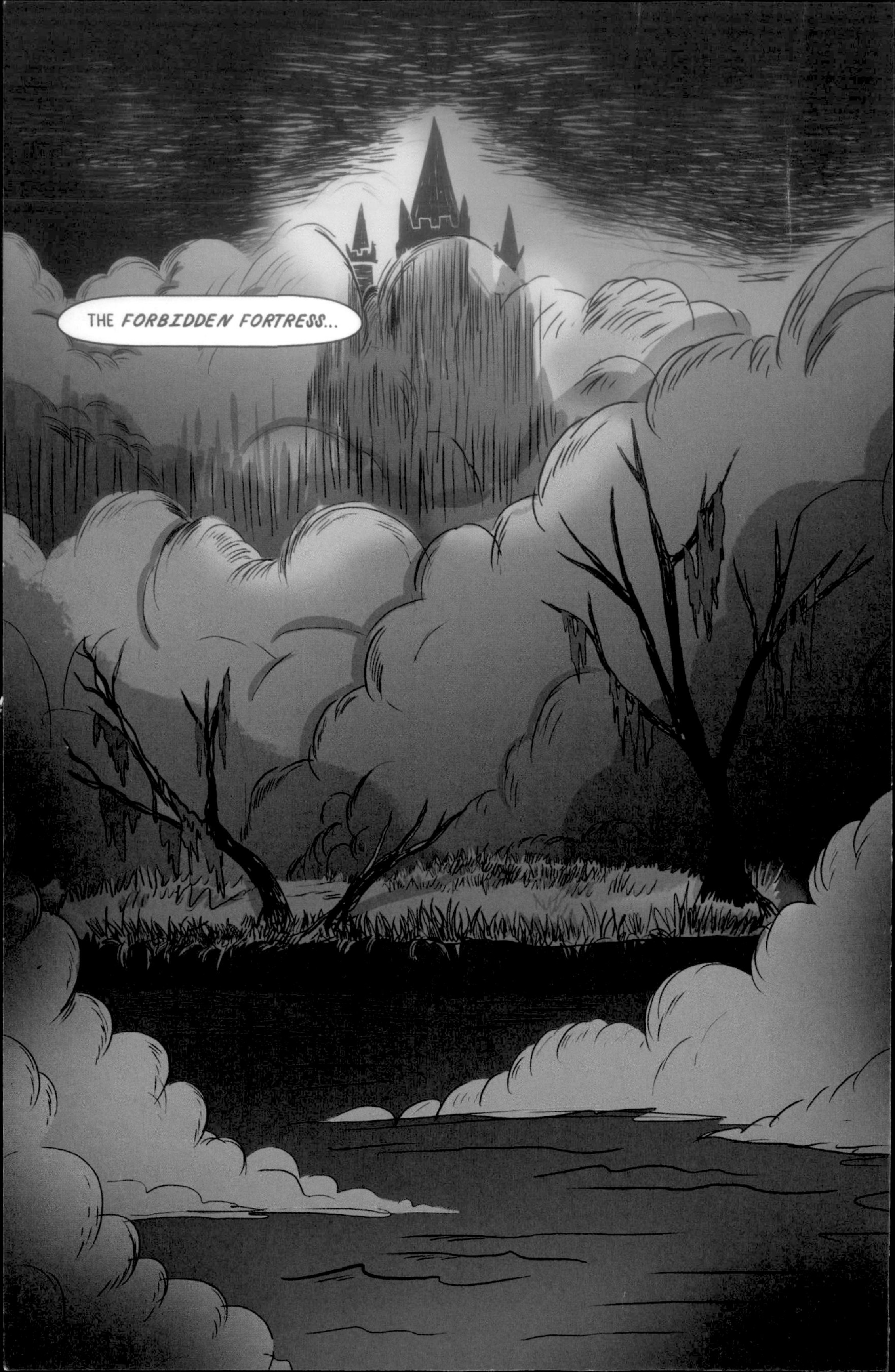
THE FORBIDDEN FORTRESS...

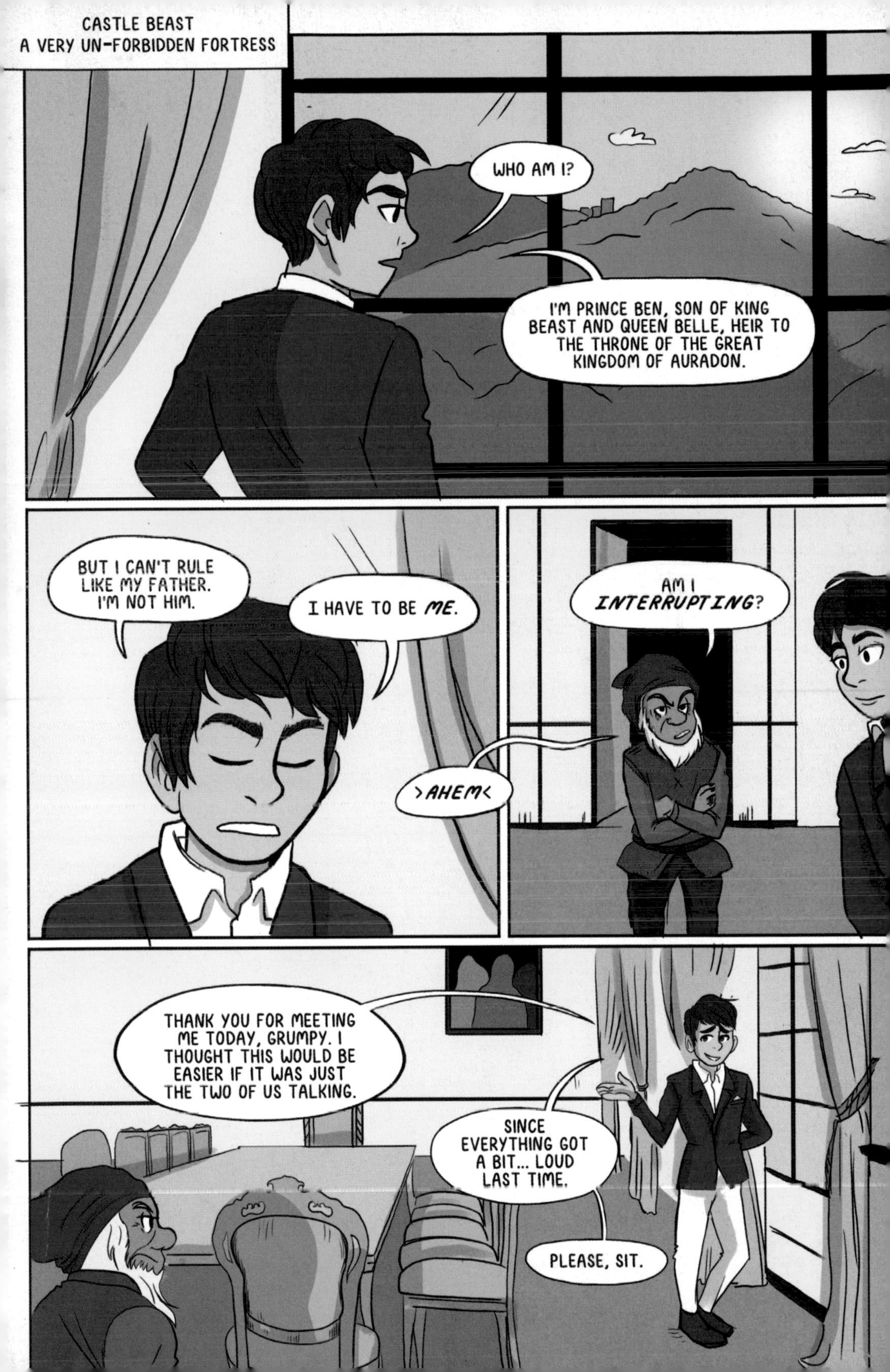
CASTLE BEAST
A VERY UN-FORBIDDEN FORTRESS
WHO AM I?
I'M PRINCE BEN, SON OF KING BEAST AND QUEEN BELLE, HEIR TO THE THRONE OF THE GREAT KINGDOM OF AURADON.
BUT I CAN'T RULE LIKE MY FATHER. I'M NOT HIM.
I HAVE TO BE *ME*.
AM I *INTERRUPTING*?
>*AHEM*<
THANK YOU FOR MEETING ME TODAY, GRUMPY. I THOUGHT THIS WOULD BE EASIER IF IT WAS JUST THE TWO OF US TALKING.
SINCE EVERYTHING GOT A BIT... LOUD LAST TIME.
PLEASE, SIT.

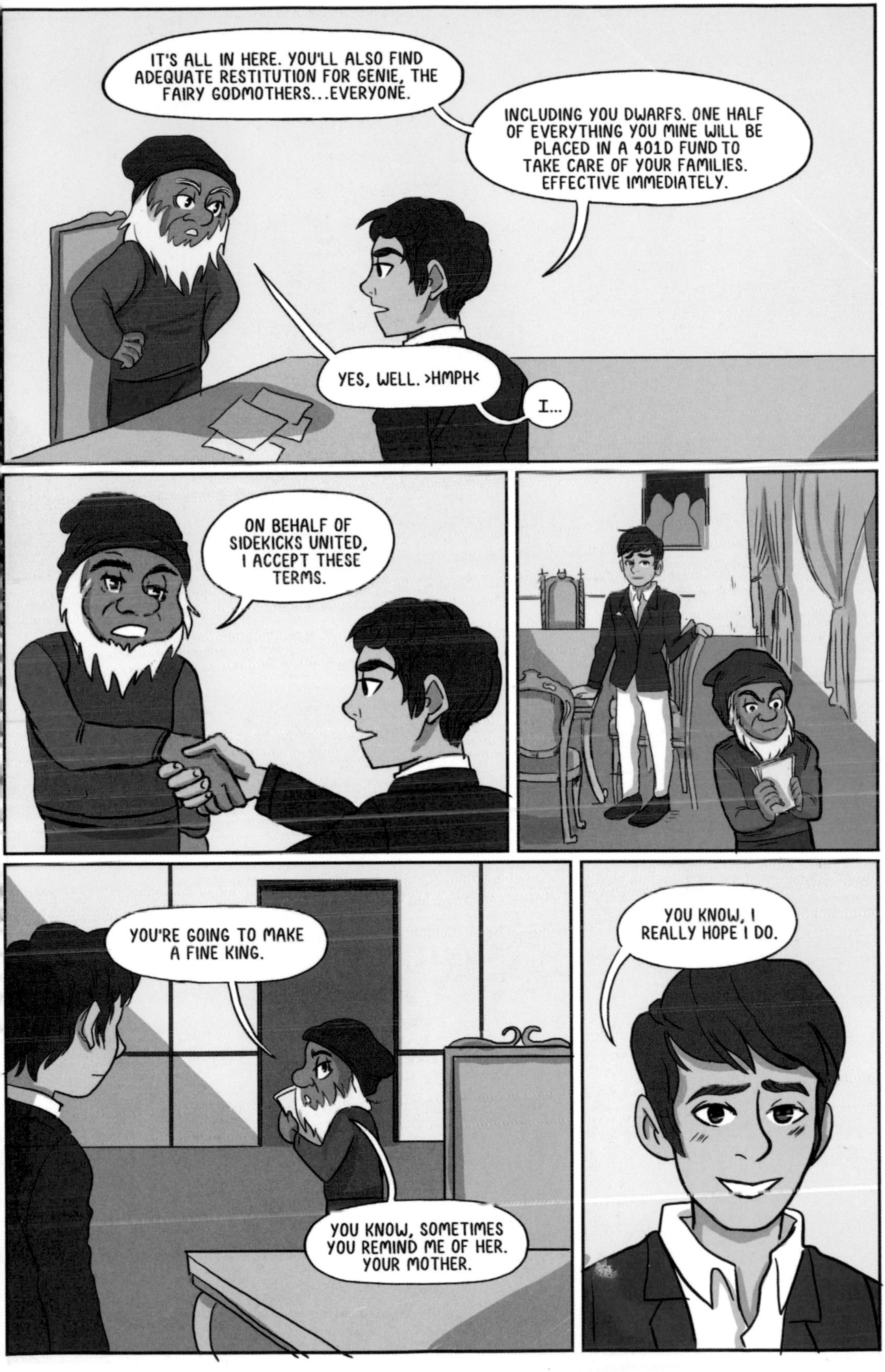
IT'S ALL IN HERE. YOU'LL ALSO FIND ADEQUATE RESTITUTION FOR GENIE, THE FAIRY GODMOTHERS...EVERYONE.
INCLUDING YOU DWARFS. ONE HALF OF EVERYTHING YOU MINE WILL BE PLACED IN A 401D FUND TO TAKE CARE OF YOUR FAMILIES. EFFECTIVE IMMEDIATELY.
YES, WELL. >HMPH<
I...
ON BEHALF OF SIDEKICKS UNITED, I ACCEPT THESE TERMS.
YOU'RE GOING TO MAKE A FINE KING.
YOU KNOW, SOMETIMES YOU REMIND ME OF HER. YOUR MOTHER.
YOU KNOW, I REALLY HOPE I DO.

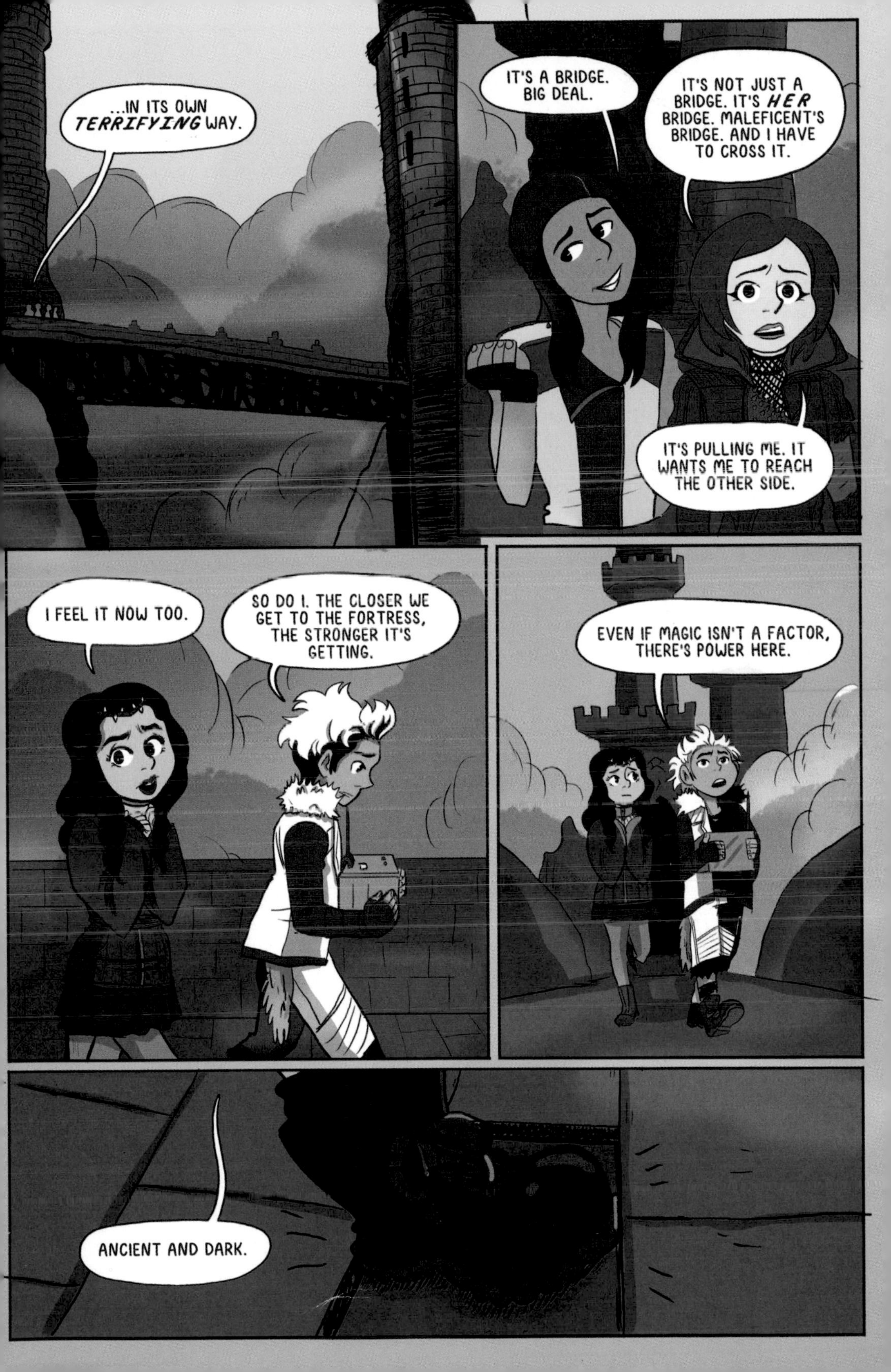
...IN ITS OWN *TERRIFYING* WAY.
IT'S A BRIDGE. BIG DEAL.
IT'S NOT JUST A BRIDGE. IT'S *HER* BRIDGE. MALEFICENT'S BRIDGE. AND I HAVE TO CROSS IT.
IT'S PULLING ME. IT WANTS ME TO REACH THE OTHER SIDE.
I FEEL IT NOW TOO.
SO DO I. THE CLOSER WE GET TO THE FORTRESS, THE STRONGER IT'S GETTING.
EVEN IF MAGIC ISN'T A FACTOR, THERE'S POWER HERE.
ANCIENT AND DARK.

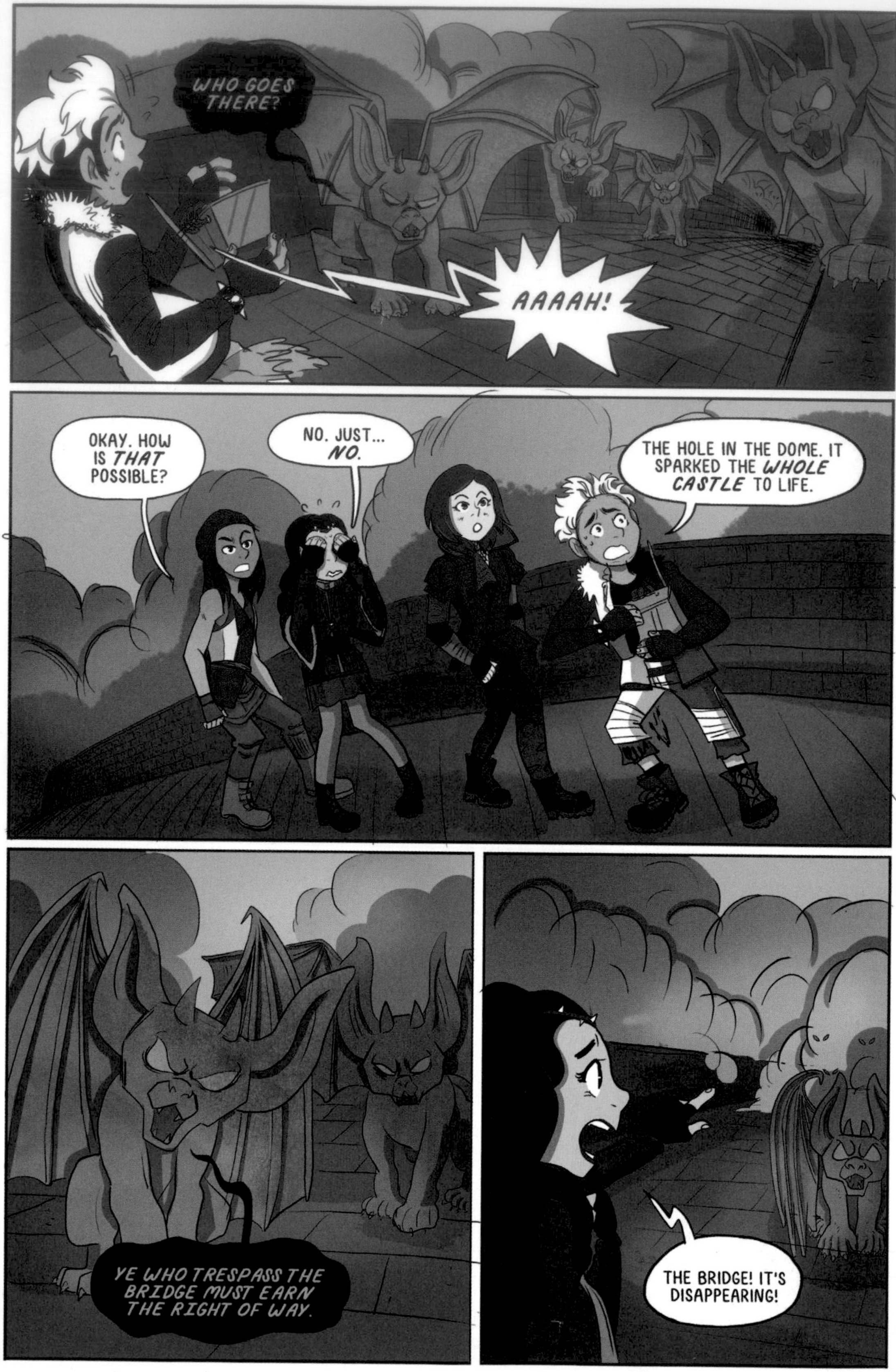
WHO GOES THERE?
AAAAH!
OKAY. HOW IS *THAT* POSSIBLE?
NO. JUST... *NO*.
THE HOLE IN THE DOME. IT SPARKED THE *WHOLE CASTLE* TO LIFE.
YE WHO TRESPASS THE BRIDGE MUST EARN THE RIGHT OF WAY.
THE BRIDGE! IT'S DISAPPEARING!

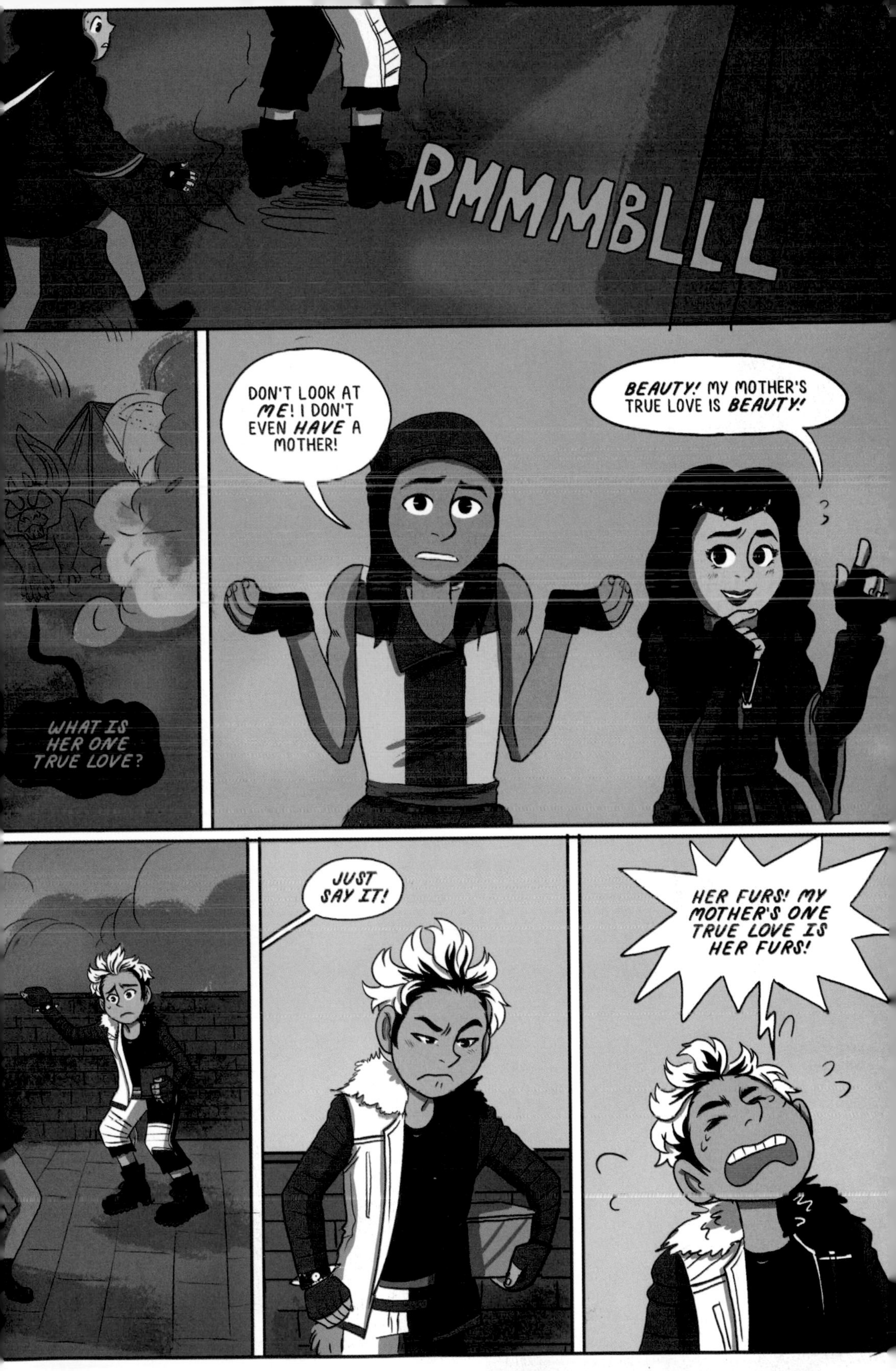
RMMMBLLL
WHAT IS HER ONE TRUE LOVE?
DON'T LOOK AT *ME*! I DON'T EVEN *HAVE* A MOTHER!
BEAUTY! MY MOTHER'S TRUE LOVE IS *BEAUTY!*
JUST SAY IT!
HER FURS! MY MOTHER'S ONE TRUE LOVE IS HER FURS!

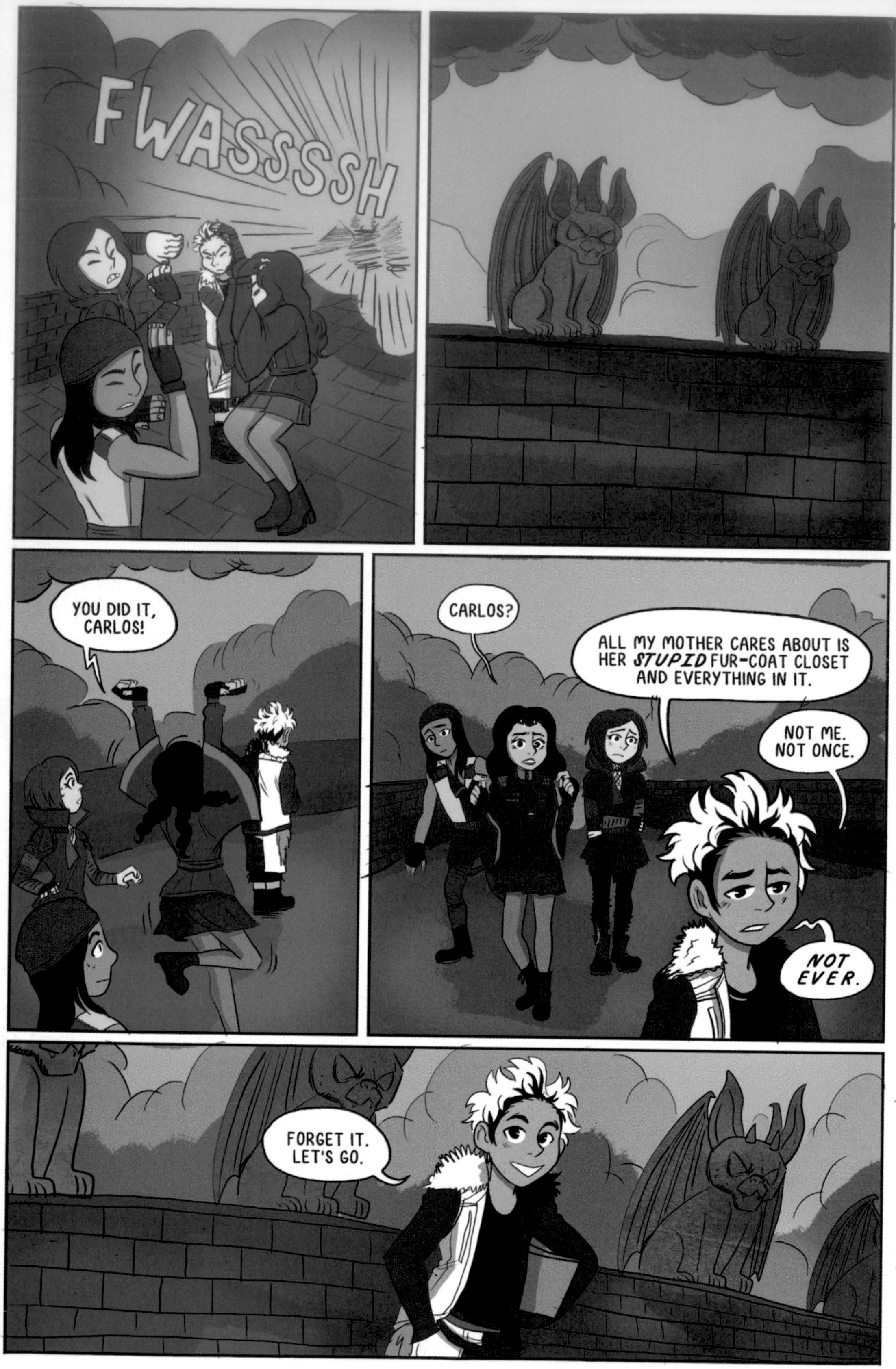
FWASSSSH
YOU DID IT, CARLOS!
CARLOS?
ALL MY MOTHER CARES ABOUT IS HER STUPID FUR-COAT CLOSET AND EVERYTHING IN IT.
NOT ME. NOT ONCE.
NOT EVER.
FORGET IT. LET'S GO.

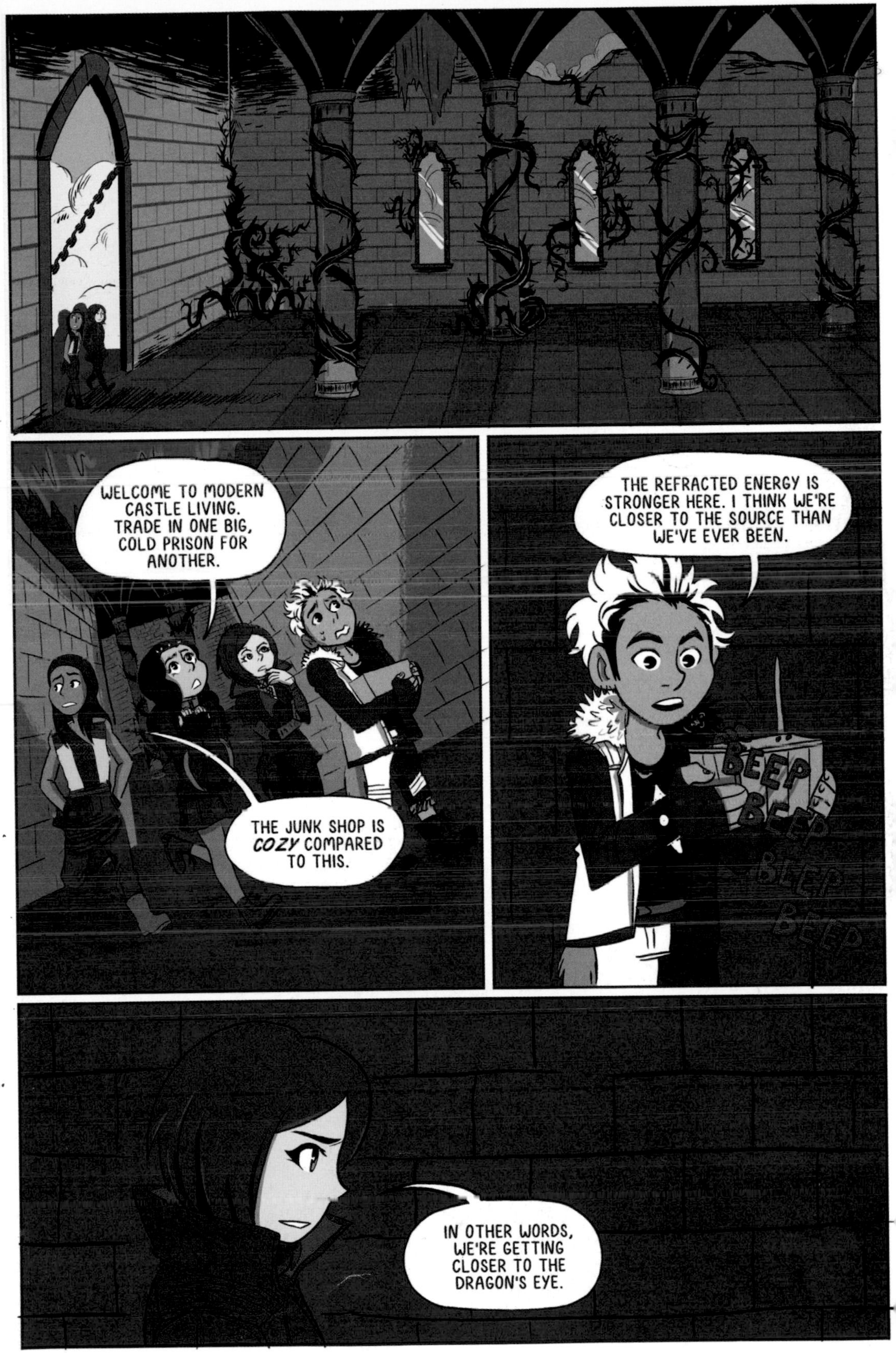
WELCOME TO MODERN CASTLE LIVING. TRADE IN ONE BIG, COLD PRISON FOR ANOTHER.
THE JUNK SHOP IS COZY COMPARED TO THIS.
THE REFRACTED ENERGY IS STRONGER HERE. I THINK WE'RE CLOSER TO THE SOURCE THAN WE'VE EVER BEEN.
BEEP BEEP BEEP BEEP
IN OTHER WORDS, WE'RE GETTING CLOSER TO THE DRAGON'S EYE.

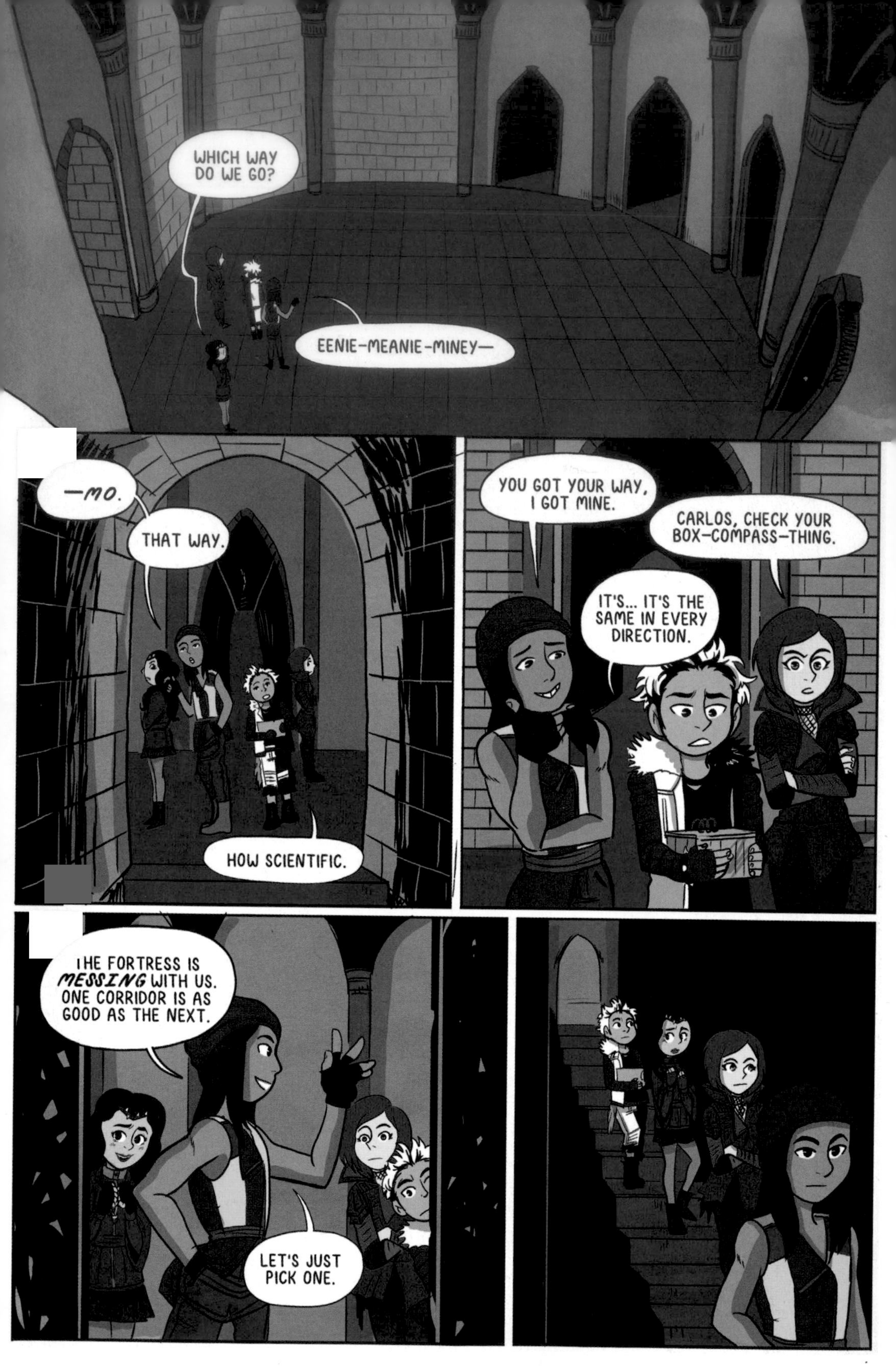
WHICH WAY DO WE GO?
EENIE-MEANIE-MINEY—
—MO.
THAT WAY.
HOW SCIENTIFIC.
YOU GOT YOUR WAY, I GOT MINE.
CARLOS, CHECK YOUR BOX-COMPASS-THING.
IT'S... IT'S THE SAME IN EVERY DIRECTION.
THE FORTRESS IS MESSING WITH US. ONE CORRIDOR IS AS GOOD AS THE NEXT.
LET'S JUST PICK ONE.

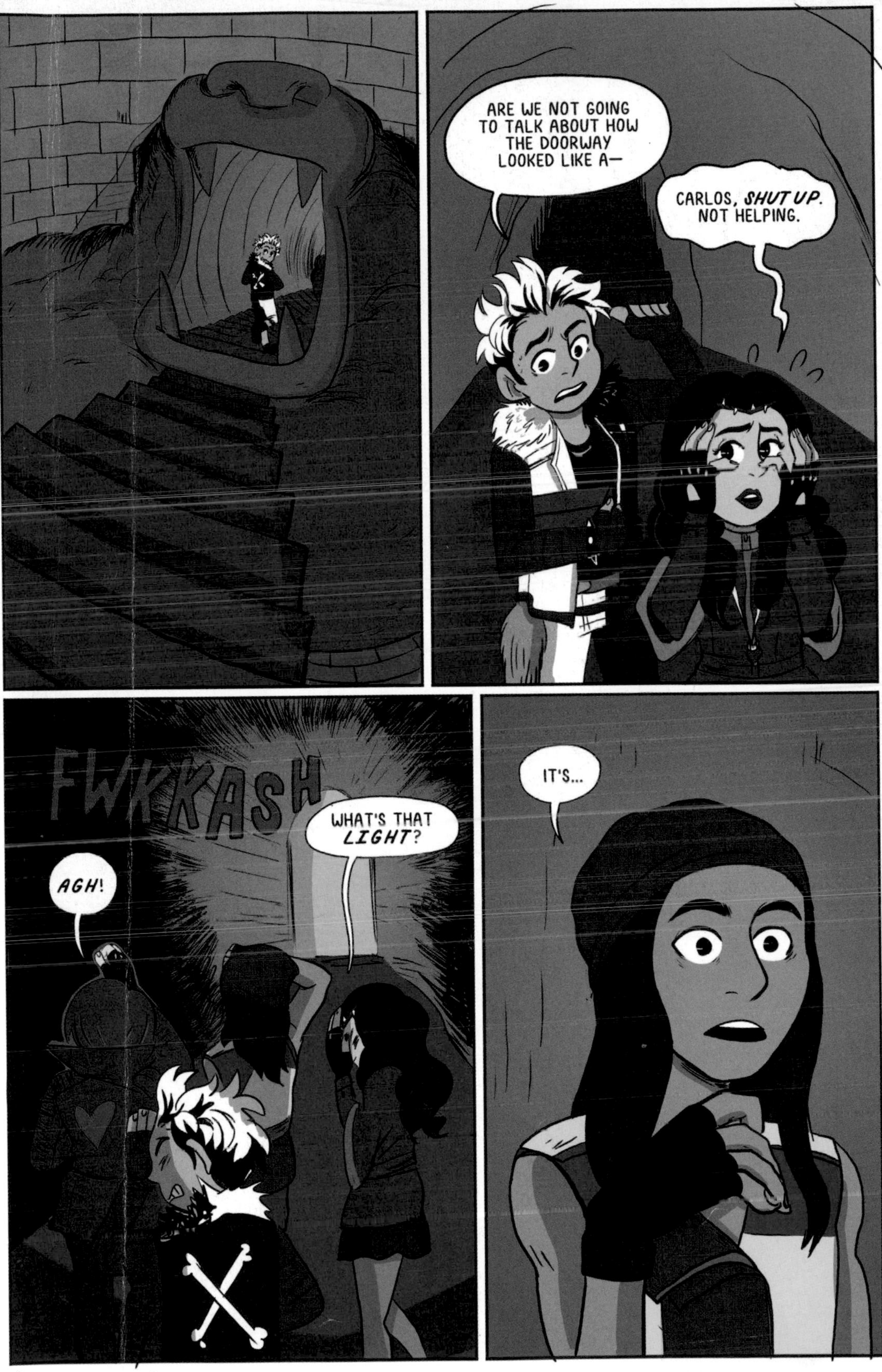
ARE WE NOT GOING TO TALK ABOUT HOW THE DOORWAY LOOKED LIKE A—
CARLOS, *SHUT UP*. NOT HELPING.
FWKKASH
AGH!
WHAT'S THAT *LIGHT*?
IT'S...

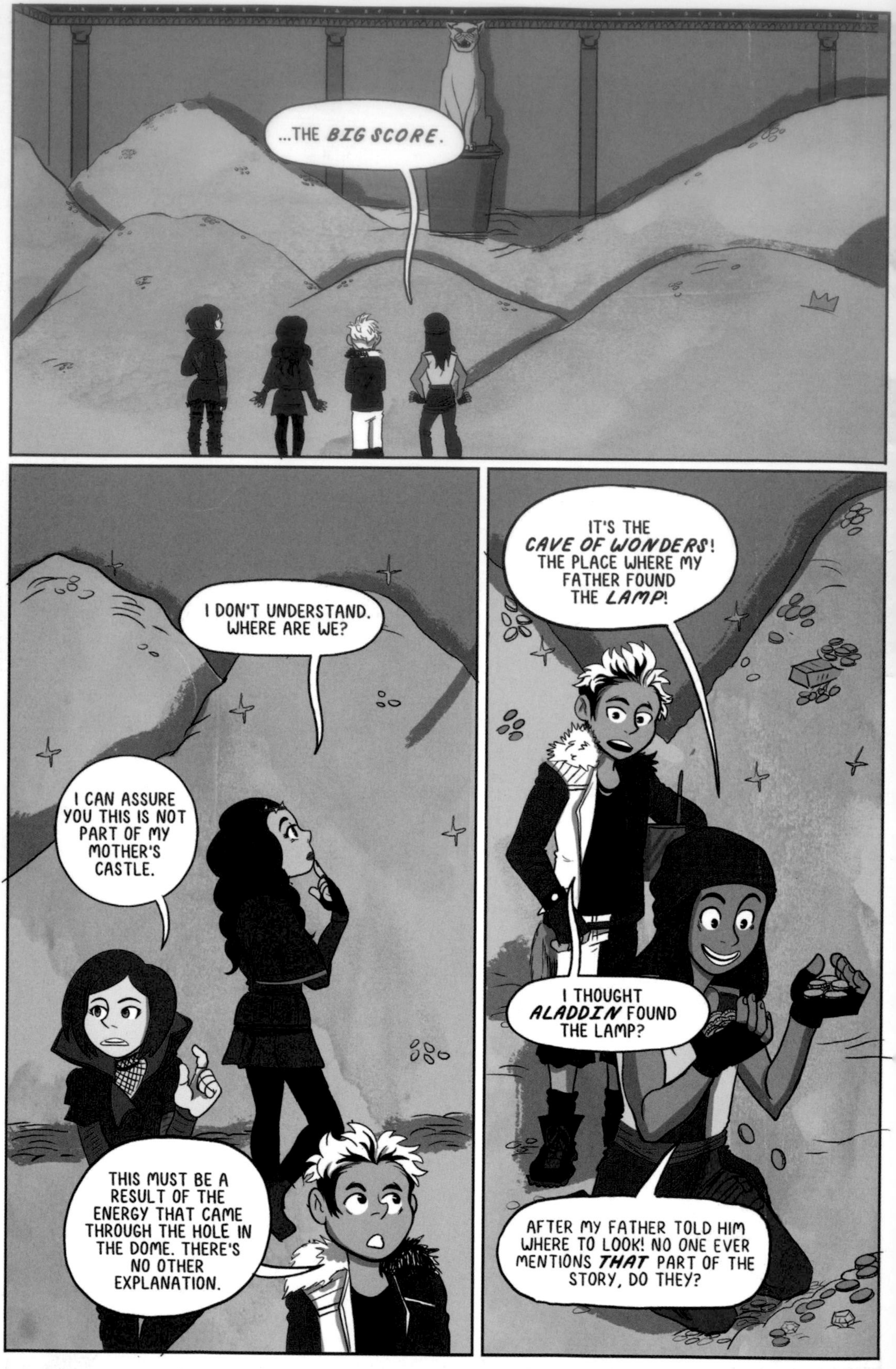
...THE BIG SCORE.
I DON'T UNDERSTAND. WHERE ARE WE?
I CAN ASSURE YOU THIS IS NOT PART OF MY MOTHER'S CASTLE.
THIS MUST BE A RESULT OF THE ENERGY THAT CAME THROUGH THE HOLE IN THE DOME. THERE'S NO OTHER EXPLANATION.
IT'S THE CAVE OF WONDERS! THE PLACE WHERE MY FATHER FOUND THE LAMP!
I THOUGHT ALADDIN FOUND THE LAMP?
AFTER MY FATHER TOLD HIM WHERE TO LOOK! NO ONE EVER MENTIONS THAT PART OF THE STORY, DO THEY?

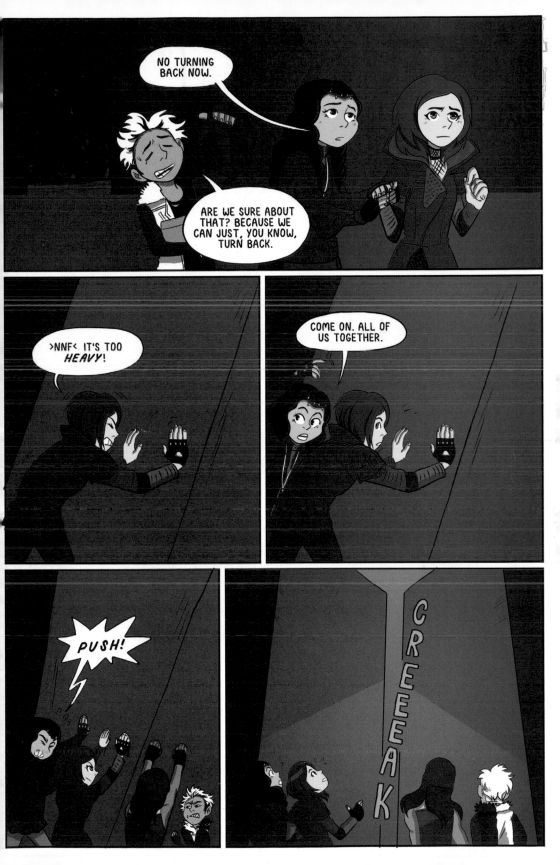

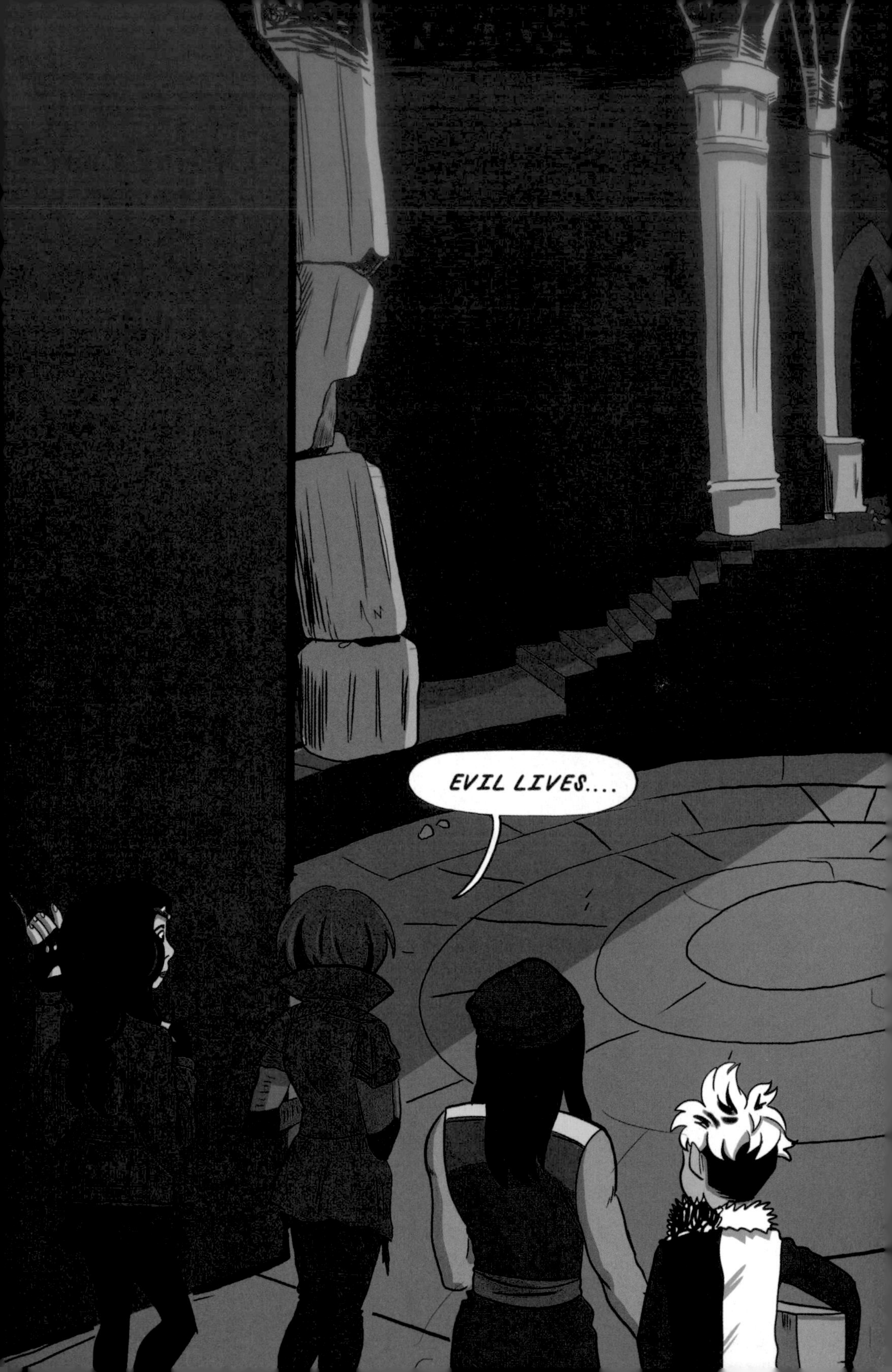
EVIL LIVES....

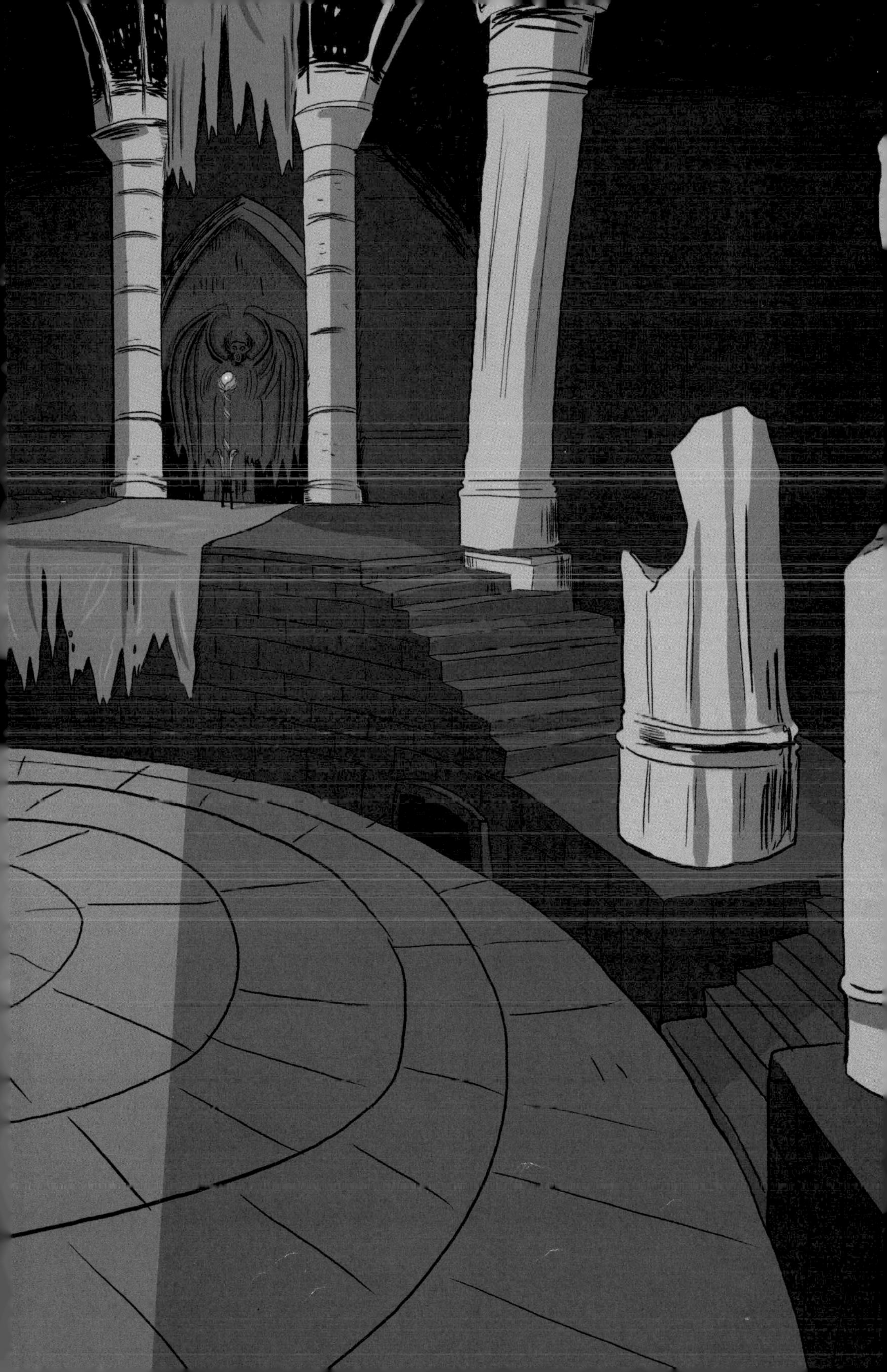

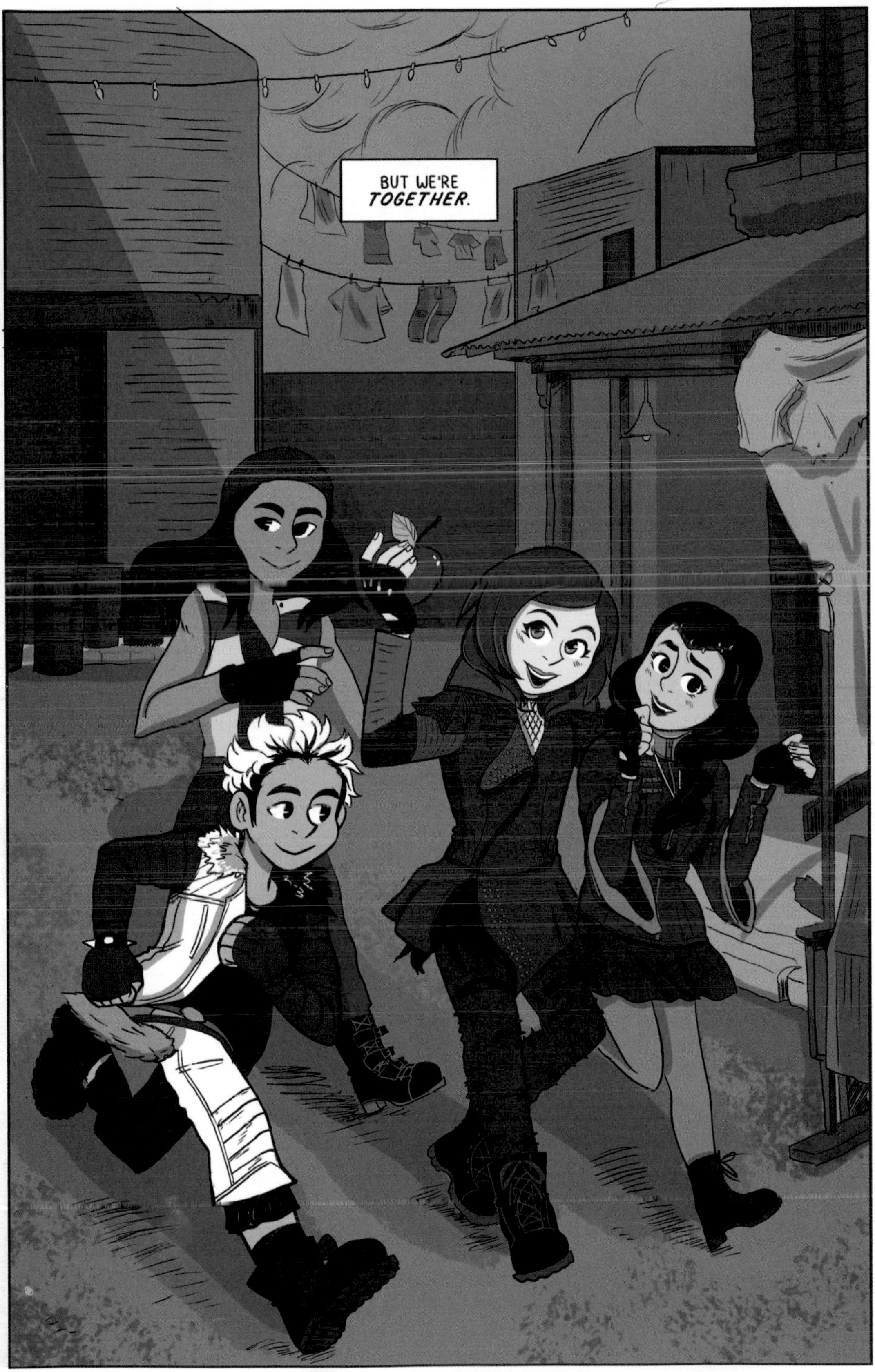
BUT WE'RE *TOGETHER*.

Sometimes being good
ISN'T SO BAD

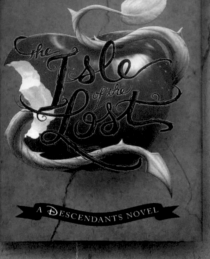

FROM #1 *NEW YORK TIMES*
BEST-SELLING AUTHOR
MELISSA
DE LA CRUZ